Oort Rising

by Magnus Victor

I0628287

Oort Rising

Published by Stonehenge Circle Press

Cover art by Emmanuel Ernel C Sapinoso

First printing, December 2015

ISBN 978-1-68012-041-7

US $14.95

Acknowledgements:

To my Family:

For your inspiration and encouragement

To my friends at Stonehenge:

For your feedback and support

Chapter 1: *Ad Astra*

"Klaus! Could you give me a hand with this?"

Klaus Ericsson sighed in irritation. As chief engineer of the freighter *Ad Astra*, he had no time to waste on baby-sitting. Unfortunately, that was exactly what he was doing. Klaus shook his head. Why had Antoniy even signed aboard as a machinist's mate? He had no real ability or experience in any of the ship's equipment.

That would have been all right by itself — Klaus didn't need an assistant, and he hadn't asked for one. However, Captain Sidonia had insisted that Klaus bring the green 'crewman' — and that was being generous — up to speed.

"What is it, Antoniy?" Klaus glided over to where the Russian crewman floated in front of a control panel. With the ship's aft reactor down for maintenance, the artificial gravity had been disabled to save power. The long, cylindrical ship's other reactor, located in the bow, couldn't produce enough power to both maintain artificial gravity and the ship's propulsion.

"I can't bring this thing's controls online."

Klaus tapped the screen, which lit up. "This reactor's an RC-37. It doesn't have built-in controls, you need the access device that I gave you earlier." Klaus gestured to where the small, box-shaped tool hung from Antoniy's toolbelt. "That one, there." He showed Antoniy how to plug it into the console, and glanced sideways at his assistant. "Where'd you say you used to work?"

Antoniy waved his arm. An unwise move – it sent him rotating away from the console. But he did grab one of the handholds quickly enough. "Oh, I shipped on my uncle's old freighter after getting my Bachelor's."

"Really? Why'd you leave? Being the Captain's brat is generally a cushy job." It would certainly explain why he didn't seem to know much about actual work.

"Well, he's getting the ship overhauled at Europa station, said it'd take a year and a half. I decided to go back to Earth for a few more classes in the meantime. You guys were the only ship leaving soon enough to get me there in time."

"You sure?" Klaus gestured at the unpainted steel walls around them. The panels were rough-made, strong and functional. It was his home, but he knew that it was far from conventional standards of beauty. "We're not exactly a fast or comfortable ride. I thought I saw a personnel carrier at the station when we were fueling up. Wouldn't they have been faster?"

Antoniy shrugged, this time holding on. "They didn't have any open spots. Luckily I convinced your captain to let me tag along as an extra hand."

Lucky for Antoniy, maybe. "That reminds me, your uncle's ship didn't have these?" Klaus nodded to the control panel. "Rockman's pretty much the only reactor supplier this far from the inner System, and I've never seen one of their models with built-in controls. No civilian model, at least."

"Well, the *Breitenfeld* was a decommissioned warship, I think."

That struck Klaus as odd – the *Thirty Years War*-class were interceptor torpedo boats. ITBs were small and fast, hardly an ideal class for conversion into a 'freighter.'

"How about that." Klaus shrugged. All the crew on the *Ad Astra* came from odd backgrounds. That was simply what life was like on an old tramp freighter. "At any rate, here's the controls. Call me again when you've run the diagnostics."

Klaus floated back across the compartment. The ship's ventral power conduit was giving him nothing but problems. It kept shorting out into the ship's keel. Not often enough to be truly useless, but enough to be a nuisance for Klaus. With the amounts of power produced by the reactor, those "shorts" amounted to melting parts of the ship's structure. An absolute pain to repair, expensive both in materials and time. Thank goodness the keel was electrically isolated, or there would have been even more damage throughout the ship's systems.

More to the point, if Klaus didn't fix the conduit before re-activating the reactor, any damages would come out of *his* paycheck.

Klaus opened up the circuit-breaker box on the reactor's power-distribution node. A cloud of ozone-tinged smoke wafted out. Completely non-functional, and the only spare high-voltage breakers were back in the spare-parts bay.

"I'm heading out, should be back in less than five minutes."

"All right. I think I've found how to get the diagnostics started."

"Gotcha." He grabbed a handhold on the wall, preparing to impel himself to the aft hatch on the other side of the compartment.

But the hull bucked, throwing his hand free. The bulkhead rushed to meet his face. What the hell—

Everything went dark.

^^*^*^*^*^*^*^*^*^*

The pain in Klaus' eyes woke him up.

Training kicked in. 'If one experiences pain (eyes or ears), dizziness, nausea, don emergency survival gear. When in doubt, don emergency survival gear.' Basic Extra-Atmospheric training manual, chapter one, paragraph one. Easy.

Squinting against the pain, Klaus groped for his helmet attached to his belt, slid it over his head, twisted it into place, and locked it closed. His eyes snapped automatically to the external pressure indicator, which, as he had guessed, showed a rapid loss of atmosphere. By the rate of depressurization, he couldn't have been out for more than ten seconds or so.

Klaus looked around, hoping that nothing important had been damaged. Antoniy drifted in the middle of the compartment, frantically waving his arms around. Was he completely disoriented, or just trying to find something to grab hold of?

He had to secure Antoniy before the kid damaged something expensive.

Either way, the kid had lost hold of his helmet, which had flown somewhere into the other end of the compartment. No time to retrieve it.

Grabbing a spare helmet from the nearby storage rack, Klaus pushed off from the floor and intercepted Antoniy. As they drifted, together, toward the far wall, he warded off the man's flailing arms with one hand, while quickly attaching the helmet with the other. Little time to waste, as the air in the compartment was too thin to convey sound now, so verbal communication would be difficult.

Klaus thudded his helmet against Antoniy's. The solid contact would easily convey sound, but Klaus shouted anyways. "What the hell did you do to my ship?" As soon as he said it, he realized he was just venting his own anger. Antoniy could not possibly have caused all this: the console only controlled the reactor. If it had been the three-point-five terawatt reactor which had exploded, they wouldn't even be here. He added, more quietly. "Ach. Never mind."

Antoniy's reply came over Klaus' radio. "I didn't do anything."

Klaus raised an eyebrow in surprise. Maybe the kid wasn't quite as inexperienced as he had thought. He pushed off to the reactor control panel. The diagnostic program was still running, nothing reported as wrong yet. Whatever happened, it wasn't this reactor. "So I see."

Unfortunately, the specialized panel could only tell him about the reactor. It could not tell him what had happened. Klaus unplugged the control device from the panel, and clipped it onto his suit. He could use it to interface with the ship-wide network.

That is, if the network was available. The thing was down half the time, it seemed. No matter how many signal repeaters Klaus installed, it never seemed to work when he needed it. A blinking red 'X' on the panel confirmed his fears. "Damn." Klaus thought for a moment, mentally reviewing the ship's schematics. They would have to move.

He motioned for Antoniy to follow him, and kicked towards the forward bulkhead of the reactor compartment. "This way. There's a spinal access node a few compartments over." The way he saw it, since the ship's spine was a hardened tube running through the center of the long ship, it was less likely to be damaged. Better bring Antoniy along, so Klaus could keep an eye on the kid. The last thing he needed was a green crewman throwing a monkey wrench into the repairs.

Antoniy's voice came shakily over the comm. "Klaus, any idea what that could have been?"

"Whatever it was, it was really big. After all, this rust-bucket masses around five hundred megatons, depending on the cargo. It must have jerked the entire ship and something broke. Explains the depressurization."

Klaus pointed to the ceiling. The unpainted steel panels hung in complete disarray. Most of the bolts which were supposed to hold them in place had sheared off completely. "An old tub like this would've blown more than a few seals from the shock." That fit most of the available evidence. "Shouldn't have killed the comms network, though..." Klaus' voice trailed off as the two men reached the hatch to the next compartment.

He hit the button to cycle the hatch open. It stayed closed, and the red 'warning' light lit: The compartment on the other side read as zero pressure. Klaus peered through the small viewport built into the hatch, but saw only black.

"Damn. Power's out ahead."

"More work, I assume?"

"Never ends on a ship like this." Klaus triggered the manual override, but only one of the two halves of the hatch slid aside, and with a loud grinding noise that set his teeth on edge. Still, it was enough to poke his head through.

For a moment, he was perplexed. Where were the emergency lights? They should have come on. Yet the supplies hold beyond was still pitch-black, broken only by small speckles of light. It was a huge compartment, yes, two hundred meters in radius, but it should be brighter than that. He couldn't even make out the hulking masses of the engineering spare parts which he knew lurked along the forward bulkhead.

Then his vision adjusted.

He blinked, staring wide-eyed. The forward hull of the *Ad Astra* floated in space, hundreds of meters from where Klaus stood. The lights he had seen were the stars, a sight so unexpected that it had taken him a moment to recognize them.

Antoniy seemed to come to the same realization only a second after. "Oh, hell."

"Yeah. There's the problem."

Antoniy's voice was surprisingly calm. "Now what?"

Just then, an explosion erupted out of the severed forward half — eerily silent in the vacuum — briefly illuminating the scene. Klaus drew in a sharp breath as he saw the rough outline of the outer hull, which had been shattered along a jagged break. He looked at Antoniy, shaking his head. "Now? We find the survivors, if any."

He pinged his suit's radio communications suite. An automated response request to any other suits in range. All that came back was Antoniy's suit.

There should have been four more — three other crewmen and the Captain. The suit transponders had the range to reach across the gap, so at the very least their suits were crippled. And unless the forward half was still pressurized, that was a death sentence. Judging by the explosions sporadically ripping through it, any atmosphere that remained was only fueling further explosions and fire. The rest of the crew were dead already, if they were lucky.

Klaus' eyes stung, but at least he could hold back the nascent tears. He fought down his emotions; they wouldn't help him now. He'd have time to grieve later. For now, he had to determine what had caused the damage, especially in case the rest of the aft part of the ship might be in danger.

The *Ad Astra* was a hodgepodge of hull sections from different classes of ship, with different design philosophies. Unfortunately, that meant that the crew sections were in the box of the ship, along with the forward reactor. While that had made Klaus' life easier for maintenance access, it also meant that the reactor was immediately adjacent to where the rest of the crew would have been.

Judging by the total power loss in the forward section, and the extreme temperature readings that his suit's sensors were taking from the forward bulkhead, the forward reactor must have gone super-critical. That would have melted the containment chamber, and then vented plasma into the rest of the ship.

But that couldn't have started on its own, and it wouldn't explain why the supplies hold was where the ship was broken apart. There were all sorts of fail-safes to keep the reactor running smoothly, ones that Klaus had personally checked.

Yet if the ship had been split into two pieces by something else, *that* could have caused the reactor to lose control. The *Ad Astra's* computer systems were as mismatched as the rest of the ship, and would have crashed when the forward half of the ship was separated. That would also explain why the communications system was down.

"Reactor must have blown. Crew quarters were right next to it." Klaus sent out another ping. Still no response. "Survivors...may not be as likely as I'd hoped."

"Shit." breathed Antoniy. "Now what?"

Klaus' mind raced. The *Ad Astra's* long-range communications array was also located on the disabled forward section. And the ship's transponder, a fragile piece of long-distance communications equipment, probably cut off when the power grid went down. It might take days for anybody to even notice that the *Ad Astra* had disappeared. Worse, the black-box's own transponder signal was lower-power, with a much shorter range. Rescuers would take weeks to find them.

They didn't have weeks. Looked like he'd have to attract attention using some more active method.

But there was something he could use in the section of the ship available to them. "C'mon, follow me. We can send an SOS with the LIDAR gear." Klaus cycled the hatch closed, shutting off the view of space outside. He pushed off toward the aft end of their chamber, but Antoniy stayed floating by the now-sealed hatch. Probably in shock at the loss of the crew. Klaus could empathize with that, but emotions were only a hindrance right now. "They're dead. Come along — we need to make sure we don't join them."

Klaus floated through a door into the ship's central passageway, checking that Antoniy followed him. They approached the next hatch, a massively heavy blast door embedded in a thick, steel bulkhead. The long access corridor beyond it would take them straight to the controls he needed. Finally, he would be able to do something useful! He launched himself towards the opening.

Suddenly, the alarms mounted on the hatch opening blared, and it began to close. He would never be able to clear the hatch in time. He flailed around for something to grab, and locked onto a protruding pipe along the wall. The hatch snapped shut with a clang he felt through his hands, bare centimeters from his helmet.

Klaus looked over his shoulder. Antoniy had barely managed to arrest his motion.

"Why'd it shut?" panted Antoniy.

"Dunno." He quickly read off the indicator lights next to the firmly-sealed hatch. "The passageway on the other side has been hit by something - probably debris from the rest of the ship.

Set off the impact triggers. The system still thinks there's air to protect." There was an emergency mechanism to crank the blast door open manually, but a few minutes of futile effort showed him that the door was jammed shut.

Klaus mentally reviewed the *Ad Astra*'s interior schematics. "From here, the passageway goes between fuel tanks. That means there's no other way through. We'll have to go EVA, get back inside further aft." He pushed off from the bulkhead, floating towards the closest external airlock.

"EVA? In these suits?" Antoniy's voice shook a bit. Klaus couldn't blame him. They were only wearing interior-service suits. They would serve to keep them alive in a vacuum, sure, but they had no thruster packs or tether lines for EVA maneuvering. If either of the two crewmen floated off from the ship, well, they'd keep floating forever.

But there was no choice. The key would be to make not a single mistake, and that meant that he needed to steady the kid's nerves. "Look, it won't be that hard - I'll go and find the next airlock down the hull, and string a tether from here to there." Klaus held up one of the lengths of high-strength carbon monofilament, part of the maintenance kit in his service suit. "Just hold on to it and you'll be fine." As long as the kid kept his protective gloves on, he'd be able to grasp the hair-thin cable without harm.

Antoniy made no reply, but just stared at the filament.

Klaus shrugged, cycled the outer airlock open, and stepped through. He gave himself a mental pat on the back for insisting on replacing the old, burnt-out airlock batteries, even though the captain had complained at the cost. The original white paint of the outer hull could still be seen in a few places, if he looked carefully.

But the hull was showing its age, scratched and pitted from micrometeorite strikes.

Klaus tied one end of the wire to his belt, and the other end to the tie-off by the airlock. "Stay here. I'll call you when I get to the next airlock."

Now safely secured, Klaus pushed off along the side of the ship's hull, floating carefully down towards the next airlock, half a kilometer distant. He used the widely-spaced handholds to correct his course, his tension mounting with each one he passed. They were installed more as an afterthought than anything else, never really intended to be all that functional. The suit itched, and he fought to keep his hands steady during each micro-adjustment needed to maintain his trajectory. Sweating heavily, and with the beginnings of a splitting headache behind his eyes, he arrived.

"I made it," he commed. "Tying off the line now. Wait for my signal before you start." Better make sure this airlock worked, first. He peered through the small porthole, but a spider's web of cracks obscured his view. He could see no detail inside, but at least there was no glow of fire, and there seemed to be nothing obviously wrong with the airlock's seal.

Taking no chances, he cycled a safety check, and was rewarded with a row of green lights. Good. The compartment beyond should be safe to enter.

He cycled the airlock open and pulled himself inside. The panel told him that the interior was depressurized, and he hit the override to open the interior lock while the outside one was still open. The emergency lights were on, but their red glow was not enough to check the compartment for damage. He switched on his suit's headlamp to fully illuminate the interior. Good. Looked safe and undamaged enough, except for the lack of atmosphere.

Some systems must still be running in this part of the ship, as he could feel the hum of machinery through his feet. But that was not as reassuring as it would normally be, as the loud rattle of the air-circulation system was absent. Just as well, as he chose not to re-pressurize until Antoniy arrived. Still, at least it was better than the near-silence of the EVA outside of the hull. About the only good thing he could say about the *Ad Astra* was that her machinery was old enough that you could judge how well it was working by the vibrations that the half-obsolete systems made.

Similarly, the slight fluctuations in the pressure of the floor against his feet told him that the artificial gravity for this ship section was failing. Judging by the frequency, it probably had a week at most before it died entirely. He'd have to get around to fix – Klaus shook his head. He had far more things to worry about before then.

More things like this almost-useless kid. He grabbed the line that he had tied off, and radioed Antoniy. "Alright, this lock is open. Untie the rope at your end, and tie it onto your belt. Worst comes to worst, I'll pull you in."

∧∧*∧*∧*∧*∧*∧*∧*∧*∧*

"Okay." Antoniy Gureivich responded, although he could tell that his voice was tight with worry. He edged his head past the outer rim of the airlock, and looked around for the filament. Grasping it, he tried to untie it from the handle. Under his breath, he grumbled "Klaus, did you really need to tie this many knots?"

"On an EVA with only that filament for safety? Of course," came the engineer's amused voice.

Antoniy jumped, and checked his mic. He could have sworn that it was set to transmit on command only. "I'll have to cut it."

He unfolded the knife from his utility tool, and thumbed the toggle to activate the blade's micro plasma emitters along its edge. He cut the filament, staring at the tiny lifeline. It looked incredibly thin, hard to see against the black of space, but Klaus had sworn up and down that it would hold a man's weight.

Antoniy smiled grimly to himself. If it was strong enough for the engineer, it was strong enough for just about anyone. He shook his head, berating himself. His mind was rambling, delaying the point where he would have to leave the ship. Attaching the thread to his belt, he stepped out onto the hull of the *Ad Astra*.

He grasped the line, his grip tightening unconsciously as he studied the row of handholds disappearing into the distance. On the plus side, at least the bright, gleaming steel, untouched by rust, promised that they would hold. On the down side, they were tiny prongs of metal weighed against the depths of space. "How far did you say it was to the airlock?"

"Just five hundred meters, kid. Only half a klick."

Only. Hah. Antoniy really hadn't envisioned stunts like this when he took the job. Well, it was too late for a career change now. "All right. Leaving now." Taking a deep breath and letting it out, he checked his tie-off one last time, and then began his journey.

As soon as his feet left the airlock floor, the shocking silence of space struck him. Sure, the vacuum back in the ship had been silent, but this was different. Maybe it was the complete absence of surrounding walls, replaced by an infinite expanse of *absolutely nothing.*

He could hear his own breathing, heavier than it should be, and his heartbeat – should it be that loud? He closed his eyes for a second, calming his nerves. He'd done spacewalks like this in training. Everybody had. It was routine, and he was — relatively — safely attached.

But did it really have to take so long? He grasped the first handhold, and half-pulled, half-pushed himself along the hull towards the next. His hands shook slightly, and he frowned at himself. Klaus had breezed through the EVA like it was a Sunday stroll, and Antoniy bet that the old engineer hadn't been on the outside of a spaceship in years. Or engaged in any other form of exercise, for that matter.

And Antoniy would be damned if he would let Klaus show him up on such a simple exercise. Besides, at least this was a physical challenge. Those he could handle. That was the part of training that he'd really enjoyed.

Antoniy grabbed the next handhold, more firmly this time. He gauged the distance towards the next handhold. Fifty meters. Another fifty to the one after that. If he skipped alternate handholds, he could move faster – could get the EVA *over with* faster – and he was securely tied off, anyways.

Gathering his feet underneath him, Antoniy kicked off towards the next-next handhold. This wasn't too bad, after all. Now all he had to do was not look down. But...which way was down?

His eyes moved to the endless expanse of stars, so many that they seemed to blur together. Oh, right. *That* was down.

He blinked rapidly, fighting back the rising feeling in his throat. No. He swallowed. He would *not* allow himself to vomit inside his helmet, not in the middle of a life or death EVA like this. He didn't even know when he'd be able to clean out his suit if he did.

He snapped his eyes back to the destination airlock. It looked closer, at least. Forcing himself to breathe regularly, he passed over the handhold, still on target for the next. At this rate, he would be done soon. That was reassuring.

Finally at the end, Antoniy half-clambered, half-was-pulled through the open airlock into the corridor. He slammed the airlock closed behind him. Air hissed into the compartment as he detached the thread from his waist, his hands shaking slightly. "Please tell me we stay inside the ship from here on."

He only half-meant it. This new compartment echoed with machinery, loud even through his helmet. If the rest of the aft portion of the hull was this loud, he'd seriously consider going EVA just to hear himself think.

^*^*^*^*^*^*^*^*^*^*^*

"Inside? Definitely." Klaus finished re-packing the filament back into his kit, using its automatic spooling tool. Gesturing over his shoulder, he responded, "The aft control center is just at the end of this corridor. There's food and oxygen there." He turned and pushed off down the corridor, throwing a glance over his shoulder to check that Antoniy was following.

The kid had actually done surprisingly well on the EVA: Klaus hadn't had to reel him in after all. He'd even been faster than Klaus had been. He hadn't expected that. Maybe Antoniy had had more experience than Klaus had suspected? He would certainly ask about that later, when they got a chance to rest.

The two men arrived at the interior airlock to the control center. With all of the high-voltage electrical lines running through the compartment, it was normally kept in a vacuum, as a fire precaution. Climbing through the airlock, Klaus took in the shiny steel walls, as unblemished as the day the ship had been launched. The isolated chamber was rarely used, and so had not had the opportunity to become dusty like the rest of the ship. Without oxygen, even rust hadn't had a chance to develop.

Now if only Klaus could remember where the environmental controls were for this compartment. The *Ad Astra* was older than he was, and had been retrofitted so many times that no two compartments were built to the same plan anymore. He started hunting around the room.

The hiss of the closing airlock told him that Antoniy had followed him through. "Doesn't look like anyone's ever been in here." Antoniy stated. "No atmosphere, either. You said something about oxygen?"

"This compartment's outfitted as a survival shelter." He opened yet another panel cover, frowning at the switches that sat beneath it. Analog switches? How old *was* this room? He flipped the main-power switch and the one labeled "ENV", half surprised that it was labeled in English and not in Aramaic or something. Had he really signed off on this compartment? Air began to hiss into the room through the grate in the ceiling. "That means oxygen, food and water supplies, the works."

"That's a relief. How long will they last?"

"Don't know, offhand." Klaus pointed towards a large, floor-to-ceiling door in one of the walls. "Food and water's in there. Could you go check how much we've got? I'll check the oxygen from here." He examined the board. The emergency oxygen supply was almost full, providing enough to last nearly a month. The ship's aft reactor even read as online and undamaged. Though it was never meant to power the entire ship, it provided more than enough juice to run the artificial gravity.

He hit the master reset button, and watched as a few of the indicator lights switched to green. The aft third of the *Ad Astra* now had gravity. They wouldn't have to worry about zero-G sickness, at least.

The grav generators spooled up slowly, and the gently-increasing field pulled Klaus' feet softly to the floor. Hearing a 'thud' behind him, he turned to see Antoniy sprawled half-in, half-out of the food compartment. Rolling his eyes, he turned back to the console built into the port-side wall. The generators came up slowly precisely to avoid that sort of thing. Had they never practiced zero-G drills on Antoniy's last ship?

His train of thought was interrupted as he saw the data readout. "Damn. The LIDAR array's offline." He ran a diagnostic – the LIDAR software returned green, but the hardware check failed. The panels must have been damaged by the explosion. "Offline for good, at that."

Antoniy's sigh drifted in from the supply storage compartment. "Any other ideas?"

Instead of answering, Klaus drew a screwdriver from one of the pockets on his suit. He carefully paced off three meters aft from the console, one meter to starboard, kneeled down and removed the screws holding a deck panel in place. He opened the seals on the panel, and lifted it a fingers'-width. Nothing happened. Good.

Antoniy looked over from his compartment. "What are you doing?"

"The main power lines for most everything in this segment of the ship run near this compartment. I can cut off power to the ship's beacon from here."

"What good is that? If you turn it off, we just disappear off the map! How would that help?"

Klaus lifted the entire panel out, and set it on the deck beside him. He drew a small knife from his boot, lay down on his stomach, and reached down into the large junction box. He pulled on a pair of insulated gloves and grinned at Antoniy. "Never try this, by the way."

Klaus carefully picked through the myriad of exposed wires, and chose the one he recognized as belonging to the proper circuit. He neatly cut it and began to strip the protective rubber coating off of the wire. "Tell me - what system did people use to communicate on Earth, before the computer, even before the telephone?"

Antoniy frowned, but went along with the seemingly pointless question. "I dunno. Smoke signals?"

Klaus held up the two ends of the cut wire and smiled. "Morse code!"

Antoniy shook his head. "Nobody knows Morse code! It's downright prehistoric! They'll just think our beacon is faulty."

"Maybe, but probably not. Worth a shot, at least." Klaus pointed at the nearby damage-control console. "Could you hand me those splice cables stowed in the console? The red-and-black striped ones?"

Antoniy handed the cables to Klaus, and the engineer spliced together one end of each to the cut wires, and then attached the other ends to the corresponding power ports on his datapad.

"Now, I've got the beacon's power cable linked — or more accurately, the power *relay* cable — so I can control the signal from my datapad." Klaus brought up a test program, and keyed it to send a series of short and long pulses, set on repeat, through the cables which he had attached.

Antoniy pointed at Klaus' pad. "Even if this works, what are the odds that anyone will see the beacon and recognize the code?"

"Well, the planet-based tracking systems follow each beacon's signal. The automated systems will recognize an SOS."

"You're placing that much trust in a system you've never tried?"

"I don't trust the person operating it, no. The programs doing the actual work, though, I trust to work. Even if they don't recognize the pattern, they should trigger an automated message telling us to repair our beacon. When we don't respond, *that* will definitely get someone's attention." Klaus' vision began to blur, and he shook his head. How long had it been since he ate? Nearly nine hours? "On another note, how are we set for food and water?"

Antoniy waved what resembled a large, multicolored energy bar, which looked amazingly unappetizing even to a hungry man like Klaus. "There's enough water for a month, but all we've got for food are ration bars."

Klaus' stomach clenched. He knew from experience that they looked far, far better than they tasted.

"That's still better than starving" he responded, although he was not entirely sure. "Back when I went through Basic, we'd go for months with nothing else to eat. Once you get past the taste, they're perfectly healthy. We'll be all right."

"Unlike the rest of the crew." Antoniy's voice was morose.

"Aye." Klaus nodded, slowly. Now that he didn't have an immediate problem staring him in the face, the loss of the crew really hit him. Some of them he wouldn't miss quite as much – Harper in particular was possibly the worst cook he'd ever heard of, the only man who could make ration bars look good by comparison.

But most of them were decent people. Captain Sidonia had been the best business partner that Klaus could have asked for. The Captain had been one of the few people willing to hire Klaus after his ejection from the Navy. He didn't have many people that he would consider 'friends', but Klaus would remember Sidonia as one of them.

He leaned back against the bulkhead, pinching the bridge of his nose as his eyes teared up. Too many good people died today, and the survivors were him and some random kid? Klaus recognized the signs of survivor's guilt, but he felt the emotional spike all the same. He didn't try to hold it back – sometimes an emotional response was necessary.

Antoniy handed him a ration bar, which Klaus peeled open. Hopefully the taste of the damn thing would distract him, give him something to focus his misery on.

Chapter 2: The Long Wait

Klaus held back a smile as Antoniy took a bite out of his fourth ration bar and made a face. Fifteen minutes of *slow* eating, and the kid still hadn't gotten used to the taste. He had probably never before tried survival rations. They'd keep you alive, regret it as you may. Antoniy paused in his eating, and looked up. "How will we know when they get here?"

Klaus carefully finished chewing before answering. Even though he could stomach the rations, he did not want any more of that taste in his mouth than necessary while he talked. "Rescuers, you mean? They'd use an all-frequencies radio broadcast." He tapped his suit helmet, sitting on the deck beside him. "The receivers built into these things aren't too good, but they're good enough to pick up a local transmission. As for how soon, well, allow twelve hours or so for the beacon's signal to reach anybody. Then assume they recognize it as an SOS within a day of receiving it, and that they divert a patrol craft or some other passing vessel over to us. Depending on our luck, it could be anything between a week and a month."

Antoniy sighed. "Sounds like we're in for a long wait, then."

Klaus nodded. "Yeah, but at least we're alive." He looked at the half-eaten ration bar in his hand. "Enough oxygen for weeks, food and water for months. A trickle of power, enough to keep the gravity in place, lights on, all the essentials." He contemplated taking another bite, but his hunger didn't quite overcome the intrinsic repulsion of the bar.

"That'll keep our bodies alive, yeah." Antoniy gestured at the compartment around them. The monolithic steel walls were devoid of any decoration. Nothing for the eye to rest on, nothing to alleviate the boredom. "What's to keep us from going crazy from the wait?"

"Whatever books you've got on your datapad. If that doesn't do it, there are some sleep-inducers in the survival kits. One of us will want to be awake, though, to hear if anybody shows up."

Antoniy grimaced. "My datapad is — *was* — back in my bunk."

"You can borrow mine when I'm sleeping, then." Klaus brought out his datapad, and handed it to Antoniy. "Hope you like science-fiction." He stretched his arms, yawning. "My advice for right now, though, is to get some sleep. Burns less calories and oxygen, and even better, burns through time." He laid down on the floor, rearranging the tough yet flexible oxygen bladders of his suit to form a pillow. Good design, that.

Klaus was about to close his eyes when Antoniy called out. "Wait!" Antoniy reached for his helmet, which sat on the deck beside him, and held it close to his ear. "Did you hear that?" he asked, and raised the volume on the suit's speaker.

An unknown man's voice now became audible, mid-sentence. "—is Lieutenant Becker of the *Tannenberg*. We saw your beacon, and we're here to look for survivors. Respond if possible."

Klaus and Antoniy looked at each other. Klaus spoke first. "Maybe they happened to be nearby?"

"No, the *Tannenberg*'s still out at Andromeda station, she's nowhere near here."

Klaus frowned. Why would Antoniy know about a naval warship? "Maybe she was heading back in-system, same as us? We'd be on about the same vector, it could happen."

"Still no." Antoniy shook his head. "She's on station for another few months."

"How do you know?"

"It's a long story."

"Uh-huh." Klaus looked askance at Antoniy. "At any rate, if the external cameras are still working, we can take a look outside from here. If our radio receivers are picking up that transmission that well, their ship can't be far off. The *Tannenberg's* a capital ship, so we can spot them with visual." He walked over to the console. "Hmm. Not all systems re-booted automatically. Cameras are still down."

It should have occurred to him that they wouldn't. But then, he'd been a bit distracted with everything else recently. Klaus tapped away at the keyboard – the camera systems would take a minute to re-start.

As long as he was re-booting that system, he may as well get the others. They might be useful. The communications system wouldn't be much help – the long-distance transmitter had been in the forward half of the ship – but maybe the bridge crew had left a message, or something. They might have seen whatever – or whomever – destroyed the ship. Unlikely, but not impossible.

The comms system would take a while to boot up, though. The software was newer than the rest of the ship, and wasn't technically backwards-compatible with the hardware that it was running on. Klaus' forced workarounds for that would take a while to re-initialize the system.

Just as he finished the appropriate commands, the camera system came online. The display switched to a view aft. "Ah, here we go."

With the navigation lights off, the gray, horizon-like breadth of the *Ad Astra*'s aft hull was visible only from its occlusion of the stars. The 'sky' was comprised of a vast array of stars, covering the rest of the view, except for —

"There." Klaus pointed to a patch of blackness, near to the hull. The camera's location tag showed that it was only a few hundred meters forward of the compartment that Klaus and Antoniy were in.

He frowned. "That's odd. They've turned their proximity lights off." He thought for a moment. "For our suit radios to pick them up that clearly, they have to be close. And at that range, that's barely the size of a cutter, certainly not a capital warship."

Antoniy had walked up next to him. "Not terribly friendly of them." He looked closer at the image, and turned to Klaus. His voice was confident now, without any hesitation. "And that patch doesn't match the outline or size of any Navy cutter." He waved his arms. "This seems off. The *Ad Astra* breaks apart inexplicably, and then these guys show up almost instantly, claiming to be Navy crew?"

"You reckon they're behind it? Now what're the odds of that?" Klaus raised an eyebrow. Why would Antoniy become so suspicious all of a sudden? Why wouldn't he want to be rescued by a Navy ship? Could he be on the run, wanted by the authorities for some reason?

Klaus discarded that idea immediately – there was no way that bumbling Antoniy could have done something to attract that much attention. But..."Who else do you think they could be? Somebody your uncle – the one with that armed starship – ticked off? Sounds like you've got an idea."

Klaus had a sneaking suspicion just what sort of low-volume, high-value cargo a decommissioned missile boat could be used for. Smuggling had always been a very profitable, and therefore very competitive, business.

"There were rumors back at Calypso station about some of the Oort Cloud rebels acting up again."

Klaus snorted. "Yeah, but we're just sun-ward of Jupiter's orbit. Light-weeks away from the Oort Cloud. Besides which, we've got nothing they could possibly want."

A realization struck him, and he shot a glance down at the neck-mounted status-display lights on his suit. The spacesuit was military-surplus survival gear, and the 'friendly-forces in proximity' light was still off.

His voice sobered. "You might be onto something – they're not broadcasting a Navy transponder."

Just then, the console chirped loudly, a three-note sequence. Klaus frowned – that was a very specific notice. He held up a hand to stall Antoniy's response, and turned back to the console. "Hold on kid, this is important."

His hands flew over the keyboard, summoning the alert to the fore. Very odd – the ship's communications system was announcing that it had finished re-booting, which was expected, but also that there was a message in the secure inbox – which was not expected. Only a few people knew about that inbox, used for some of the off-the-books work that Klaus and Captain Sidonia had used the ship for. The only people that Klaus was aware of who knew the commands to send to that inbox were either in the Navy, or in 'Legitimate Business.'

And one of them had messaged him. That was either very good, or very bad. He brought up the message itself.

"First responders are hostiles. Help on the way. " Okay, so that was both very good *and* very bad. There was no sender listed, but then this inbox was set up so that it didn't require a stated originator for each message.

Antoniy must have read over his shoulder. "So it *is* pirates, then. Could there be someone on board that they want dead?"

Klaus shook his head, puzzled. An odd question. One hell of a jump to an unlikely conclusion. "Not bloody likely. This isn't the movies, kid." Could this be some sort of botched sting operation? A Navy ship shadowing the *Ad Astra,* waiting for pirates to show up? Who else would be nearby enough to assist? "If they wanted to kill they wouldn't have approached this close. They'd stand off and bombard us into wreckage. My guess is they're just pirates operating out of the Asteroid Belt."

"But they *did* shoot out the crew quarters! We're the only ones left, and that's mostly just dumb luck on our part!"

The kid had a point, except that he clearly didn't understand cargo ships. "Most freighters have the manned sections amidships. But this old thing" he patted the bulkhead "has 'em all the way in the bow." He frowned. "Well, *had* them there. These pirates probably just thought they'd only disabled the forward reactor."

"That's still terrible! What do we do?"

Klaus laughed. "On the contrary, it's good news. For us, at least. Pirates are out to make money, they're here to loot the ore. This tub carries her contract cargo externally. Mark my words, they won't even board the ship. Just strip the cargo off. The crew – us – aren't the target. We'll just sit tight in here and stay out of their way. They won't trouble us." Even better, if the loss of the *Ad Astra* was ruled to be due to piracy, Klaus wouldn't be held accountable. With the *Ad Astra*'s cargo taken and her surviving crew not pursued, there was little question as to how a review board would rule.

"Are you joking?" Antoniy threw his hands in the air. "They've destroyed your ship, killed the crew and you're not going to do anything? Not going to fight them?"

"With what?" Klaus retorted, his voice rising. "We're outgunned and outnumbered. Nothing to do but hide." He jabbed Antoniy in the chest with his index finger. "I don't like it either, but we're not the Marines, it's not our job, and we couldn't do it anyways."

Antoniy leaned away, defensively. He seemed about to respond, but then double-checked the display of the pirate ship. "You said something about pirates not boarding us?" He pointed at the display. "How close to us is that?"

Klaus looked at the screen. A half-dozen or so man-shaped black smudges were trekking along the *Ad Astra*'s hull, towards an airlock. The same airlock which Klaus and Antoniy had exited through only recently. "Very close."

The pirate ship was nearer now, undoubtedly so that they could deploy the boarders. Klaus could now make out the highly enlarged engines on the enemy vessel. The sort of over-built engines used only in the far reaches of the Solar System. "I'll be damned — those are from the Oort Cloud. Not ordinary pirates."

"Shit. Can you lock the airlocks from here?"

"No, not when we're on emergency power. It's a safety measure, in case of an accident." Klaus snorted. "I don't think the designers expected 'hostile action' to be worth planning for."

Antoniy's voice was tense. "Well, can we delay them, then?"

"We can seal the bulkhead hatches manually." Klaus looked around the compartment. "But we can't stay here, too many ways in." He paused, thinking. "Quick — grab as many rations as you can, and follow me. We'll make our way to the number-five lifeboat bay."

"The lifeboats? They'd just run us down. These guys are after us, not the cargo."

"Just trust me — I'll explain on the way." As Antoniy and Klaus hurriedly left the compartment, Klaus keyed a set of commands into the control pad by the bulkhead door, which closed behind them. "There, that'll hold them."

Klaus hurried aft to the next bulkhead door. "Ah, good. This is the aft blast door – it'll take them ages to pry it open after we lock it."

Klaus reached for the controls, but before he touched them, the door slid open.

A spacesuit-clad figure stood framed in the round opening. The jet-black suit did not match any of the *Ad Astra*'s crew.

For a moment, Klaus and the newcomer simply stared at one another, motionless. Then, the unknown figure drew something from his waist, and began to raise it.

Klaus hurled himself to the side. He had barely begun to move when Antoniy flew past him. The pistol fired.

Rapid-fire impacts walked across Klaus' chest and head. He was knocked back, hard, too stunned to move his arms and arrest his fall. A spider's-web of cracks now covered the faceplate of his helmet, completely obscuring his vision.

For some seconds, he couldn't breathe. It was a struggle to force his chest to move, to bring air into his lungs. His head was fuzzy. It was difficult to focus. Forcing himself to concentrate, he managed to finally take in a rasping gulp of air.

Okay, no pain. Might be a good sign, might just be shock. Or he might be dead.

Dazed, he slowly felt around on his chest and arms. No holes. He needed more air! The pressure indicator on his helmet read positive, so he ripped his helmet off.

The gunman!

Klaus' head shot up, and he looked around the compartment, ready to move. Then, however, he relaxed. Slightly. The gunman lay unmoving, slumped against the rough metal wall, right arm twisted far beyond its natural range of motion. Two closely-spaced holes in his helmet showed why he wasn't moving. Klaus stared dully, as if it were nothing more than a scene from some vid. Antoniy stood over him, examining the enemy's gun.

Klaus managed to croak, "Where the hell did you learn to do *that*, kid?"

Antoniy snapped his head up, eyes wide in surprise. "Forget that – how the hell are you still breathing?" He gestured to the four small dents on the upper chest of Klaus' spacesuit. "Four rounds center mass and you're *alive*?"

Klaus grinned, and thumped the front of his suit with one gloved hand. "Military surplus. Two centimeters of reinforced steel. Keeps me alive when things fail explosively." He grimaced at his cracked, now-useless helmet. "Helmet's dead, though. Thank God there's pressure here."

Antoniy nodded. "Told you these guys were dangerous. They must have landed troops ahead of us, bypassing all of those sealed bulkhead doors of yours."

"We'd best hurry, then." Klaus stood, still somewhat unsteady. "Have to get to the lifepod bay before they close in on us."

Antoniy stepped past Klaus. "I'll take point. We must assume they've landed more troops ahead of us."

Chapter 3: Raven

Three tense minutes later, they passed through the last hatch and entered the lifepod bay. Antoniy covered the corridor behind them as Klaus docked the hatch closed. His shoulder muscles ached with tension, and the inside of his suit was sticky with sweat. "There's only this entrance to the bay, and it's shut for good now. They'd have to cut through ten centimeters of steel to get in, and I doubt they would have brought an arc cutter just to board a freighter."

"Well, they do seem to be unusually well-equipped." Antoniy indicated the pistol he had liberated.

"Good point. We better hurry. I'll get her warmed up right away."

Antoniy turned around, frowning. "Get what warmed..." His voice trailed off.

Antoniy stared, open-mouthed at the craft parked in the bay. In stark contrast with the *Ad Astra*, this vessel was polished and sleek. Its long, thin fuselage and wide delta-wing-shaped heat radiators gave it a predatory look, reminiscent of atmospheric craft from the days when mankind was limited to Earth. A pair of rocket nozzles, charred from use, jutted from the rear, at odds with the smooth curves of the rest of the craft.

It barely fit within the twenty-meter length of the bay.

Antoniy pointed at it with one hand. "What the hell is that?"

"This is my Raven." Klaus beamed with pride, not breaking stride. "Isn't she beautiful?"

"Sure. What's a Raven?"

"It's our escape plan." He called over his shoulder as he caressed an indentation in her hull. The bow hatch of the craft slid open, and he paused at the entrance, smiling.. "Follow me. I'll start the engines." He ducked inside.

He didn't waste time. Before Antoniy could crawl in through the narrow hatch, Klaus was already strapped into the pilot's seat, studying a trio of large screens.

He patted the seat next to him. "Just strap in. The weapons console is deactivated." Klaus almost wished that the weapons were still installed, but he wasn't sure if he could have trusted Antoniy with them anyway. The kid seemed to have gained years' worth of competence in the past hour, but he was still an unknown quantity.

He paused. "Damn, I forgot – bay doors won't open remotely on emergency power." Klaus pointed out at the bay control console near the entrance. "You know how to open them from there, right?"

Antoniy shook his head.

"Of course." Klaus sighed, and unbuckled. "I'll go, then. Don't. Touch. Anything."

As he was partway across the bay, a high-pitched hiss came from the compartment entrance. A bright spot of light appeared at the top of the hatch, spraying molten metal into the bay. The light began to move, tracing along the outline of the hatch.

Klaus' jaw dropped. There was no way they could have deployed a plasma-arc torch *already*, but they had. He'd better make this fast. He ran to the bay-door control console, and entered the launch command.

The console flashed up a message: 'Personnel detected outside bay entrance. Launch aborted.'

Klaus gritted his teeth. Goddamn safety feature. No sooner had he thought that than he heard the bay hatch break off and hit the deck with a loud clang.

Time to go.

Klaus brought his fist down on the large, red button labeled 'Emergency Launch' and threw himself towards the Raven.

The bay doors flew open, and the artificial gravity re-oriented so that 'down' was towards the vacuum of space. A hurricane howled out through the open bay doors as the atmosphere, the Raven, and Klaus — minus a helmet — shot out of the *Ad Astra*.

Immediately, Klaus felt the pressure rising within his head, and precious air trying to force its way from his lungs. Panic set in. He was in a vacuum *without a helmet!*

His pulse jumped, and he barely stopped himself from reflexively trying to breathe. Breathing out now would be a very bad idea. His eyes pressed painfully, threatening to explode from their sockets.

The suit contracted around his body, quickly reaching standard pressure. That let him hold his breath without lung damage, and he forced himself to lock his throat closed as if swimming. He relaxed his muscles, to conserve what oxygen he had left.

He felt some blood vessels in his nose burst, but tried to ignore the pain and focus on his situation.

At least he was drifting toward the Raven. He compared his distance with his velocity towards it, running some quick calculations. He had, at most, a minute and a half before losing consciousness.

That would have to be enough.

The seconds passed with agonizing slowness. Klaus willed his heart to beat slower. He only had so much oxygen, and didn't dare waste it. At last, he was close enough to grasp the Raven's hatch, when something grabbed his arm.

Alarmed, he spun his head to find himself staring into a mirrored faceplate. No doubt one of the boarders — either he had been waiting outside the dock, or had been thrown out of the bay along with Klaus.

Startled, Klaus did the only thing he could think of — grabbed the oxygen hose leading to the man's helmet, and yanked as hard as he could. The tube came loose, and instantly, his assailant released his grip and scrabbled for the thrashing hose. The thrust of the escaping gas caused him to rotate as he attempted to re-attach the lifeline, and Klaus gave him a hard kick to get him away from the Raven.

Huh. That shouldn't have worked on a military-grade suit. Poor reaction as well. No soldier would have panicked like that. Typical pirates. Klaus toggled open the hatch and clambered inside. It sealed behind him automatically, and the airlock quickly re-pressurized. He could breathe again!

He stumbled into the cabin, still gulping down air. The pressure behind his eyes was gone.

Antoniy looked at him in surprise. "What the hell happened?"

How could the kid have missed all that? Ah, Antoniy must not have seen the fight. With the internal screens only showing the view directly ahead of the Raven, Antoniy wouldn't have been able to see anything else. And since the Raven's internal gravity would have dampened the acceleration, he might not even have noticed that they had launched.

Klaus drank the wonderful oxygen back into his lungs. "Boarders got in. Had to launch." As his pulse returned to near-normal, he strapped into the command seat and brought up the pilot's display. Hopefully the pirates would be too busy recovering their spaced crewmen, and would let the Raven slink off.

Suddenly, red flashed around the edges of the screen, and a warning tone blared. Apparently that had been too much to hope for.

"We're being targeted!" Klaus quickly toggled the flight controls. "Hope you're strapped in, kid!" He redlined the engines.

The Raven roared forwards, the power of its twin fusion engines reducing everything behind them, anything ejected from the lifepod bay – including boarders – to cinders. Banking hard towards the enemy spacecraft, Klaus fought the g-forces that crushed him into his seat, leaking through the best efforts of the Raven's gravity-management systems.

Another warning strobe flashed on the screen: incoming ballistics. Klaus reflexively threw the craft to the left, dodging the stream of high-velocity shells that ripped through the space where the Raven had been. He smiled grimly. Someone over there's got good reflexes, too.

"What the hell are you doing? Why are we flying towards them?"Antoniy shouted. "We've got no weapons, you said it yourself!"

"We can only dodge so long, and we can't hide. The Raven's stealthy, but the enemy is tracking us. We need to distract their sensors to make them lose contact." Klaus looked ahead at the enemy ship, using his craft's sensors to examine the enemy vessel. "Good. It's a converted asteroid. Not very maneuverable. Probably just has a civilian-grade sensor suite, too. Should be easy enough to get away from."

"Away from?"

"Watch." The Raven skimmed along the enemy ship, clearing it by a bare handful of meters. The uneven surface of the 'ship' made it the maneuver extremely dangerous, but Klaus knew there was no choice. They flew right at an array of sensor globes mounted haphazardly on its exterior. Just as they reached them, he threw the Raven into a ninety-degree turn, so that the twin torches of the Raven's fusion engines melted the sensors into so much useless slag.

"Wa-hoo!" Klaus exclaimed. "I've always wanted to try that, see if it works!"

He turned to beam at Antoniy, who was looking back at him with an ashen face. Klaus could see the marks on the armrests where Antoniy had gripped the plastic hard enough to deform it. Antoniy blinked. "Where the hell did you learn to fly like that?"

"Simulator." Klaus shrugged. "In my spare time, I run the Raven's systems in combat-sim. I'd always figured that the fusion torches could slag sensors like that." He wouldn't yet mention exactly *why* he'd gotten into that train of thought. If Antoniy didn't want to talk about his actual background, then Klaus wouldn't divulge his. "Hard to believe, but everything just worked just according to theory!"

He reached overhead and flipped a large red switch. The eye-searingly bright fusion engines spooled down. With those extinguished, the Raven would be difficult to re-acquire even if the enemy had operational sensors. Klaus pointed to the sensor icon for the blinded pirate ship, and then ticked off points on his fingers. "They're blind now, so they'll never find us. No other ships nearby. All we have to do is wait. They'll run off any minute now; after all, by now we could have sent out an SOS to the nearest Navy ship."

The Raven didn't have that sort of Navy-spec long-distance communication ability, unfortunately. He'd never needed it, in fact never wanted it before. But the pirates didn't know that.

After the Raven had drifted for a few kilometers further away from the enemy craft, the low-signature fricsim engines deployed to stealthily dump the Raven's relative velocity. Grabbing hold of the warped gravity well of Sol, they acted as an anchor, slowing the small craft. This far in-system, the relatively strong gravity gradient afforded them excellent traction.

Antoniy nodded. "Well, while we're waiting, mind explaining just how you've got this?" He gestured to the ship around them. "It doesn't seem to have quite as much, er, rust as the *Ad Astra*."

"Well, *technically* it belongs to Sidonia," Klaus replied, patting the console in front of him. "Of course, I subscribe to the old pre-spaceflight Air Force rules of ownership."

"Which was?"

"The planes belonged to the mechanics. The pilots only borrowed them for missions." Klaus grinned, and leaned back. "Who do you think keeps the rust out of here?"

"Oh, I get it." Antoniy winked at Klaus. "And what kind of 'missions' did pilots borrow this thing for?"

Before Klaus could organize a response, a loud chime rang out from the cockpit speakers. He ran his hands over the keyboard. That wasn't an alert he was expecting. At least not this quickly. "Oh, you've got to be kidding me."

"What?"

Klaus' hands were scrambling over the controls. "FTL sensors found something incoming." He shut down every non-essential system, making the Raven even harder to detect. "Something huge, at that. Too fast for a freighter. No idea what it is, but I'm assuming it's hostile. Should be coming in any minute now. This should be interesting to watch — I'll clear the hull."

He flipped a switch, and the hull turned translucent. Only the controls and screens in front of Klaus remained opaque.

He heard Antoniy's sharp intake of breath, and grinned at the inexperienced crewman. "Holoprojectors on the inside hull, cameras on the outside. Best view possible. Keeps the boredom at bay."

"Jesus Christ! Warn me next time!"

Klaus chuckled. He pointed at the sensor display. "At any rate, that contact should be coming in any second now."

For a moment, nothing happened as the two men peered out at the stars. Then, there came a soundless flash of crimson and white, and the unique shape of a fricsim-drive warship materialized. A dark sphere, at first visible only by the stars occluded behind it.

The image-resolution software of the Raven went to work, revealing more details. The skin was slate-gray, and two arrays of sails each stood out, glowing a dull orange as they shed heat. In the ship's side, a small docking port glowed light blue.

Klaus frowned. The gravity footprint — the 'bow-wave' — had indicated a much larger ship.

Then he gasped as the Raven's sensors pointed out that the warship — which he had assumed was closer — had come to a stop over ninety kilometers away. "That thing's got to be five klicks across!"

Even the *Ad Astra*, an unarmored high-capacity freighter, had only measured four kilometers from bow to stern, and her cylindrical shape had had a much smaller volume. There was only one ship that Klaus knew of that could be that large, and there was no way that she would be sent this far from Earth.

"Who the hell would build such a monster?" added Antoniy.

On the plus side, regardless of exactly which ship it was, this newcomer had to be Navy — nobody else could possibly have the resources to launch a ship of that scale. The Raven's IFF system registered the newcomer as neither friendly nor enemy, which is about what he would expect with a Navy ship. The IFF in Klaus' suit didn't register anything - it just didn't have the range to see the ship.

Still, what was a Navy gunboat doing out here so quickly? Klaus zoomed in until he could see, in letters large enough to be visible, the name *Overlord* emblazoned on the matte-gray hull.

Well. So *she* had been sent all the way out here. But what in blazes was her mission? Klaus appreciated the rescue — albeit the timing could have been better for his crewmates — but there was no way the Navy would divert such a ship for just him and Antoniy.

Then again, there was the old saying about looking a gift horse in the mouth. Klaus would ask later, *after* being picked up by that ship.

"I'll be damned! It's a Navy ship!" exclaimed Antoniy.

The pirates, in their converted asteroid, seemed to have drawn the same conclusion. Their cobbled-together vessel turned to flee, flinging off the repair-crew clinging to its outside. It had barely begun to move when all of the exterior lights on the pirate vessel suddenly went out, as did every other energy emission that the Raven's sensors could detect.

Klaus drew a strained intake of breath. Most likely a microwave beam from the warship. Must have fried everything electronic aboard the enemy craft. Klaus' eyes widened. A high-power beam like that would also have cooked any EVA crew from the inside out. Of all the ways to die, that was among the worst. "Lieber Gott..." His voice drifted off.

Antoniy slowly turned to Klaus, and blinked. Did the kid understand what had just happened? The Russian whispered, "How about we tell them—" he pointed to the massive warship, now closing towards the disabled pirate vessel "—that we're friendly. Before they assume we're hostile."

Klaus shakily nodded. Smuggler or not, Antoniy had the right instincts on this one. "Aye." The Raven's stealth systems were top-notch, at least when it had rolled off the factory floor. But Klaus was willing to bet that such a new warship would have an equally new sensor suite. He opened a whisker-laser communications link with the warship on the standard emergency frequency, and brought the Raven out of stealth.

Chapter 4: *Overlord*

As the Raven entered the docking facility, Klaus had to keep himself from nodding off. The adrenaline was draining out of him, and with it, his energy. He realized with a start that he had not gotten any real sleep for nearly twenty-four hours. Then again, that may have been a simple result of having had his ship — his home and workplace for the past year and a half — shot to pieces with him aboard it. Klaus looked over at Antoniy. The kid didn't look stressed, though. The resilience of youth, he supposed.

The Raven nudged against the docking clamps, which then secured the small ship. Klaus laughed to himself. After more than a year of sitting in its jury-rigged docking mount in the *Ad Astra,* the Raven finally got to lie in a dock which she was designed for. Must be like home again.

Klaus opened the hatch, and then climbed out into the hangar. The open space was large enough to house the entire production line of Ravens — and the factory that built them! Stranger still, it was almost empty, with Klaus' own Raven sharing the expansive room with a mere three Fleet cutters docked below.

It looked wrong. Even more, it smelled wrong. A bay like this should be filled with the reek of oil, of coolant, of half-a-dozen different chemicals. There should be the smell of ozone from welding, the shouts of repair crews. This utterly clean, empty bay felt more like a display model than an active military hub.

Klaus and Antoniy had stripped out of their space suits in the Raven, and in the antiseptic, military-grade cleanliness of the docking bay he felt out of place in civilian clothes. To compound the issue, a smartly-dressed ensign was waiting, 'Marius' printed on the name-tag on his chest. "Welcome aboard the TNS *Overlord*, Mr. Ericsson. And welcome aboard, lieutenant!" The ensign saluted.

Confused, Klaus began to protest that he was not a lieutenant – never had been, even when he'd been in the service – when he realized that the ensign was not looking at him, but rather past him. Turning, he saw that Antoniy was just exiting through the hatch.

Antoniy drew himself up and returned the young officer's salute smartly. "Thank you, ensign." His voice was tinged with friendly sarcasm, accompanying the grin on his face. "Glad to see that the Navy's timing is as *excellent* as always."

Antoniy? *Antoniy* was Navy? Klaus quickly thought through the day. He couldn't remember getting a concussion, much less one serious enough to explain this. He must have simply forgotten hitting his head on something. Maybe several times.

Or possibly it was just sleep deprivation, making him hallucinate. Imagine - clumsy Antoniy, a military officer? The idea was preposterous! Then again, at least this promised to be interesting, so Klaus decided to play along.

"Captain Conagher's compliments, sir, " the ensign enunciated carefully, "and she would like to speak to both you and Mr. Ericsson in her quarters. Follow me, sir."

"Conagher, you say?" Antoniy raised one eyebrow. "Lead on."

Antoniy and Klaus fell into step behind the ensign, who led them through a maze of intersecting corridors, always making sure they kept to the right-side wall. For their safety, he had said. Klaus barely registered the Navy personnel streaming past, or the drab metal walls, his thoughts lost in the events of the past day. There was precious little that made any sense. He leaned over and whispered, "You're a naval officer? Why didn't you tell me? *And what in blazes were you doing on my ship?*"

Antoniy smiled. "Marines, actually."

That made a bit more sense. It would explain why he was so out of his depth on-board a ship. God only knew Marines could get dizzy playing checkers. Three dimensions was just asking too much of them. Klaus chuckled to himself.

Antoniy continued, "Sorry for not telling you, but it never became important on the *Ad Astra*. I feel for the loss of your ship, especially as it's sort-of my fault she was attacked."

"What?"

Before Klaus could erupt into a tirade, Antoniy held up his hand. "Calm down. Let me explain. I was assigned to the monitoring team out in the Oort Cloud, keeping eyes on one of the rebel groups among the miners. We had picked up rumors that they'd managed to get their hands on some military-grade equipment."

Klaus snorted. "You don't say. I take it that these rebels are the reason we had such a bad day." Then again, they'd certainly gotten the worse end of it. Klaus raised his voice and addressed Marius. "What happened to their ship, anyways?"

"We've got boarding crews picking through the ship. When they're done, I imagine they'll scuttle the wreck."

Antoniy followed the ensign through a hatch which snapped open ahead of them. Much faster than the old doors on the *Ad Astra*, and quieter too. Klaus paused halfway through the opening, noting the large gap between the hatch and the bulkhead into which it retracted. Must be nearly two centimeters. Nodding, he continued through. It was a warship, he reminded himself, so that made sense. That much room meant the slab of reinforced steel was much less likely to jam open or closed if damaged in battle.

Up ahead, Antoniy continued, "I'd say you're correct. At any rate, my station manager figured nobody would watch a lowly grunt too closely, so he sent me back Earth-ward on the next tramp freighter to swing by."

"And that just happened to be the *Ad Astra*." Klaus nodded. The three men rounded another bend in the corridor. "Why didn't they just send a message? Seems like that would have been faster."

"They must have thought that the rebels had our communications tapped, so if they sent a message that would just alert them. But if I went undercover as a sailor, nobody would notice." Antoniy scowled. "But I figure they must have had the whole station's troop complement under surveillance, and guessed who I was when I left." Antoniy shook his head. "What I *can't* figure out is where a bunch of grimy rock-rats got the guts to come this far in-system. Or a ship which could take them this far without being spotted."

Klaus smiled thinly. "I see Marine training still doesn't cover enough about spacecraft. Think about it: What do you get when you hollow out an asteroid, add life support and stick an engine on one end?"

"A suicidal deathtrap?"

"True enough." Klaus laughed. The party paused at a cross-corridor, as a pair of maglev carts flew by. "But it'll get you from point A to B. Most of Earth's early starships were built that way. And since it's still basically an asteroid, with most of the systems shut off it would just be another comet coming in-system from the Kuiper Belt."

"I see. But what about those point-defense cannons they fired at us in your Raven?"

"Probably the same as are used to protect mining operations against flying debris. Anybody with determination and some technical skills could re-purpose them as weapons."

"Ah. That didn't occur to me. Makes sense, though." responded Antoniy.

"What do they teach you at the Academy, then? What good is an officer out in deep space who doesn't know the basics of starship design?"

"I signed up to lead strike teams, not poke through data like some fobbit. I'll leave all that boring crap about spaceships to the Navy squids. Just give me dirt under my feet and a gun in my hand!"

Klaus snorted. They were millions of kilometers away from any 'dirt' which didn't require knowledge of vacuum operations to survive. "I see the jokes about 'Marine Intelligence' really do have something to them."

"Who said anything about Intelligence?" began Antoniy, as ensign Marius halted before an unmarked door, holding up his hand to stop them. The junior officer tapped the intercom pad next to it. "Two to see the Captain." The hatch opened, and the three men walked through.

They found themselves in a well-appointed anteroom, perhaps four meters on a side, paneling hiding the ship's dull metal. A leather couch was bolted to the carpeted floor, and Klaus was briefly tempted to rest, but they remained standing. An ornate door dominated the wall ahead, bright golden Navy insignia stood out from the deep-blue of the door itself.

Two crisply-uniformed guards flanked a door at the far side of the room. One of them stepped forward, shone a light into their eyes, and then ran a wand up and down their bodies. He stepped back and mumbled something inaudible into his throat mic. After what felt like only half an eternity, the buzzer mounted by the guarded door sounded. A woman's voice with a slight Dixie twang spoke from it. "They check out. Send 'em in."

The two halves of the door snapped aside, and air hissed out. They thought of everything, Klaus mused, even positive pressurization. He was used to positive pressure isolation in some of his old labs, but it seemed like overkill this deep inside a warship. Exactly what kind of threat were they guarding against, anyway?

Without a word, Antoniy walked through the opening, and Klaus followed. It closed behind them with an audible, deep 'thump' as pressure was restored. In front of them, behind a desk, sat the Captain. Blonde, athletic, mid-forties by Klaus' estimation.

She spoke first, voice matter-of-fact. "Gentlemen. Glad to see that you survived. I trust that my message arrived in time?"

What message? Klaus wracked his brain for a moment. Could she mean the one that only arrived *after* the *Ad Astra* was destroyed? That was really the only candidate.

He opened his mouth to ask, but Antoniy beat him to it. "Captain Conagher, ma'am. This is a long way to come to save a former student."

"What?" Klaus blurted, too tired to think first. "Never mind, my ears must not be working today. Anyway, it's a good point. Not that I'm complaining, mind you — far from it — but how *did* the Navy know to be out here so quickly?"

Conagher steepled her fingers and said nothing, face impassive.

Klaus paced. "And with the *Overlord*, at that? Last I heard, she was still going through her trial runs in cislunar space. Trying to work the kinks out of that experimental new drive system, supposedly."

Captain Conagher raised an eyebrow. "That *new drive* is supposed to be classified material, Mr..." she glanced pointedly at the display screen on her desk. She evidently knew who he was already, but then the Navy did teach a person to follow protocol. "...Ericsson – how did you come to hear of it?"

"I wrote my thesis on the applications of quantum multi-positioning machinery, and I served on the board which approved it for construction," he pointed at the captain's screen. "As that box probably told you already. Come to think of it, most likely I've met whoever you've got working on it belowdecks." He could think of a few of his colleagues who would have jumped at the chance. Heck, he had managed to have himself placed on the fast-track to that position, before the Navy threw a fit at him getting advice from a friend. Some friend.

The Captain held Klaus' gaze for a few seconds, and then nodded slightly, as if to herself. "Doctor Johann MacDougal is part of our engineering team. He's aboard until the new drive works reliably."

Klaus snorted, surprised. He'd never have guessed *that* name. Or maybe he should have. After all, the day had started quite badly. "Johann's aboard? Someone managed to pry him out of his comfy deanship? And now he's loose aboard a warship, no less?"

Out of the corner of his eye, he spotted Antoniy staring at him. Let him stare. Apparently, the Marine wasn't the only one with surprises today.

Klaus shook his head. Of all the people, Johann. That rules-lawyering tweed-jacketer who'd gotten Klaus drummed out of active duty? Who'd gotten him banished to the *Ad Astra*? "Ma'am, Johann's a researcher, not an engineer. Oh, he can describe the *theory* of the thing better than anybody else." Which was *why* Klaus had asked him for advice on the schematics. Sure, they were classified, but..."I think Johann's the only person who actually understands how *and* why the underlying theories work.

Even so, he couldn't build a working mousetrap, much less a warship drive."

He wanted to say more, but snapped his mouth shut. He'd never been very good at when to keep silent. Of course, Johann also couldn't keep his damn mouth shut. Without considering the consequences for Klaus, the man had cluelessly revealed their conversation to the harpies over at the Intelligence Directorate, and they'd had Klaus thrown into 'reserve status.' With years left on his service tour, that kept him on reserve-pay and still obligated to report his location to the Navy.

He blinked his eyes and exhaled slowly, willing his jaw to unclench, trying in vain to banish the growing migraine. A headache was the last thing he needed, on top of his exhaustion.

Maybe his tired mind was playing tricks on him, but he thought he saw a hint of a smile as the Captain answered, "That certainly matches how the trial runs have been going." She glanced again at her desk display. "But I see that you have some applied experience in the field?"

She damn well had more information than that. The one overarching rule of the Navy was that paperwork and records never die. But still, he may as well be polite. He may have hated being "reserve-d," but at least he wasn't in prison. No sense pissing off Navy officers any further. "Yes, ma'am. I've worked with designs to move small objects a few meters away – say, a lab animal across a room. But I haven't done anything larger or further than that."

"That'll have to do. How would you like a job as a contractor? We're not heading back in-system for a while yet, so you're stuck aboard for the foreseeable future. I need that drive working before we reach Andromeda station."

"When will that be, er, ma'am?"

"Classified. Let's just say I want it yesterday."

"What's the rush?"

"Classified."

Klaus hesitated. Same old Navy. Of course, it would be a great opportunity for him. On the downside, he'd have to work with Johann again, but on the upside he'd get to play with the biggest QMP system ever made. That was quite the prize, one heckuva carrot.

Apparently, the Captain misread his hesitation, because she added, "Or you can spend your time under guard until we return to Earth. As you know, much of the ship is highly classified. We can't have a non-verified civilian looking around."

And there was the stick. "Ach, you don't need the threats." He smiled. "When do I start?"

"Immediately." The Captain pressed the intercom button on her desk. "Ensign Marius, please escort Mr. Ericsson to med bay for chipping, and then to his quarters. He is assigned to Dr. MacDougal's project under Lieutenant Ranjit starting first thing tomorrow, so also show him where the auxiliary engine room is located."

Well. That was fast. He had expected a long wait while he was verified. Or rather, re-verified. Had the Navy always worked this quickly? Or was everything just being distorted by his migraine? Well, so long as it got him to a comfortable bed soon, he could deal with it.

^^*^*^*^*^*^*^*^*^*

Antoniy watched Klaus leave the office. He turned back to the Captain, a faint smile on his face. "Thank you again, ma'am, but really, though — how *did* you know to be out here in time to save my skin?" He frowned, glancing at the door through which the older engineer had left. "*My* skin, right?"

Wait. That had come out much more familiar than he'd intended. He was getting sloppy. He ran his fingers through his hair, and straightened, "Sorry, ma'am. I just nearly got killed without being able to defend myself." If Klaus hadn't pulled him off of his lunch break – in the kitchen, adjacent to the supplies bay of the *Ad Astra* – he would likely never even have felt the blast coming. "It's got me a bit on edge."

The Captain grinned. "Regretting transferring to Intelligence section already?"

That snapped Antoniy out of his woolgathering. "No, ma'am."

This felt entirely too much like one of Captain-Instructor Conagher's classroom 'discussions.' The ones where she taught students to watch their wording by embarrassing themselves in front of the other cadets. He decided to watch what he said.

"Good." She nodded, her expression still unreadable "Please sit down." She drummed one finger idly on her desk. "I'd hate to think that one of my best students was having second thoughts."

Antoniy, if he was being honest, knew full well that he was *not* one of the top cadets at the Academy. He was good, yes, but not *that* good. Therefore, the Captain must either be testing him, or she must want something.

Best to turn the tables, then, and go on the offensive, ask questions of his own. He gestured to the office around them. "I have to say, for a ship of this scale, I expected the Fleet Admiral himself in command. On-board, at least. Never thought he'd miss a deployment like this." Or a photo-op this grand.

"Captaincy assignments are need-to-know, and you already knew that."

"Fair enough." Basically, she was telling him to try again. "Do I need to know why the *Overlord* is here?"

"The Admiralty ordered us out to Andromeda station. We're to rendezvous with Commodore Petrakov, and take further orders from him."

"Petrakov? The cowboy?" Antoniy leaned back in his chair, fully aware that Conagher had not really answered his question. But what intrigued him was the Commodore. He grinned.

"I take it you don't like his leadership style?"

"The opposite, actually. I have to admire his style. Admittedly, the proper way to raid an uncovered enemy facility does *not* involve having the sector commander personally kick in the door." He laughed. "I can't really fault his initiative, though –

our best operatives could barely keep up with the old man. But as they say, if you're under his command, best prepare for an interesting experience." He paused a heartbeat, then added, "So why do I need to know this? Er, ma'am?"

Conagher tapped her console, and leaned forward. "You heard my conversation with the surprisingly well-informed Mr. Ericsson." She raised an accusing eyebrow at Antoniy.

He held up his hands. "Don't look at me. I said nothing to him. Besides, I was never briefed on your mission."

She nodded, continuing in a neutral tone. "Until recently, this was just a shakedown cruise, with a skeleton crew and far too many civilians. Our Marine contingent is thin, most of them green. Well trained and highly recommended, yes, or else I would not allow them aboard my ship. But green."

Antoniy leaned forward in his chair. "And you could use my help?" She must really be desperate, if she proposed putting a spook back in charge of real Marines.

Conagher leaned forward. "Exactly, Lieutenant."

Still seated, Antoniy saluted. "Aye, ma'am. What are my orders, ma'am?" Not strictly protocol, but he wanted to make a point.

Conagher paused, then gave a thin smile and steepled her fingers. "As you said, Lieutenant, prepare for an interesting experience."

Chapter 5: Marius

Klaus found a small vehicle waiting for him outside the Captain's office. It looked rather like an elongated, open-topped golf cart, except for the way it floated a few centimeters off the deck. Maglev, interestingly. Expensive technology, and for a golf cart, yet! After the *Ad Astra*, he found it hard to get used to the utter waste of resources here. He glanced over the light-brown deck, spying the telltale silvery strips embedded into its smooth texture.

He laughed at Ensign Marius, perched in the driver's seat. "You brought a maglev cart for me? Those are reserved for well-connected civilians and senior brass!"

The ensign sat at attention, looking uncomfortable. "Nevertheless, sir, it's the transportation which we have arranged." He gestured to the passengers side. "Please have a seat, sir, and we'll head over to the med bay."

Klaus climbed aboard and settled back. His knees ached, and his headache just wouldn't quit. Despite his words, he was grateful for the chance to rest. "Huh. Bit more comfortable than I'd expect on a warship. This vehicle can't possibly be fast enough to get around a ship this size, though."

"These are for the VIPs, normally." The ensign swiveled his seat to face Klaus. "The crew just goes superman." He paused. "Uh, that means we use the grav systems to 'fly' down the corridors."

"Ach, I know what supermanning is." Klaus growled at the ensign, who could not have been past his early twenties. "I've been working on starships since before you were born. I *invented* supermanning." So far as the kid knew. Klaus rapped the base of his seat. "Now, if it's designed for some soft desk-jockey, this crate must be damned slow. So why don't we just save time and fly instead?"

"You'd need to be re-chipped, first, sir, before you can fly." The ensign tapped a command into his datapad, and the cart took off down the corridor.

"Chipped?" Klaus asked. "What's wrong with my own chip?"

"Yours lacks several necessary systems, sir."

"What? It's only six years old! An implantable beacon doesn't go obsolete *that* fast!" Even though he was talking with Marius, Klaus' attention was on the corridor as they flew past. The brown-and-blue color scheme wasn't surprising, by itself – all spacecraft used a similar interior color scheme. What was surprising was the size of the corridor – Klaus estimated that it must be three meters square, far more room than could possibly be necessary. "And stop calling me 'sir'!"

Ensign Marius swallowed, "Yes si—ah, well, chipped persons are tracked by the ship's systems. It's so that the ship can tell friendlies from enemies in case of a boarding action." he grinned. "Not that anybody'd be dumb enough to try that on a Fleet cruiser."

Klaus scowled, "I know that." The ensign's grin disappeared, as Klaus turned his head to face him. "You still haven't explained why mine won't work."

The ensign sobered. He drew a deep breath, and answered in a steady monotone, eyes straight ahead. Clearly a well-practiced speech. "As part of their security function, modern chips are all but impossible to remove by force without being destroyed. They also tell the computers where you are, how fast you're moving, and in what direction. That lets them control the grav systems to maneuver individual crew through the corridors." The ensign waved a hand towards the capacious corridor around them. "Where most ships have separate passages for cargo and personnel traffic, we use a single corridor for both. Sir."

"Ah." That explained these plus-sized corridors. Klaus pinched the bridge of his nose and closed his eyes, the imminent headache drawing closer. He berated himself. Tired or not, he should not have barked at the kid. "Look, I appreciate your help, but —."

He stopped talking. They were approaching a T-junction at speed, and Klaus braced for the cart to decelerate. But it didn't. Klaus shifted and leaned into the turn to account for lateral acceleration.

The cart turned right, suddenly and sharply, around the corner, and Klaus almost toppled off the cart, *into* the turn. "What the—?" He exclaimed, clutching the grab-bar to keep himself from falling. He had felt no lateral acceleration, even though the sharp turn ought to have thrown him back into the cart.

Klaus peered below his seat. "Hm. Small gravity generators in the vehicle here. Why not just hold your passengers in place with Krugerrands? It'd be cheaper."

"What VIPs want, VIPs get." The ensign shrugged, hiding a grin. "Can't have Admirals or senators falling off the cart." Admirals with a capital letter, senators without, Klaus noticed.

"Ah."

After several more hairpin turns, Klaus relaxed enough to release his death-grip on the cart's grab-bar. A few moments later they pulled to a halt at a featureless stretch of the corridor. At first, Klaus could see no reason why they had halted at that specific location. Only when the ensign stood up from the vehicle and approached the wall did Klaus spot the hatch.

Like all of the others they had passed, this one bore no label or distinguishing mark at all. Only its slight protrusion from the wall betrayed its presence.

Ensign Marius keyed it open, and stood aside for Klaus to enter. "Go on in, sir. I'll wait out here."

Klaus stepped through, and stared. It was Frankenstein's laboratory! The compartment, perhaps ten meters on a side, had its walls lined with machinery of all shapes and sizes. Four large operating tables were stowed in the corners of the room, with rails on the floor ready to move them, he supposed, into position for use. Each one sported a rack of robotic arms , which looked capable of re-building a Marine using nothing more than his dog tags. Would probably be an improvement, too.

The door at the other end of the room opened, and a tall, thin man stepped through. His white lab-coat was the uniform of a medical specialist, but in this lair of a laboratory it lent a certain 'mad scientist' air. He held his datapad in front of him with both hands, like a shield. "Mr. Ericsson, correct?"

"Yes."

"Good. I'm Lieutenant Baker. You're here for an exam and a new chip, right?"

"Yes on the chip." Klaus frowned. "But I don't need any exam."

"It's mandatory for anyone coming aboard, I'm afraid. It only takes a minute, though. No need for worry."

"If it's necessary, then go ahead.." Klaus sighed. He was tired, and wanted his rest, but the exam would probably take less time than arguing about it.

The corpsman reached into a pocket on the front of his uniform and attached a square-tipped probe to his datapad. "Ah, here we are. Your hand, please." He placed the flat tip against the inside of Klaus' wrist, and held it there for five seconds. Klaus' wrist tingled as a mild current ran up his arm. But it wasn't all that painful, and he was too tired to ask about it.

Lieutenant Baker withdrew the probe and glanced at his screen. He nodded crisply. "Very good. DNA matches your file. All readings within normal body parameters. Pathogen scan returns negative." He looked over the top of his 'pad at Klaus, and added, "You're good. No issues detected."

"Of course," Klaus answered. He always passed his physicals. He eyed the probe. Apparently, the thing couldn't detect anything about being dead tired. "And the chip?"

The Lieutenant held up a syringe.

Klaus eyed the needle. "A hypodermic? That's it? I'd hoped for one of the larger chips."

"Not necessary. This is easier, cheaper and safer." The corpsman looked at Klaus, one eyebrow raised in question. "You're a Marine? Miss the scars of the old models?"

Klaus opened his mouth to respond, but Baker interrupted him He looked Klaus up and down, pausing at his mid-section. "Hmm, no, you don't have the build of a Marine." He paused, then snapped his fingers. "Ah, I see. You must be from Engineering. In that case, I'm sorry to say you can't play with the needle-inserted chips. Not re-programmable and all that. They stay in the muscle, so it's all but impossible to get at them anyways."

"So it'll stay with me for life?" A waste, if he couldn't tinker with it.

Lieutenant Baker shook his head. "Oh, no, they biodegrade after five years or so."

"Get on with it, then, doc." He rolled up his sleeve.

A few minutes later, Klaus exited the medical bay, gently rubbing at the sore spot on his right shoulder.

Marius stood by the cart, exactly where he had been when Klaus had gone in. Klaus grinned at Marius, and pointed to the cart. "Now you can send this *kinderwagen* back to wherever you got it. It's been a long day, and the sooner we get quarters sorted out, the sooner I can get some sleep."

The ensign nodded, tapped at his datapad, and the empty cart sped off down the corridor. "Fair enough. Repeat after me,

please: 'Computer, request standard flight to civilian cabin…'"
Marius glanced at his datapad. "…E37. Execute." He vanished
down the corridor in a blur of movement.

Klaus blinked. Either he was getting groggy, or the flight
was faster than the transit corridors he remembered. He repeated
the proper phrase, and instantly the corridor walls were blurring
past him. He grunted as the two gees of acceleration hit him, but he
grinned nevertheless. He really missed this form of transit. The *Ad
Astra's* grav systems probably would have killed him if he ever
tried to get around this quickly.

After the initial acceleration, the familiar feeling of free-
falling was reassuring, even though he was moving much faster
than he was accustomed to. Fast enough to make even a veteran
feel a slight twinge of nervousness. Furthermore, when he turned a
corner, he was surprised to feel several gees of lateral acceleration.

He had expected that the gravity systems would
compensate fully, to make for a more comfortable ride. It made
sense, of course, that a warship would prioritize speed over
comfort, but why spend the money on grav systems for the golf
carts, and then skimp on those same compensators for the people
who actually work for a living? He clucked reprovingly to himself.
Typical Navy.

Less than a minute later, he felt the forward tug of
deceleration. While he knew that he must be hitting several gees,
the gravity systems let through only a single gee, no more than
normal standing upright. This prevented blood from pooling in his
feet, which he appreciated, given how close he was to falling
asleep anyway. He landed gently outside yet another nondescript
hatch, where Ensign Marius stood waiting.

"Here's your room, sir." He said. When Klaus did not answer, the Ensign coughed to draw Klaus' attention, and repeated, "Here's your room, sir." He checked his Navy datapad again, and nodded. "It's already keyed to your chip, so you can open the door by addressing the ship's computer."

Klaus shook his head to clear the cobwebs. It didn't help. He was a bit angry with himself for having lost focus, making the young ensign repeat himself. He was supposed to set a better example than that, after all. He tried to keep the gruffness out of his voice, and failed. "I'm very familiar with this sort of system, kid."

"Okay, sir. If you have any questions, you can call me by—"

"Very. Familiar."

Marius got the hint, and grinned sheepishly. "In that case, goodnight sir." He took off down the corridor.

Klaus shrugged, dismissing the conversation. He supposed Marius was a decent enough sort, for the Navy. He was just too tired to care. He voiced the door open, fully expecting a basic cabin, about the quality of his old one on the *Ad Astra*. He did a double-take. The room was enormous, and elegantly appointed, like no military bunkroom had any business being. It had wall-to-wall carpeting, no less, and ambient lighting in some shade of orange that he presumed was supposed to be relaxing. The king-sized bed along the far wall pulled at him, but he took a deep breath and pushed his tiredness aside. It might not be his room for long, but for now it was his corner of the giant ship. Best see everything that was here.

The closet was stocked with uniforms, although he was too tired to catalog them other than noting that they were Navy, and that there was nobody hiding behind them to jump out and kill him in his sleep. Why had he thought that? No matter. He opened the door to the head, and was surprised to find a spacious shower. The room belonged in a five-star hotel! He wondered what lucky civilian bastards the room was normally reserved for. Then again, the ensign had mentioned that the ship was designed to carry VIPs. That just left the question of why *Klaus* was given a luxury stateroom.

He'd worry about that later. Maybe after he slept, and his mind could think.

There was even a small kitchenette, off to one side! His stomach growled, telling him to inspect it more closely. The *Ad Astra* had, to no great surprise, an extremely limited menu when it came to food. And he hadn't eaten in what, forever?

He padded over to the faux-marble counter, leaned on it for support, and then rapped the surface with his knuckles. Good. At least the Navy hadn't wasted weight on real marble. He examined the odd-looking wall oven, puzzled at first. He blinked a few times, and then it came to him. It was a full auto-kitchen. He'd always wanted to experiment with one of those, but he was just an engineering tech on a rust-riddled freighter, and those auto's certainly weren't cheap.

He paged through the auto-kitchen's product display. Fancy stuff, but a bit too exotic for his taste. He couldn't even pronounce half the stuff there. Where was pizza? Where was peanut butter? Where was the speckpfannküchen?

Ah. Here was something he recognized, at least. Klaus punched in his order, and checked the time required for processing. Ten whole minutes? Auto-kitchens were pretty new gadgets, so he had thought they should be much faster than that. What was the machine doing, catching the fish first? His stomach growled again, and he silently promised it the best sandwich ever.

He straightened up from the display, and his vision swam. He should probably sit down to wait. May as well test how soft the bed was — in a suite like this, it was probably ridiculously soft.

He sat down on the bed, and sure enough, sank a good four inches into the mattress. Typical. The room was probably meant to be for politicians, well-heeled VIPs and other ground-sider wimps. No true spacer would trust a bed like this – too much of the room was wasted, and it was too soft. If gravity were lost it wouldn't be a good surface to push off of.

He leaned back, testing the pillows. As expected. Ludicrously soft. It was downright unnatural. If the crew of the *Ad Astra* had seen him in a bed like this, they'd have laughed themselves sick.

He could never sleep in a fluff-pit like this. As soon as he finished his sandwich, he'd have to find something to place on top of the mattress, to make it hard enough that he could—

He slept.

Chapter 6: New Day

A sharp beeping woke Klaus the next morning. Eyes closed, he fumbled his hand toward the nightstand, trying to find the source of his annoyance. And kill it.

His hand connected, hard, with a solid bulkhead. He sat up, nursing his bruised knuckles. At least now he was fully awake, but he no longer heard the alarm. Come to think of it, he didn't remember setting any alarm last night.

He found a clock mounted next to his bed. Seven in the morning, ship-board time. The same time he had woken up every morning for what seemed like forever, working on the *Ad Astra*. But this wasn't the *Ad Astra*.

That brought his thoughts into focus. Had yesterday really happened? He half-remembered the *Ad Astra* being destroyed, escaping on the *Raven*, and some gigantic warship appearing out of nowhere. It was either the weirdest day he could remember, or the strangest dream. He rapped on the wall next to him. Solid enough. No dream, then.

He wrinkled his nose. Something smelled bad, like stale sweat and old fish. And dreams didn't smell bad, did they? Fish? He remembered something about ordering a sandwich last night, and opened the door of the auto-kitchen. He wished he hadn't.

"Ach." The acid bite of hours-old fish attacked him, and he turned his face away. He grabbed the sandwich, holding it as far from his nose as he could, and searched for someplace to throw it away. Preferably, someplace airtight. He found a recycler set into the wall, toed it open using the foot pedal, threw in the old sandwich and slammed it shut. But the damage was done. His stomach remembered it was hungry, and complained loudly.

First, though, he had to get out of his old clothes. He stripped them off, and was tempted to throw them in the recycler with the fish. After all, they smelled almost as bad. But then he stopped. They were his only physical reminder of his time on the *Ad Astra.* It was logical to throw them out, because even as a contractor, the Navy would surely want him in uniform. But at least he knew his old clothes fit. Besides, somehow it seemed wrong. As if he were somehow discarding the memory of that ship's crew. He carefully folded up the old clothes and placed them on his bed.

After a lengthy-by-military-standards five-minute shower, Klaus felt human again. Wrapped in a towel, he opened the closet, remembering the Navy clothes he had spotted there the night before. This time, he took a closer look, and found two sets of crisp Navy uniforms. They were Engineering-duty issue, and the shoulders and sleeves were bare of any insignia. Civilian spec. He checked the size and length, and as he had expected, they fit him exactly. Impressive. The Navy must have found his file from the last time he was in the service.

Well, the uniform should have fit him exactly. Something must have been recorded wrong, as it was rather tight about the waist. He squeezed himself into it nevertheless, and decided he'd get it fixed in the evening, when his shift was over. After all, maybe the uniform was just new and would stretch out to its correct size through the day, if the waist button held. At least the shoes fit. Klaus stepped outside his stateroom. "Computer, request flight to nearest mess hall. Execute."

As the *Overlord*'s gravity system snatched him off of the deck and down the corridor, he reflexively shifted himself into his preferred position for supermanning – reclining, legs extended out front, hands interlaced across his stomach. After a few abortive tries, anyway. It took a bit of doing to get the arm movements just right to position himself. Every person had their own preference – the gravity systems didn't care what position you chose – but Klaus felt more comfortable going feet first.

The speed of the ship's system no longer surprised him, and he idly wondered just how fast the system would go. "Computer, request flight speed increase to maximum safe velocity."

Now he *really* felt the acceleration. Because of his feet-first orientation, blood rushed to his head as his speed increased rapidly, and the corridor around him flashed by in an unreadable blur of motion, too fast for Klaus to even begin to guess how rapidly he was moving. He shot around a corner, grunting against the g-forces that squeezed the air from his lungs.

"Whoo!" He looked around, hoping that nobody had overheard him. That must have been close to five gees!

He was just beginning to settle in and enjoy the ride when it abruptly ended. Blood rushed to his feet as he decelerated violently. He groaned absently, and then grinned to himself. Well, that's one way to wake up. Better than a cold shower, even.

The gravity systems deposited him outside a large, open hatchway. His stomach growled as the welcome scent of food – real food! - wafted through the wide opening. Two long rows of tables, each lined with sailors eating and talking, sat on highly polished, black-and-white checkered floor. Beyond them lay the serving area, backed by actual *trained* cooks. Maybe it was wishful thinking on his part, but at least they *looked* trained. None of them looked like the part-time machinist's mate aboard the *Ad Astra,* whose only talent lay in heating pre-cooked meals in a dangerously antiquated microwave, while simultaneously scratching himself, chewing tobacco and coughing over their food.

Having never served on a Navy ship with a complement greater than a few dozen, Klaus was overwhelmed by the sharp clicking of cutlery and the loud murmur of voices from at least a hundred people in the mess hall.

He blinked, and leaned on a table to steady himself. His blood hadn't quite returned to his head yet, and he hadn't eaten in what felt like days. On top of that, he could certainly do without the noise. Or the crowd. Especially the crowd – Klaus couldn't remember the last time he'd been in a room with this many people. The "mess hall" on the *Ad Astra*, converted from a single bunkroom, rarely sat more than three at a time. This sort of bustling crowd was just...unnatural.

But the food on the tables! Proper meals, cups, glasses, plates and all, not MREs. Hopefully that would be worth having to put up with the crowd.

He made his way through the diners to the serving area. The serving counter was lined with an assortment of hot and cold foods, vegetables, even fresh fruit, if he were any judge. On the other side of spotless glass and gleaming stainless steel, a staff of cooks were hard at work over stoves and grill-tops. He couldn't see a single pre-packaged food container.

He left with a half-pound hamburger, an omelet, and a lasagne on his tray, along with side dishes of pad thai and some naan bread. The plates overlapped each other, and threatened to spill over the side. But it was worth the risk. He was astonished at the variety of food available, and wanted to sample as much as he could, especially when someone who actually knew what they were doing was cooking.

And what a variety it was. God bless Navy cooks. Serving anything you want, around the clock.

"Klaus! Over here, lad! I'd heard you were aboard."

Crap. He knew that voice. Should have expected it, he realized, remembering his conversation with Captain Conagher. A tall man waved at Klaus from one of the tables. Two crewmembers sat opposite him, their suits bearing the bright-yellow shoulder-patches of the engineering crew.

Klaus would have to work with him, back-stabbing bastard or not, so he might as well start right away. Still, he had hoped to finish a nice, glorious breakfast first. No changing that now, though. He took a deep breath, and reminded himself not to frown. He carefully threaded his way over and set his tray down. "Johann, great to see you." He lied. "I'd heard you were aboard."

"Aye, that I am. Must say, living on a bloody warship of all places has been better than I expected." Johann waved a ruddy, big-boned hand at the platter of food in front of him, which held a burger much like the one on Klaus' platter. "However, I must say I miss proper food. You'd think I was the only Scotsman in the whole bloody Navy – none of yon cooks have the slightest idea how to make a decent meal. No haggis, or proper meat pies! All they make are these bloody Americanized dishes!"

Klaus smiled in spite of himself, glancing pointedly at his side dishes. If it wasn't Scottish, it was "Americanized". Apparently Johann hadn't changed a bit, either. For better or for worse.

"Och, but where are my manners?" The tall Scotsman gestured to the two figures sitting across from him. One solid and light-haired, the other with reddish-brown hair and - Klaus blinked - curves. "Meet my assistants, Petty Officers Jim North and Roberta Murphy."

"Murphy, eh?" Klaus groaned to himself. Had he really said that? He must not be fully awake yet.

She snorted, smiling guardedly, with one eyebrow raised. "Don't start. I assure you that I've heard every joke known to mankind about an engineer named Murphy."

"Ah." Klaus grinned back, glad she had not taken offense. He liked the subtle lilt in her voice, the slight roll of the r's. "You got me there."

Johann took a bite of his burger, waved it in Klaus' direction, and spoke softly. Well, softly by comparison to his usual standard. "The Navy gave me their best and brightest: these two." He paused, another bite. "They're bloody good mates, don't get me wrong, but they don't have a PhD between them."

"Johann," Klaus began, "the *Overlord* was only on her trial runs, and she's a warship to boot. They probably couldn't spare anybody more qualified." He heard a sharp intake of breath from North, and realized what he had just said. He chastised himself. What he had said was true enough, sure, but not everyone reacted well to plain facts. He turned to the two engineering ratings. "No offense."

"Oi!" replied the Scottish physicist. "But they should have at least found me more. The QMP is cutting-edge! You don't give a groundbreaking new drive mechanism like that a crew of three!"

Johann really was the same as he'd been back at MIT. Always insisting that his project, his team must always take priority over any others. Priority funding, best lab allocation, and first choice of grad students. At university, the man's ego had been a minor annoyance. Johann's work was important enough that he usually got the labs and the funding, and interestingly enough there had always been a long waiting list of grad students applying to work on his projects.

But a warship was not some academic lab. There was no way that his project could be the center of the universe. There were literally hundreds of other systems all more crucial to its combat effectiveness, every one of them probably still going through tests. And on a shakedown voyage, Klaus suspected that many of those systems would be demanding a lot of attention.

Klaus remembered all too well how difficult it had been to work with Johann's ego, with his inflated expectations, even if he had to acknowledge that the physicist was brilliant. Since he would now have to work closely with him, he decided he had better knock the situation into Johann's head the only way he thought would be effective: loudly and aggressively.

"I would bet that half the systems on this ship are 'cutting edge'!" Klaus began, his voice rising. "She's got three times the displacement of any warship before her, and probably uses those other 'cutting edge' systems all the time. And you wonder why they can't spare more manpower for some *untested* and non-critical experiment?"

Klaus saw a couple of sailors at the other tables looking at him, and realized that he had spoken louder than he should have.

North mumbled, "Yeah. We haven't even seen the L-T in days."

"Not a bad thing," chuckled Johann, "That Ranjit lad hasn't shown much interest. Keeps him out of our hair."

"Exactly," Klaus cleared his throat and started over in a quieter voice, "Bet his boss is also more interested in the other stuff on this ship. For instance, take the reactors. This ship's got eight of 'em, each one individually enough to power any *other* ship ever conceived by man. Line up the three tallest buildings on Earth end-to-end, and they'd all fit inside the hull. The armor and shielding on this ship's enough to run over a good-sized planetoid! Everything onboard this damn ship's practically experimental – they can't spare more crew for just another prototype."

"I thought you just came aboard," interjected Murphy. She met and held Klaus' gaze, as if daring the older engineer to deny her a part in the conversation. "How could you know something like that? Most everything about this ship is classified."

Heh. Boy, did Klaus ever know about *that*. "Because, God help me, I advised the board that approved this ship's construction."

"Huh. And you still don't like it?"

Klaus smiled. "The board approved the ship. I didn't. For the price of building this great big showcase of a ship, we could have fielded another entire squadron." He tapped his finger on the table with each word. "Five. Entire. Warships. Would have been much more useful than this one tub – there's nobody anywhere, except the Fleet itself, who could pose any sort of threat to the *Overlord*. Always building bigger and better weapons, to fight the last war. It's a powerful vessel, sure, but she can only be in one place at a time."

He stopped, glaring back at some sailors who were once again looking in their direction. No, he told himself, he absolutely was *not* bitter. Not about his sincere effort to improve this ship. Not about his friend getting Klaus' career shot in the foot. And *especially* not about how that same colleague had the job that Klaus had been wanting, even if he *had* advised against the whole project in the first place.

Johann cleared his throat, interrupting Klaus' thoughts. He spread his hands wide, his voice loud, as if imparting the wisdom of the ages. "Well, that's what the QMP drive's for, isn't it? So we *can* be in more places at once."

Chapter 7: QMP

Johann led Klaus and PO Murphy into the QMP compartment. The door whooshed closed behind them, making Klaus grin. The doors on the *Ad Astra* used to groan like damned souls, when they *did* close properly. This ship just felt so...*new*. It was downright refreshing.

And then there was Johann.

"I still canna get this damn thing to work!" He waved his arms in the air angrily. "Every time we run the test, the code comes back garbled all to hell!" He took a seat at a stool in front of a metal desk which was heavily bolted to the wall, and powered-up his computer. "Full-function state-of-the-art quantum standalone, this is," he explained loudly, tapping the case. "Fully isolated from the ship's network, and not some stripped-down access point."

Swiping his finger across the security scanner, Johann opened a file, and the screen filled with complete gibberish. He pointed an accusing finger at the random symbols. "And totally bloody useless! Have a look for yourself – it just can't be done. A quantum computer simply can't work unless it has a determinate, physical presence!"

Klaus pulled a stool next to Johann, and looked more closely at the 'text' on the screen. There were occasional strings that he recognized as programming code, but these were far outnumbered by a confused babble of symbols, many not even native to the programming language. Klaus raised an eyebrow. He swore that some of them were clearly not native to this universe, since his eyes hurt just from looking at them. "This, I take it, is what you get back?"

"Aye. Complete bloody quantum decoherence. We can send the computer into incorporeality and bring it back again just fine, but the code goes all to hell and it can't find its way home. My theory is the probabilistic liberties we take with QMP play some sort of hob with the algorithms in the quantum initalization — Och, don't look at me like that, Murphy, this makes perfect sense — leaving this bloody damn ... nonsense." He pounded one thick finger on the table, "And then we have to scrub the system and re-load the code, all over again from scratch."

PO Murphy cleared her throat. "That is, *I* have to re-load the code over again from scratch, sir. It takes the better part of an hour, and that is just for this simple computer, which makes the whole idea unusable for the Navy. At least we haven't had the physical circuits fried. Yet."

"Hmm." Klaus could certainly see how that would be a problem. "You mean the collider guidance, the plasma containment programs, stuff like that?"

Murphy nodded. "Glad to have a Navy man aboard, Mr. Ericsson. Perhaps you can explain that to Dr. MacDougal."

"Just Klaus will do," he answered, tapping his shoulder. "I'm a civilian, after all."

Johann paid them no mind. "But the thing is, you see, if I can just discover exactly how the probabilistic collisions between the QMP and the quantum code are fighting each other, then we would really have something to write up for the journals. Why, we would —"

Murphy shook her head and smiled at Klaus. "You see what I have to put up with?"

Klaus just chuckled, tapping the computer screen in front of Johann to get his attention. "I'll bet that your Navy brief did not include the words 'probabilistic collisions' or 'quantum decoherence' anywhere." Johann just glowered at him. "In fact, I'll bet that they said something on the order of 'just make it work.' Am I right?"

"Ach yes, but just think of the research we could do, my boy!"

Klaus gave him a sharp look. "I've already been down that road, Johann, and look where it got me." He waved his hands to forestall Johann's retort. "But look, why don't we just do what the nice Navy pays us to do, and find some way to make it work?"

Murphy looked at the ceiling, and added in a sing-song voice, "Only what I've been telling him for months."

Klaus paced, hands in his pockets. "Captain Conagher says we have to have this working by the time we get to Andromeda station. You've been puttering around with this for months now, so why the sudden rush?"

"I don't know, she said it was —"

"Classified, I heard." Klaus tapped on the computer's casing. "Have you tried sending a non-quantum computer, instead?"

"Are you daft?" Johann stared at him. "The operations to keep this ship from exploding are measured in yottaflops! Have you forgotten, man? That would take hours, if not days!"

"Ah." Klaus nodded, face reddening. Of course, he should have guessed that Johann would have already run the calculations.

Murphy said nothing, just sat stiffly at her console, staring intently at the screen.

"The irritating bit is," continued Johann, his voice calm again — or as near to calm as his voice ever got — "not all of the code gets corrupted, so it should be possible to find something that isn't bloody garbage, and make it work." He shrugged, patting the top of the computer casing. "So, we change the parameters and keep running test after effing test."

"I see." A surprisingly practical solution, for an academic like Johann. "Given enough data, you hope to see a pattern in what code survives."

"Exactly." Johann rose from his seat, and walked over to a hatch located directly opposite the one leading to the corridor outside. Tapping a command into the keypad next to it, he looked over his shoulder, and waved Klaus closer. "And to keep the Captain happy, let's start the first test of the day."

With a loud hiss of in-rushing air, the hatch slowly retreated inwards towards the testing chamber. After traveling a full thirty centimeters, it halted and receded sideways into the wall of the corridor linking the control and testing compartments. The movement was almost silent, but the vibrations that rolled up through Klaus' feet betrayed how heavy the blast door really was.

The chamber beyond was long and narrow, about four meters in width and at least a dozen in length. Three meters of height kept it from feeling cramped, though.

At the far end of the compartment stood the test rig: a white-painted metallic cube standing atop a sturdy table. Perhaps fifty centimeters on a side, the cube's surface was marred only by carrying handles and access ports.

"First, we inspect the rig, to make sure that nothing's shifted, and it's ready for the next test." Johann started across the room without even a backwards glance.

Murphy stopped by the entry, and added "And check the overpressure relief valve, sir." She knelt down to inspect the valve's intake, which was covered with a plastic cap. She checked off a box on her datapad.

Klaus nodded. "Vents to outside, I assume?"

"That it does, sir, er, Klaus."

Good to see that the Navy had seen to it that the compartment was made safe for testing. The unpainted steel gave the room an industrial feel. After the pristine, smoothly-painted feel of the rest of the ship, Klaus felt truly at home again. "This looks solid," he remarked, tapping the wall with a dull thud.

"Aye, titanium-reinforced ceramic with a carbon-lattice backing. Stronger than anything has any business being. Would probably stop a nuke. See, those officer types don't think that my little experiment is safe. So I have to go through the whole bloody routine of 'check the rig, close the hatch, lock the hatch, run the test, and then do it all in reverse." He rolled his eyes. "And the two assistants won't let me stay in the room to watch."

Klaus glanced at the Petty Officer, who gave him a 'spare me' roll of the eyes, and then studiously returned to her checklist.

Klaus suspected that Murphy might be the only reason that this test chamber wasn't already lined with little bits of Scottish physicist. "Well, you are messing around with some rather high-energy physics."

"Bah, it's perfectly safe." Johann waved dismissively over his shoulder, not looking up from his test box.

"In theory. And what if the whole rig botched the translation back to corporeality? Say, if it tried to fit too much mass into too little space?"

"Bah, that's impossible. QMP theory clearly states that matter won't emerge in densely-occupied space." Johann gestured around the room. "In any case, we pump this room as close t' a vacuum as it'll get for each test. Nowhere near a perfect vacuum, but less than fifty pascals of pressure. Easily below the danger limit."

"Isn't that the same theory that failed to predict that translation would mess with your computer's data?"

Johann completed his inspection, and stood. "All right, lad. Fair point." He patted the top of the test rig, his voice once again energized. "Regardless, let's get this piece of tripe ready, then." He attached cables to the open ports on either side of the cube. As each cable was inserted, PO Murphy would verbally confirm it and check off a box on her datapad.

"Osmium input, check. Computer IO, check. Trigger pulse input, check."

While the two completed their pre-test checklist, Klaus studied the receiving rig, nearer to the entrance hatch. If the experiment worked correctly — and from what it sounded like, that was unlikely — the test cube would be teleported from its current position over to the receiving rig. Just as importantly, the high-power quantum computer contained within the cube would still have all of its programming intact and ready to function. Not a long jump at all, but that wasn't really the point.

"Primary vacuum sensor, check. Emergency cutoff valve, check. Main power bus, check."

The walls of the compartment were lined with cylindrical capacitors, reaching from the deck to the ceiling. Klaus was no Luddite, but the thought of just how much power was stored in those metal cylinders, less than an arm's reach from him, made the hairs on the back of his neck stand up.

Johann stepped back from the test rig, clapping his hands once. "And that's that. All ready for the next test."

"Not quite, sir. The compartment integrity has not been confirmed." The Petty Officer stepped quickly over to a series of lights embedded into the bulkhead.

Johann sidled over to Klaus, and muttered under his breath. "Y'see what I have to put up with? Nothing *happened* last test, or the dozen before it. The room's as pristine as the day the ship launched, not a single mark on it. But don't try telling that to my resident rules-monkeys."

"Every check has its purpose, Johann." No sense tempting Murph - er, fate, after all. Klaus shuddered to think of what would have happened to the *Ad Astra* if he himself hadn't been thorough, some of his crew had called it pathological, in his system maintenance. Probably would have come apart at the seams just leaving port.

Not that it helped the ship — or the crew — in the end. He shook off the negative thoughts with a force of will. He needed to stay focused on this experiment. "We've already got one Murphy in the room, Johann. No sense inviting the other."

"Ahem," Murphy cleared her throat , "Compartment structural integrity, seals, and data recorders check clear, sirs."

"Bloody finally." responded Johann, walking out through the entry tunnel back to the lab.

Klaus followed, and Murphy stopped outside the tunnel, and tapped a command into the control panel outside. She spoke softly to herself. "Close the test seal, Murphy. Test seal closing, aye," as he checked off another box. She winked over her shoulder at Klaus. The hatch plug slid back into the tunnel and slowly advanced to seal the test compartment. It was tapered, larger at the interior side, so that any overpressure would push it tighter into its seals. When it reached the fully-closed position, a row of lights — two green, one orange — came on underneath the control panel.

Murphy tapped each of the lights in turn. "Compartment seal verified, pressure within acceptable limits." She un-clipped a keycard from a lanyard around her neck, and inserted it into a slot next to the control panel. The last light switched from orange to green. "Cleared to proceed with next test iteration. Sir."

Ah, good, Klaus thought. Maybe the Navy did indeed know Johann. At the very least, they had ensured that the physicist couldn't run the test until someone more...*practical*...verified that it was safe to proceed.

Johann patted the seat next to him. "Have a seat, lad; this'll take just a bit."

Klaus took the proffered stool, but his attention was locked on Johann typing away at the computer. The mess of symbols were quite rapidly being replaced by recognizable, albeit complex, code. "Shouldn't it take longer to overwrite all of the junk software?"

"Nay, although it used to. After the first dozen iterations or so, I figured it'd save time t' divide the code into sections. Very, very small sections, a few bits each. That way, the command overlay can quickly compare the software to the periodic checksums we planted, and over-write only when necessary."

"Isn't that all of the time?"

"That's the odd part, lad. Some of the code comes through okay, but it's never the same code. Ruins the program as a whole, but the bit-patterns themselves are often still there."

Interesting. "How much surviving code are we talking, here?"

"Eh, usually about twenty to twenty-five percent." The blue glow of the display made Johann's ruddy face look downright pale. "Enough to cut down on the time required t' re-load everything, thank God." He pointed at a progress bar creeping along the bottom of the display. "We're about a quarter done. It's mostly automated by now."

"If the recovery is automated, couldn't we have the functional code sections re-build the software by themselves after transition?"

"Tried that already, Klaus." Johann shook his head. "There's no way to predict which bits come through unchanged. No matter how redundant I make them, they just refuse to re-connect to each other without manual input. It's the damndest thing, too. The code's there, everything should work, but it just doesn't."

Very odd. "Still, at least it works as a drive." In theory.

"Aye. Except we would have t' manually re-boot all of the ship's systems afterward."

Murphy turned toward them, from her seat at the observer's desk. "Which defeats the purpose. The QMP drive is needed for tactical maneuvering, not travel. If we have to spend ten minutes with no grav, no reactor containment, no life support, no shields, no nav, all the while getting shot at, then the drive is useless to us. Too dangerous to use in combat, too expensive to use anywhere else."

She looked at Klaus, catching herself. "But of course, you already know that." She turned back to her console.

Klaus nodded. Leave it to the PO to put her finger on the truth. Osmium remained one of the most expensive elements in the system, absurdly difficult to obtain, and the QMP drive burned it like diesel fuel. "I see," Klaus said quietly. Murphy had a good head on her shoulders. Maybe she was here to supervise Johann, not the other way around.

He was at a loss regarding the code, though. No ideas on how to fix it. Maybe some other tack. He thought back to his student days, back to the other issues he and Johann had worked on. "Any progress on just *where* the cube goes between disappearance and re-materialization?"

It was the kind of question that would fascinate Johann, full of unverifiable theory. When Klaus had last worked with the technology, nobody had any idea where objects actually *went* while being teleported. Or whether they went anywhere at all recognizable to human perception. In theory, they were reduced to oscillating between thousands of superimposed quantum states, none of them with any certainty, meaning that they didn't technically *have* a location. Quantum machines that were teleported came back with their data corrupted and so couldn't answer the question of just where they thought they had been. Standard machines recorded nothing.

It sounded counter-intuitive, yet there had been no negative effects on the various living animals which had been sent through. The few humans who had gone reported various types of discomfort on the trip, but nobody had any idea where they had actually *been*. It was all quite strange.

"That's still a mystery for the ages, despite my research. It would be another one for the journals, if we only knew." replied Johann, then sighed. "But on t' other hand, if it'd make the bloody thing work properly, and soon, it could route everything through hell itself for all I care." He shook his head. "At any rate, let's just get on with this test."

Murphy called over her shoulder, hands on her console. "Aye, sir. Beginning test alpha-27, iteration twenty-three." She typed in a command. "Test run initialized."

Klaus' eyes were glued to the display fed from the cameras in the test room. No matter how many times he'd seen a QMP rig in action, it was still an amazing sight.

For a moment, the camera feeds showed perfect stillness. Then, the image rippled as heavy-duty capacitors discharged, pouring exajoules of power into the test cube's lattice of tubes. Much of the power was diverted to high-power lasers running through the center of the tubes, bent into the shape of the cube by focused gravitational fields.

The lasers ignited the gaseous osmium in the tubes, boiling it into a plasma. The last gasps of the electrical current ran through this plasma conduit, stripping off loose electrons.

Less than a heartbeat after the capacitors activated, the cube disappeared. There was no slow transition, no fading afterimage.

One instant the cube was there. The next, it was gone.

"Test vehicle launched." recorded PO Murphy.

Despite himself, despite his history with Johann, Klaus felt his lips pull into an ear-to-ear grin. This, now *this* was what he'd missed when drudging on the *Ad Astra.*

He held his breath, counting. QMP transitions rarely took longer than ten seconds. If Johann's assurances were anything to go by, then the cube would re-materialize in the target zone instead of back at the test rig, but Klaus wasn't getting his hopes up, not yet. After all, he hadn't had a chance to fiddle with the setup himself.

"And there goes our latest test." Johann sighed expansively.

Seven, seven-point-five, eig— the cube popped back into existence.

In the test rig, as expected.

"And the prodigal robot returns." Johann's resigned voice was beginning to get on Klaus' nerves. "A failure like the others."

"Maybe the code survived, this time." It came out more snappish than Klaus had intended. "After all, we still have to check it."

"Nope." Johann held up his datapad, waving it at Klaus. "The test program is made to send an audio file to my 'pad and play it. If you ever hear bagpipes after a test, *then* we've succeeded."

^^*^*^*^*^*^*^*^*^*

Two long days later, after a series of similarly non-productive test runs, Klaus was growing frustrated. They'd tried running multiple parallel computers, they'd tried altering the energy parameters of the plasma field, and they'd tried sending massively redundant processors.

PO North had even managed to convince one of the machine shop techs to fabricate enough non-quantum computers to brute-force the ship's operating calculations. They came through just fine, but even slaved together, they were useless for the calculations the ship would need when it emerged. Life support maybe, but never reactor control or firing solutions. Nothing that Murphy would call mission critical.

He handed Johann one of the sodas that he had gone to fetch, during their most recent test. "Is it back yet?"

The Scottish physicist nodded, chin resting dejectedly on his hand.

"Still not working?" Klaus asked, knowing the answer. "I feel like Edison, but do we really have to find ten thousand things that don't work?"

Murphy mumbled something under her breath, something about how much osmium they were using on each of the trials.

Johann ignored her. "Speakin' of which, have ye got any interesting ideas for what to change to make this work? Less osmium? More computers? Throw a virgin crewman in as a sacrifice?"

Klaus didn't think the idea was practical, and opened his mouth to say as much, but shut it when Johann's computer chimed. Johann read the message, and groaned.

"It gets even better, lad. That was Lt. Ranjit. The Captain wants to see us in her office."

Murphy looked up from her console. Her eyes looked tired. North had gone off-shift, and she had volunteered to stay on. The junior crewman's voice was slightly tense. "Us?"

"Him and I." Johann pointed at Klaus.

The Petty Officer nodded, let out a breath, and turned back to the display.

Klaus couldn't fault her. Maybe she had been tasked with containing the budget, as well as keeping Johann alive. No sailor that junior ever met directly with the captain, unless there was either very good news or very bad news to report. And there was an unfortunate lack of good news with the QMP testing thus far.

"Now?" asked Klaus.

"When else? Don't they know we have bloody work to do?"

A scant minute of high-g transit found the two standing outside the Captain's office once more. Johann looked a little green — probably not used to the speed of transport that Klaus had spec'd — but he took a deep breath, straightened his back, and commed the office.

The hatch snicked open, and the two men stepped through. It closed behind them, bolts sliding home with a series of audible thumps. Klaus and Johann were the only guests in the room. No Lt. Ranjit. No senior engineering officer. That spoke volumes to Klaus. The meeting was clearly *not* going to be about giving them the resources they needed. He tried to signal the physicist to be careful with his words, but Johann was not paying any attention to him.

The Captain looked up from her desk display, and spoke without preamble. "My apologies, but I'm rather pressed for time. I'll be brief." She fixed her gaze on Johann. "Can you get the QMP drive working in less than four days?"

Johann drew a deep breath to speak, and for a moment Klaus was afraid he would say yes, but then his shoulders slumped. "No. Not a single machine we've yet tested has come through as anything more than a lump of brain-dead circuits. I've got a theory that I'm workin' on, about getting the probabilities to cancel each other and —" He stopped, regarding the Captain a moment, "but, ah, it'll take two weeks at least before I get a definitive answer on it."

The Captain shifted her gaze to Klaus. "And do you agree?"

On second thought, that was more of a glare than a mere gaze. The Captain seemed as frustrated with the lack of progress as Johann and Klaus were. "Yes, ma'am. Unfortunately."

"I see. Well, in that case I'm sorry to say that it'll be delayed longer than that. We just got a message from Commodore Petrakov – we're to ready the ship for combat. That means we're shifting petty officers Murphy and North back to their normal duties, the machine shops are working on fabricating more spares and equipment, and we can't spare the energy for your tests."

Johann scowled. "So what in blazes are we supposed to do? I was on the verge of a bloody scientific breakthrough, at the very least!"

Klaus mentally rolled his eyes. Johann's complete inability to demonstrate any level of respect for his superiors, or at the very least for the people who supplied his paycheck, was one of his less...endearing aspects.

Conagher's expression did not change an iota. "Your breakthrough can wait. In the meantime, as a civilian, you are allowed to leave the ship when we arrive at Andromeda station. Until then, feel free to find something to do that doesn't get in the way of the crew. You are dismissed."

Johann stood silent for a moment, mouth opening and closing. Then without a word he turned and walked out of the door, just managing not to stomp his way out. Klaus shrugged and turned to follow.

"Mr. Ericsson, could you wait a minute." It was not a question.

He turned back, a knot forming in his stomach. There was something about how she had pronounced 'Mr. Ericsson', with the emphasis on 'Mr.', that brought back memories of his time in the regular Navy.

Bad memories. "Yes, ma'am?"

Captain Conagher gestured to the datapad on her desk. "I see here that you're ex-Navy yourself."

"Yes, ma'am. Reactor crew chief."

"Correct. As it happens, part of the reason we had to suspend your friend's experiments has to do with the ship's reactors. They aren't performing to spec, and the fitting-out crew we've got aboard doesn't seem to include anybody who knows what's wrong."

It figured. The Navy threw some kid through barely two years of training, and call him a 'reactor tech.' "And you want me to take a look at it, ma'am?"

"Do you have anything better to do?" Was that *amusement* in her voice?

Klaus grinned. She must have read his voice wrong. Truth be told, he was tired of beating his head against the wall with Johann's experiments. Especially as nobody would tell him what the urgency was. "Not anymore, no, ma'am. When do I start?"

"You'll need some rank, first. What grade did you...*retire* at?"

"Technically, I'm on reserve, but I left as a CWO-5."

The Captain nodded. "That'll do, Chief Warrant Officer. You're off unpaid leave for the time being, Captain's authority. Pay by standard scale. Head down to central engineering, meet up with Commander Ryves. He'll get you sorted where you're needed. I'll have a rank patch sent down for you."

"Thank you, ma'am." Finally, after only-mostly-metaphorically beating his head against a wall for days, he had some *real* engineering work to do. No more bloody guesswork, no more eye-straining poring over every line of garbled code. Klaus turned to leave the compartment, eager to begin.

Behind him, the Captain coughed pointedly. "You are dismissed, Chief Warrant Officer."

Klaus froze. Ah, yes. Military punctilio and all that. He turned around again. "Yes, ma'am. Thank you, ma'am." He gave his best rusty imitation of a proper salute, and then hurried out as quickly as his dignity would allow.

Chapter 8: Same Old Navy

Klaus chuckled to himself, mulling over his briefing from Commander Ryves, as he approached the reactor compartment. True to form, the Navy had not disappointed his low expectations, had not changed a bit. Officer first, engineer second. The lobotomy that comes with an officer's commission was still mandatory, apparently.

Commander Ryves, titular head of the Overlord's drive engineering, had filled him in on the problems the ship had been experiencing with the reactors.

'Filling in', though, was a gross overstatement. All that Ryves had been able to tell him was that the reactors weren't producing the amount of power which they were stated to be capable of. All of the Navy's by-the-book inspections of the reactors had shown no faulty systems, nothing out of the ordinary.

Klaus shook his head. And they called that man an engineer? Of course, he really should have expected no different. Real-world problems never showed up on inspections. These systems were so complex, that it was statistically impossible for some elementary-school test procedures to find their faults. The way he saw it, at least he now had a great opportunity. Or a great pain in the ass, depending on how it played out. It fell to him to find some way of making the reactors perform as they should.

With a sigh of mixed resignation and anticipation, he entered the number-five reactor compartment, ducking his head to squeeze through the tight ten-centimeter-thick hatch. As an engineer, he wasn't worried about radiation; the fusion reaction itself was perfectly safe. But the gravitational energies that supported it were not. If the reactor's control systems glitched, and the fail-safes didn't work, all hell could break loose. Hopefully, the reinforced armor that lined the reactor room would save the ship from catastrophic damage, but that would be little consolation to the unlucky techs, such as himself, working inside it.

The compartment itself was perhaps twenty meters across, its vaulted ceiling giving it an imposing cathedral-esque atmosphere. The echo of his service boots, even with their traction soles, bounced off of the hard walls, completing the image.

At its center, a column of high-power gravitational control nodes channeled a stream of ions into the reaction chamber, which was a sphere of overlapping artificial gravity waves fifty centimeters in diameter. The reactor was filled with water, which flash-boiled into steam from the enormous heat released by the fusion. In a design little changed over the centuries, the steam ran a colossal turbine which occupied much of the remaining space within the compartment.

Old, proven technology. Old enough that it could be run steady-state with old-style computing. Yet according to the Captain, it had somehow still found a way to malfunction. To look at it, everything seemed to be running smoothly. But, if that had been true, Klaus wouldn't be here.

One of the technicians in the room had noticed his arrival, and hurried over. "Glad you're here," he glanced at Klaus' still-civilian dress, "Ah, Officer Ericsson. How can I help you?"

No time like the present to get started. Klaus pointed at the reactor. "Well, let's start with a review of exactly what problems you've been having with this reactor." Commander Ryves hadn't been able to give him any specifics, or at least not any specifics that meant anything.

The technician tapped the console next to him, which instantly displayed a detailed schematic as well as a diagnostic readout of the reactor's critical points. Klaus nodded, happy to be among people who worked for a living. The man must have been briefed about Klaus' inspection of the ship's reactors, and had had the good sense to prepare.

"Nothing wrong that we can find, sir. No power fluctuations, no escaping heat, no coolant leaks or anything else. So far as we can see, this reactor's working as well as the day she came off the factory floor."

"Uh-huh." Klaus answered absentmindedly, tracing through the schematic on the console. Like all Navy displays, it was technology older than fusion itself – an LED touch-screen display. Reliable, but basic. Holographic emitters were simply too prone to damage, and their higher energy drain meant that it was difficult to give them enough backup power supply in case of emergency.

His eyes drifted to the reactor information panel. Specifically, the reactor model code. "R57?" It was worse than he thought. "The Navy's buying crap from Rockman? No surprise, I guess. The lowest bid strikes again."

"Sir?"

"I had enough trouble with their products on the *Tabellarius*. I can't count the number of times we were late on a delivery because the reactors couldn't keep the engines running at speed." He shook his head, remembering his first ship after the

Navy. "This is a waste of time - there's no way you can get a Rockman reactor to deliver its stated power output."

"What!?" The crewman's voice was sharp now. Either puzzled, or irritated, or both.

"Unfortunately. Rockman's only sold on the civilian market, so I guess the Navy hasn't had to put up with their crappy products until now." Klaus looked at the technician, one eyebrow raised. "You've never heard this?"

The technician shook his head. "Not a word."

"Huh." Klaus chuckled. "Guess the ol' rumor mill's slipped since I was in the service. At any rate, I see the Navy's gone with aneutronic reactors instead of a deuterium-deuterium reaction."

"Well, they're cleaner. No more slag byproduct."

Good answer. Not valid, really, but at least plausible. "Yeah, that was the argument they used to get it approved by the Senate. It's still a stupid idea – the fuel's too pricey. Out of curiosity, what reaction sequence are you using on these reactors?"

"Helium-3 – Helium-3."

Klaus pinched the bridge of his nose. "Helium-three? Really? What idiot politician decided that? You couldn't find a more expensive fuel if you fired the engines with solid gold!"

"Well, yes. But it's much more fuel efficient."

"But it's a real pain to find enough fuel mass. We're trillions of kilometers from anything – efficiency is nice, but I'd prefer a *reliable* source of fuel."

His voice trailed off. No sense getting worked up about things he couldn't change. He dug his way through the control schematics and diagnostics, enlarging one area after another, looking for something out of line, or at least something that he could tweak to perform better. "Show me where you are, you bastard," he grumbled at the screen, willing the problem to surface. Still no luck, but he still had millions of data points to check. He was so absorbed that he did not notice as the outer door opened, until someone behind him cleared his throat.

Klaus blinked, startled. It almost physically hurt to have his concentration broken like that. He stood and turned, ready to scold the technician. Instead, he bit his tongue. Ensign Marius stood to attention, and saluted. He held something out in his hand. "For you, sir."

By its feel, Klaus knew what it was. He held it up. The shoulder patch of a Chief Warrant Officer, Fifth Class: three vertical stripes, two broad and white, one thin and dark-blue sandwiched in between.

"Your insignia, sir." Marius stated, unnecessary but by-the-book. He glanced at the reactor, and then scurried out of the compartment.

"Don't tell me," Klaus asked, pointing at the closing door. "The rest of the crew still avoids the reactor compartments."

"Yes, ah..." The still-nameless technician looked at the insignia in Klaus' hands, and stiffened to attention. "Yes, they do, sir."

Klaus sighed mentally. This crap was why he had grown tired of the service. "You don't need to 'sir' me. This isn't a damn parade ground…" he studied the technician's insignia for the first time. "…CPO Wallace."

Chief Petty Officer Wallace didn't relax his posture. "Yes, sir."

"Uh-huh." Klaus admitted defeat. "Back to ... where were we? Did the tanks at least get filled?"

"To fourteen percent capacity, sir."

"Jesus. Fourteen percent?"

"Helium-Helium reaction, sir. Four times as much power per unit of fuel."

"So that's what, fifty-six percent equivalent? Still low."

"Yes, sir."

Klaus looked again at the console display. "Well, at least we can still tamp these down and use deuterium fuel when we need it."

"Yes, sir."

"Hm." At least CPO Wallace did not bother him with fool questions, and there were *some* things they could do to improve the damned systems. But the captain had given him some very specific specs to meet. He waved at the fusion chamber. "What's the power output you're getting from the reactors?"

"We've achieved a maximum of only eighty-three percent of spec, sir."

Not surprising. Eighty-three percent was about all that could be expected from the Rockman piles-of-junk. Their factory specs were about as reliable as an election speech, so eighty-three percent actually sounded more honest than usual.

"Thank you for the help, CPO Wallace." He sighed, lost in thought as he tapped the display screen. He turned to leave the compartment, and heard the Petty Officer follow behind him. Right, Navy. He didn't bother to look back. "Might as well come along, CPO. I expect the other reactors won't be much different, but maybe you can tell me otherwise." He didn't hold out much hope.

Hours later, after inspecting each of the *Overlord*'s reactors, Klaus sighed and scratched his chin. Everything checked out. Which meant, it didn't. He certainly had his work cut out for him. For whatever reason, and he knew full well what those reasons probably were, the ship had been saddled with near-useless reactors, made by the lowest bidder.

The whole issue was not that some malfunction had caused problems with the design of the reactors. That, he might be able to fix. The issue was that the design itself *was* a malfunction. So the only thing he could possibly fix would have to be the design itself.

He combed his memory, trying to recall what the engineers he'd served with had done to make their Rockman reactors work. They must have found something, because nobody except the

Navy could afford to run at eighty three percent of what they had paid for. Unfortunately, at the time Klaus hadn't been assigned to the reactor crews, so he had never seen the solution first-hand.

But at least he had some ideas. He could get some more grav emitters made, and mount them around the feed channels. It wasn't in any of the manuals, and it wouldn't last for more than a year or two, but at least it would get the reactors up closer to their on-paper specs. How long had the Captain said he had - a week? Better hurry. A warship with crap reactors was about as useful as a cardboard submarine.

Chapter 9: Petrakov

Captain Conagher watched the shuttle enter the docking bay, maneuvering to position its personnel hatch level with the unadorned walkway on the platform jutting out into the center of the open area. A grav-shield kept the space eighty percent pressurized, the thin air carrying the smooth hum of the maneuvering drives to her ears. She admired the skill of its pilot. Not a wobble or correction in the whole procedure.

Normally the ship's Marine company would have mustered out to formally welcome the Commodore aboard. Petrakov's record, however, mentioned his disdain for any ceremony of the sort.

That thought didn't make her feel any better, though – perhaps he had just been looking for something to criticize. Any officer experienced at least one superior who was in the habit of complaining about whatever their subordinates did. Maybe he would cite her for not receiving him with the turnout which his rank warranted.

Not that she could change anything now. Nor would, for that matter. Petrakov's record certainly didn't show that he was that type of commander, but then again that sort of note rarely made it into official paperwork.

The portside hatch opened, and the traditional shrill piping accompanied Commodore Petrakov as he stepped out onto the gangway. The piping of course wasn't real. It came from a speaker mounted overhead. Tradition only goes so far, after all.

He stopped and saluted."Permission to come aboard, Captain?"

"Granted." She answered the salute.

"Excellent. Follow me." Without any other acknowledgement, the Commodore strode past her, foregoing the traditional greetings of a flag officer stepping aboard a new flagship. Not even the courtesy of asking to be escorted to the bridge.

He was certainly living up to his reputation for impatience and brusqueness. His pace was brisk as well – fast enough that she almost had to run to catch up. But she had anticipated that, and matched his stride.

His voice was steady and even, despite the pace. "You were diverted from trials - is the *Overlord* ready for combat?"

They passed through the docking bay personnel gate into an adjacent corridor, and the air pressure reverted to standard. The Captain double-checked that they were alone before answering. "Twelve hundred crew aboard, out of a full complement of fifty-five hundred. Skeleton complement of Marines, mostly green. Reactors are struggling to hit eighty-five percent capacity, but I've got someone working on it; they say the reactors can hit one-hundred percent for a short while if needed." She shrugged. "The usual maiden-voyage troubles. Weapons and deflectors are fully online, limited by power generation. The *Overlord* was designed to fight off a fleet. Even with our limitations, we can handle anything up to squadron-strength."

Petrakov nodded. "Good. Let us talk in private, then."

"Aye, sir." At her command, the gravitational systems picked them off the floor and they took off down the corridor.

After they arrived in the Captain's office, Captain Conagher took her seat, while the Commodore paced back and forth instead of sitting down himself. "The *Overlord* won't need to fight a fleet, nor will there be any full naval engagements." He almost sounded disappointed. "We're going to be intercepting a weapons shipment to one of the insurgent groups operating in the Oort Cloud. The same chaps that you ran into on the way out here, we believe. Did you get anything out of the rebels you captured there?"

"Not much, I'm afraid. We disabled their ship with a microwave beam before boarding. Their gravity system didn't have any backups."

"So?"

"It spiked before failing. Hit nearly a thousand gees."

"Ah." He grimaced, face paling slightly. "All the crew painted the walls?"

"All those inside, yes. Those outside were cooked in their suits."

"Damn. Waste of intel." The Commodore's expression was neutral. Conagher studied the commodore, taking note of the tightening at the corners of his mouth. As much as the man may have wanted to project a facade of combat nonchalance, his face betrayed him.

Conagher took a deep breath to dispel a knot high in her own gut, and continued. "Most of the bodies were pasted beyond recognition. We wanted to test DNA samples, but that equipment had not been installed before we left Earth. None of their electronics were shielded, so we couldn't mine their databanks, either."

"So how'd you identify which group they were?"

She keyed her datapad, displaying a red-speckled ball of white — a human eyeball — lying in the middle of a corridor. This time, the commodore didn't even blink.

The green paint of the corridor was barely visible underneath the reddish paste speckled with bits of bone, all that remained of the eye's former owner. "One of the Marines found this. We slaved one of the security retinal scanners and ran the eye through it. Matched a certain Pravin Adbal. Arrested three years ago after a raid on an insurgent camp in the Gallic wastelands."

"Three years? What the hell is he doing out of prison, then? For that matter, why wasn't he hanged?"

Captain Conagher raised an eyebrow, giving the commodore a wry smile. "Interesting question, isn't it? He wasn't listed as released, executed or escaped – his file said he was still behind bars."

"Hmm. Did you mention this to HQ?"

"Yes." A pause. "Haven't heard back from them, though."

"Probably some low-level SNAFU, not germane to our mission. Although it'll be rather uncomfortable for some prison bureaucrat." He leaned forward in the seat. "Did they get a message off before you hit them?"

"We didn't detect one, but since their computers were mostly destroyed, we can't confirm that none were sent."

"Damn. So we'll have to assume that they know the *Overlord*'s in the area." He sat back, and tapped his datapad. "We've intercepted communications of theirs — a smuggling operation will be handing off stolen weapons in a few days. Heavy weapons. Their planned handoff is near an active mining operation, planetoid 908377 Worzik. I've sent you the coordinates."

She checked her own pad. "Received. They're using the mine as cover for traffic?"

"Looks like it. Confirmed by the Union. They've had their eye on it, and they have better humint." His voice softened slightly. "I should add that Intelligence doesn't believe that the miners know they're being used. Poor rock-rats can't pull their noses out of their dig-sites long enough to see what their bosses are up to."

"So they might not be actively hostile?"

"Chances are, no. So we keep collateral damage to an absolute minimum." He looked the Captain in the eye. "You've got no combat experience on your record. I know that inner-system, wet-behind-the-ears newbies love to paint anybody outside the Belt with a broad brush. Avoid it."

"Aye-aye, sir." She kept her tone neutral and matter-of-fact. She did not need that kind of lecture. After all, she was a professional. But it made her re-assess the Commodore, and wonder what his motives were for saying something so obvious. Perhaps he had been on-station too long, relying far too much on the locals. Or maybe he was hedging his political bets. If so, against what, exactly?

"Good. If we come down too hard, all that does is drive them into the rebels' hands." He snorted. "Mind you, they're no saints. Anybody working as far out as Worzik is likely hiding from *someone*. But they're just low level, not worth the effort to hunt down."

Ah. That answered that question. Or at least, it was *meant* to.

Now it was her turn to ask questions, to find out what the Commodore knew. "What sort of opposition are we going to be facing?"

"Intel says a dozen ships or so, mostly converted asteroids like the one you fried on the way out. Even so, they might also have a proper warship, sort of." He leaned in, his voice quieter. "The *Verdun* was hijacked on her way to be scrapped."

"Really? I had not been notified of that."

"Well, technically she was reported as Disappeared Class II, not-from-hostile-action, . It's been chalked up to a reactor failure, but I'm assuming the worst."

The Captain nodded, thinking. It *was* plausible that the *Verdun* had just blown up. After all, the *World War One*-class cruisers had been the last naval design to utilize antimatter power plants, instead of the far, far safer — albeit less individually powerful — fusion reactors which were now universally employed.

Unlike a fusion reactor, intensive damage to an antimatter reactor would almost certainly have resulted in the near-complete destruction of the ship, due to the inherent instability of antimatter as a fuel. The sort of wreckage that a disaster like that would have left behind would have been difficult to trace. The *Verdun* could reasonably have been destroyed by reactor failure, her wreckage reduced to particles too small and too spread-out for search parties to recover.

Still, though, Murphy dictated that she assume the worst. The *Overlord* was the most powerful ship she had ever sailed on, but she had only a skeleton crew and was minimally outfitted for a shake-down voyage. If she met a fully functional warship, the outcome would not be certain.

There had been plans to simply retrofit modern fusion reactors to the old vessels, since the standards for naval weapons systems had not changed much over the years. But between the cost of such extensive refitting and the age of the hulls themselves, the plans were scrapped. The *World War Two*-class would completely replace their aging predecessors. But those predecessors were still very dangerous.

The Commodore must have read her mind. "She'd had her weapons and shielding stripped out first, of course. But that's still a very well-armored hull, and a good engine. That is why I'm pulling the *Tannenberg* off of her patrol to accompany us. She'll join up with us just before the ambush."

"The *Tannenberg*? She's a sister of the *Verdun*! Isn't she a bit...old?"

"Scheduled for scrapping next year, yes. But a warship nonetheless. Back to the plan…"

Chapter 10: Worzik

The *Overlord* and the *Tannenberg* dropped out of FTL transit near 908377 Worzik, weapons charged and ready. Captain Conagher braced against the usual brief wave of nausea as her stomach and eyeballs tried to keep moving forward out of her body. The shipboard systems flickered briefly as they reset from emergence, then powered up. The two-ship squadron probed the surrounding area with their sensors, seeking the rebel transports.

Conagher studied the holo-map of their emergence zone as it flickered back to life above the bridge. The bright lights she had expected were not there. Where were the target ships?

The tactical officer beat her to the obvious conclusion. "No transports, ma'am!"

Ambush!

"Stow sails!" cried both the Captain and Commodore Petrakov, simultaneously. The fragile sheets of tubing provided nearly half of the *Overlord*'s heat dissipation, an absolute must in a vacuum. By necessity they were large, projecting well beyond the ship's deflector screens, and therefore vulnerable when deployed. The engineer hit the emergency retract, which would ship the enormous sails in a matter of seconds.

Too late.

A group of bright flashes erupted in the center of the display, overlapping the green and blue icons of the *Overlord* and the *Tannenberg*. Red lines denoting high-power lasers flashed toward the blue icons.

"Kiloton-range nuclear mines, ma'am!" Reported the tactical officer. "Right on top of us!"

The bridge lighting flickered, and Captain Conagher felt her stomach jump into her throat. The artificial gravity was out, too. "Take out those mines!" she ordered.

"Tactical systems have already returned fire, Ma'am. Enemy targets at zero."

She gritted her teeth. Too little, too late. "Damage report!"

"No hull damage, ma'am!" replied the engineering officer. "Sails retracted but heavily damaged. Sail effectiveness reduced to eight percent."

Damn. Those had to be military-grade weapons, mines by the look of them. Their bomb-driven lasers were designed specifically to destroy heat-venting sails. But they could also penetrate a military hull if they were close enough.

Not the most up-to-date weapon, most likely left over from Earth's Unification Wars. Those mines were older than any of the *Overlord's* crew.

But they still worked. The *Overlord* was powerful enough to withstand the ambush, and she was still dangerous, but the *Tannenberg*...well, they'd have to see what happened next.

After all, she suspected that the ambush was far from over. Only a fool set a minefield without active combatants to take advantage of it.

^^*^*^*^*^*^*^*^*^*

Klaus hung suspended in the suddenly-darkened room, trapped like a beetle on its back. The straps of his chair tightened automatically, pulling him back into the seat. Blood rushed to his head, tingeing his vision red. "What the hell have those idiots done now?" he cursed.

"Emergency reactor choke!" called one of the engineering ratings in the compartment. "Sails are gone!"

Damn. He pulled up the reactor scram schematic, his datapad eerily bright against the dark around him, to make sure that the overrides were working. As the heat-sinks approached maximum capacity, it was absolutely critical that the reactors should automatically throttle their power output.

The choke was holding. Good.

Now the distribution board. With the reactors' lowered output, power should be prioritized to the deflectors and weapons systems. Check.

He let out a sigh of relief. At least the reactor fail-safes were working as they should, unlike those brass-holes on the bridge. Who enters a combat zone without furling the sails first? It's like they *want* the engineering crew to hate them. It would require hours of sweat-work in uncomfortable vacuum suits to replace the sails!

He secured a loose datapad that floated past him. Of course, the artificial gravity power had been diverted. At least the crew had been ordered to action stations. All suited up and strapped into their seats. Well, most all.

There's always one, Klaus thought, watching some green tech float past. The drifting crewman transcribed a steep arc through the room, just as Klaus felt his own security straps pull tight against his chest. Interesting – the ship must be maneuvering, and without any gravity compensation. The lights flickered back on, went out, and then shone full force.

"What's happening?" yelled the floating crewman.

Rookie. Who did he think could tell him?

^^*^*^*^*^*^*^*^*^*^*

Captain Conagher fought to keep her face impassive, but her knuckles were pale as she squeezed the arms of her command chair. She should have brought the *Overlord* out from superluminal speed with the sails already stowed. It would have taxed the heat-sinks, but they were factory-new and could have taken the strain.

She forced herself to breathe out. There had been no way of knowing that they would be ambushed, and there were of course solid reasons to enter combat with sails out. For one, it made pursuit of fleeing targets much easier, and the heat-sink reserve might also be needed in combat. All the same, it was a risky tactic. A risk she would not have taken, had the decision been hers alone.

It was the commanding officer's job – in this case, Commodore Petrakov's, not hers – to decide on the proper balance between safety and effectiveness.

A difficult choice, and he had chosen wrong this time.

She pushed the line of thought from her mind. There was nothing she could do about it now. They just needed to fight their way out of the trap.

She scanned the tactical display – empty. No contacts in sight. Yet.

Commodore Petrakov might have reached the same realization. "Sensors? Do we have a target?" he called.

"No, sir." The tactical officer shook his head. "Nothing on optical or LIDAR, and the grav sensors haven't recovered from the blast yet. Should be up any second, sir."

"Shift weapons power to deflectors." ordered Captain Conagher. No targets in sight, but who knew what more weaponry the enemy might have? Turning to Commodore Petrakov, she added in a lower tone meant for him, "They'll come to us, sir. No point in an ambush like this if they don't follow it up."

The Commodore merely nodded, his gaze locked on the tactical display. She noted the hard set of his jaw, muscles moving under the skin, as if he was grinding his teeth.

"Contact!" called out the tactical officer. "Multiple drive signatures, count sixty-seven." Another flurry of red dots appeared on the display. "Correction, count one-oh-eight. Small craft, by the readings. They're standing off, ma'am. Range five-hundred-fifty thousand kilometers."

The weapons officer looked at the Captain. "Orders, ma'am?"

Captain Conagher, in turn, looked at Commodore Petrakov, her eyebrow raised.

To her surprise, Petrakov nodded. "Your ship, Captain. Just keep the *Overlord* in one piece, and I'll stay out of your hair." A small smile tugged at the corner of his lip. In a lower voice that wouldn't carry to the rest of the bridge, he added, "My experience lies in attacking, not defending. Consider yourself in command."

"Aye, sir." An unusually wise move for a senior officer. *Very* unusual, and not at all in line with what was in Petrakov's records. Could he know—?

That could wait. Must wait. Captain Conagher turned her attention back to the holo-display. The enemy ships were waiting, in position, with their drives off. And yet they made no attempt to close to weapons range with the *Overlord* or the *Tannenberg*. What could they be planning?

"Drive spikes!" called out the tactical officer. "Enemy craft closing on us! Moving at five-thousand KPS!"

The weapons officer called the sitrep in a steady cadence, "They'll enter effective main battery range in sixty seconds, ma'am!" His targeting console beeped, as a red warning light flashed. His hands flew over the console's controls. When he spoke again, his voice was sharp, less steady. "Enemy ECM - we can't get a lock!" He leaned closer to his screen. "Correction, enemy craft have Navy IFFs. Targeting computers refusing to designate them as valid targets!"

Someone muttered, "Where the hell'd they get those? They're supposed to be —?"

"System malfunction, lieutenant?" demanded Conagher. She would not permit idle chatter on her bridge, especially not in the midst of a battle.

"No, ma'am. Triple-checked."

That meant that those ships out there had the proper encryption. Supposedly impossible to duplicate, especially illegally. But she was certain they were hostile, and was willing to bet her career on that. Better than betting the lives of her crew on the opposite. She called to her weapons officer. "Can we work around the programming?"

The officer glanced up from her console and grimaced. "No, ma'am. It's base-level."

Conagher chided herself. She already knew that, of course. A good safety precaution under most circumstances, but a critical block now. "Authorize the gun crews to go to independent targeting." The basic targeting computers built into the ship's batteries were little better than aiming the guns by eye, but they were better than nothing.

"They're closing the range!" The tactical officer's voice came through loud and sharp, clearly surprised. "Ma'am. Ninety-three enemy ships, now closing at ten thousand KPS. Seventy-two closing on us, the rest are going for the Tannenberg."

Conagher frowned. That made no sense. Why would the enemy want to advance to such a close range, when the *Overlord* could neither aim her guns effectively at long range nor dodge incoming fire? The ship's deflector shields were strong, yes, but not invincible. Even relatively simple weapons would be effective against the crippled warship, if fired *en masse* and from a safe distance.

But at closer ranges, even the individually-aimed guns of the *Overlord* would be deadly. What were the enemy thinking? Captain Conagher would certainly not complain about her foe making such a critical mistake, but she also doubted that they were that stupid. They certainly had not been stupid so far.

"Range closing to four-hundred fifty thousand klicks, eighty-two ships remaining under power. One disabled and floating without power. Intercept in forty seconds." He looked more closely at his screen. "Enemy ships match Navy design specs." The officer glanced up, meeting the Captain's eyes. "Ma'am, it sounds crazy, but they show as boarding craft from the *Verdun*!"

"They are, crewman," She confirmed. She locked eyes with Petrakov. No more doubt that the *Verdun* had been captured. Surprisingly capable, these rebels. "Treat them as hostile."

"Aye, ma'am."

Petrakov leaned toward the Captain, his voice low, "So they stole the IFF tags from the Verdun?"

"Not possible," she answered, "No way to break the encryptions in time." She gnashed her teeth, and added to herself, "Not without help."

But still, were they really aiming to *board*? Board a Navy capital warship? That would be outright suicide against a ship of her size!

Would be. If the *Overlord* had had her full crew complement, especially her full Marine loadout. As it was, things could easily get somewhat touch-and-go.

Commodore Petrakov barked, "Rotate ship, max velocity. Shift power to the deflectors facing the enemy. Ready the crew to repel boarders. Copy the order to the *Tannenberg.*"

At least the *Tannenberg* had her full troop complement.

^^*^*^*^*^*^*^*^*^*^*

The blare of the klaxon pulled Klaus' attention away from the heat-distribution layout. What now? He frowned at the tone— that couldn't be right. But that alarm pattern was very specific, if his memory was correct.

Boarding?

The hatch to the compartment hissed open, and a troop of Marines spilled in, clad in full power armor. One of the hulking figures waved to Klaus and cleared his faceplate.

"Antoniy! Haven't seen you in, what, four days, now?" Klaus said, gesturing outside the hatch. Several of the other Marines were setting up a series of mines to cover the entrance. "Shouldn't you be setting up closer to the hull?" He waved at the machines behind him. "Away from the important bits?"

"No can do. We've only got less than a quarter of the normal Marine complement aboard, so can only defend the key parts of the ship."

Klaus frowned. "Wouldn't the ship's integrated defenses be enough?"

"Nope. The bad guys' ships have stolen Navy transponders, so we're assuming that their boarders got 'em as well."

"What the hell? Those are supposed to be absolutely secure!" Doubtless the technology itself still was. Some idiot must have sold off the codes. "So the automated defenses won't target them?"

"The higher-ups say they can program around it." He grimaced at Klaus. "Of course, Murphy says they can't. And *that* means they have access through all the exterior hatches, and ship's systems can't even keep them out of the damned transit corridors. All we can do is shut off transit power to the corridors for everybody." Antoniy un-slung four duffel bags from his shoulder, and tossed them to the deck. The bags clanged as they landed.

Klaus opened one of the bags, and pulled out segments of hard blue plas-ceramic, which clattered to the deck. Low-profile body armor.

"So," continued Antoniy with a wry smile on his face, "you get to join in the fun!"

Klaus opened his mouth to protest, and then closed it again as Antoniy emptied the other bags. The armor was lighter than he remembered, and thinner. He hoped it was just as effective. Below the armor was a military-issue coilgun. Full spec, fully charged. Kudos to whomever came up with anti-boarding ready-packs. Still, though, close-quarters fighting was not his idea of 'fun.' Sure, he'd gone through basic training, and had even been in a few firefights with pirates during his early Navy career, but that was *ages* ago.

He was getting too old for this shit.

His voice was deadpan. "Joy." He fastened the breastplate on. The two centimeters of alloy would stop a coilgun round, but it only covered his chest. The arm & leg plates which he strapped on next were less than half as thick. They would barely stop shrapnel, but better that than nothing. He could only hope that the boarders were good shots.

"Look on the bright side! At least we get to shoot back, this time." Antoniy grinned.

Klaus shook his head. On board the *Ad Astra*, Antoniy had seemed way too eager to fight it out. And now, the youngster seemed positively happy about imminent combat. That was crazy. "All in all, I'd still rather it wasn't necessary."

"Can't blame you for that. All the same, we're looking for materials we can use for fortifications." Antoniy nodded over Klaus' shoulder, and pointed to the crates of spare parts stacked against one wall. "That's replaceable, right?"

"Yeah." Sort of.

"Good. Let's move those into a barricade outside, then. You have grav-lifts?"

The Marines wasted no time, and quickly wrestled the crates to build a makeshift wall across the corridor. It gave the soldiers a field of fire down the long hallway, which ran for nearly twenty meters before dead-ending in a T-junction. At the wall's center stood a twin-mount railgun, its two-man crew crouched behind the gun-shield, checking the ammunition feed. Further down the corridor, another team had placed half a dozen shaped charges.

With a grunt, Klaus helped stack the last crate in place. He was thankful, for a change, for those long months sweating on a tramp freighter. At least he had learned to use the 'lifts effectively, and not his back. He easily outpaced any two of the others when it came to moving the quarter-ton crates, although his back ached despite the assistance of the grav-lifts.

Now he felt marginally safer. The long, narrow approach would force the attackers to advance head-on, and the lighting was being redirected to aim over the shoulders of the defenders, directly into the face of any attacker.

"All right." Antoniy commed. "This is good enough. Everybody check your rifles, contact expected in under five minutes."

Klaus examined the weapon Antoniy had issued him, running through the standard drill that had been drummed into him long ago. A standard-issue military-grade coilgun. It felt familiar in his hands, like the ones he had trained with before, but it was newer and smaller.

Hopefully, it would work the same. Capacitor charge indicator where he remembered. One hundred percent. Good. He removed the cell and visually checked it. Very nice – the capacitor itself was bundled with the ammunition magazine into one unit. An excellent improvement, although the whole thing looked undersized for this class of deadly weapon. Only one way to test that, though.

Thumbing the capacitor back into the weapon, he cycled the diagnostic program. Indicator green and good to go.

He found a spot on the barricade where he could fire without exposing too much of himself, and burrowed into it. The Marines around him seemed calm enough, running through their prep routines, but that did not help his nerves. They were *specifically* trained for this situation. He forced his hands to steady, and then looked over his own lines of fire.

Antoniy scurried over next to Klaus, grinning. "Ready to get revenge for the *Ad Astra?*"

"And her crew." Klaus growled. He hefted his rifle. "Y'know, I haven't fired one of these in anger for years."

"Well, hope you're still in practice." Antoniy tapped the side of his helmet. "Just got news – they've boarded the ship." He paused. "Dammit. Where'd they get those?"

"What?"

"They've got priority-tagged transponders, the whole lot of 'em. The ship registers they're on-board, but won't let us track them."

Hell. Klaus looked down the corridor. They'd have no warning of the enemy's advance.

Antoniy must have realized the same. "Gutierrez! Get up to the corner and keep an eye out!" One of the Marines dashed down the corridor.

A soldier to Klaus' left pushed on the barricade, which swayed ominously under the power of his armor. "Hope they don't have weapons to match those transponders." A logical worry – the barricade wouldn't be worth much against heavy weaponry. But...

Klaus groaned under his breath. "Goddamnit, did you *have* to say that?" Never tempt Murphy like that.

^^*^*^*^*^*^*^*^*^*

Captain Conagher peered intently at the holographic display which flashed bright pinpricks and lines in the air in front of her. It showed a comprehensive three-dimensional overview of the battle in neighboring space, and she used her controls to zoom in on one sector after another, yet she could not find what she sought. "Sensors. Any sign of the *Verdun?*"

"Nothing at all, ma'am."

It would be a mistake for the rebels to hold back the only true warship they have, she though, and yet they were doing just that. Their fifty-two remaining boarding craft were just reaching the *Overlord's* effective weapons range.

If those boarders wanted to reach the ship in enough numbers to matter, they needed covering fire. Yet nothing had appeared. The enemy vessels were dodging, of course, but they kept charging headlong into the teeth of her defenses.

Another volley of individually-aimed main-battery fire burst forth from the *Overlord*. Eight more enemy ships disappeared from the display, their icons changing color from hostile red directly to destroyed black. No orange of 'damaged' — the

Overlord's railguns were designed for ships far larger and better-protected than the flimsy craft.

The secondary batteries accounted for another dozen shattered wrecks, although each of those guns needed several hits before they took out a ship.

And then the icons for the rebel craft overlapped the *Overlord* on the display. The ship was far too large for Conagher to actually hear the thumps and clanks of the boarding shuttles, but she could imagine them.

"Board count?" Commodore Petrakov asked. "How many of them have trapped themselves on-board?"

An interesting way to view the situation, very in-line with his reputation. But not in-line, she feared, with the actual situation. The rebels must have spent hundreds of lives in order to get their soldiers onto the *Overlord*. She could not bring herself to believe that they had merely thrown away those lives without a greater plan in mind.

"Twenty-three enemy craft reached the hull, sir." reported the tactical officer. "We can't track their troops individually, but their boarding craft cannot carry more than a dozen troops apiece. A total maximum of two hundred and seventy-six boarders. Half that if they are in heavy armor."

^^*^*^*^*^*^*^*^*^*^*

"Contact!" shouted the Marine lookout, as he leaned around the corner. He raised his weapon.

Next to Klaus, Antoniy jerked his head up above the barricade. "Hold your—"

A drawn-out ripping noise echoed as the lookout poured fire down the corridor.

"—fire." Antoniy pounded the crate he knelt by. "Damnit, now they know we're here."

The lookout ceased fire, the 'ping' of his emptied capacitor cutting through the echoes of his fire. He dashed back to the defensive line, hurdling the barricade. The barrel shroud of his coilgun glowed a dull red, hot enough that Klaus could feel it nearly a meter away. "Got two of 'em, sir!"

Antoniy shook his head. "Good shooting, at—"

Bang!

The first of their defensive landmines detonated, the sound harsh even around the corner where the defensive bulwark was located. Klaus reeled at the concussion, ears ringing even through his helmet.

Antoniy's Marines, less affected in their heavier armor, opened up before Klaus could regain his bearings. The roar of coilgun fire cut through his deafness, pierced by the sharp reports of the railgun.

Coilgun in hand, he poked his head above the crate, trying to see through the thick smoke, unable to make out any targets. The coolant on the railgun's barrels had vaporized, filling the corridor with an acrid haze. It looked like something out of an ancient black-powder war documentary.

The Marines on either side of him, though, kept up their fire, their helmets' integrated IR sensors providing them with a much sharper picture.

But there! Blurry shapes showed through the smoke – more of a mist, a corner of his mind detachedly noted. He triggered a half-second burst at the target. No visible effect!

An instant later, the railgun walked its fire onto Klaus' target, sending the figure collapsing to the ground.

There came a brief lull in the firing, the smoke clearing enough to reveal a suit of powered armor. A rather sloppy green paint-job didn't quite cover the Federal blue underneath. Captured equipment? It looked much more solid than the armor Klaus wore.

More to the point, two smoking holes through the figure's chest meant it wasn't a threat. That armor hadn't helped him, in the end.

Behind the dead man, a flash of movement as another suit retreated back around the corner. Another suit of military-grade heavy armor. These could not be run-of-the-mill rebels – not with that armor. Where the hell had they gotten that?

A small cylindrical object flew out of the smoke and clattered towards them. Klaus ducked behind the crates, just as Antoniy shouted "Down!"

But it was no explosive. With a loud *pop*, a thick plume of black smoke filled the corridor, thick enough to look downright solid. Streams of fire tore through the dense smoke from both sides.

The gas was IR-refractive, which eliminated the Marines' advantage. It also told Klaus that the rebels must not have IR vision in their helmets, so their theft of military gear was not complete. Both sides were firing equally blind. That still gave the Marines a small advantage, since they had cover. Ricochets sparked off of the crates, the walls, and even – someone was truly panicking – the ceiling. A shot whistled past Klaus' head, close enough that he felt the displaced air more than he heard the sound.

The Marine to Klaus' left dropped like a marionette with cut strings, a hole punched neatly through his visor. Cover wouldn't save you if your number was up.

Klaus returned fire through the cloud, trying to guess where the shot had come from. No effect, at least nothing which he could hear or see.

Right. Armor.

He thumbed the selector to over-charge, and fired again. The surge of power which ran through the coils singed his left hand even through the barrel shroud. This time, an armored figure stumbled out of the smoke, clutching an arm held on by only a few fragments of his shattered armor. Two of the heavy railgun rounds caught the enemy soldier square in the faceplate, severing the helmet and knocking it flying back into the smoke.

Good shooting, that, thought Klaus as the headless corpse collapsed to the floor.

A moment later, a grenade detonated at the base of the hastily-built fortification, right under the railgun. Lucky throw. The railgun's full-throated suppressive fire stopped instantly, and the dual-mount weapon flew through the air to land next to Klaus. There was not much left of its crew.

Tensing his back muscles against the shot he feared would kill him, Klaus quickly reached out and tugged the heavy weapon closer. As he did, the deck began to shake. Someone, he didn't know who, shouted. "Here they come!"

The railgun's tripod had been bent into modern art, so Klaus unclipped it. He wrestled the barrel up onto the crate in front of him. He had no idea where the ammo indicator was on the thing, but he prayed it wasn't empty. And it had two triggers. Which one?

The enemy was coming. No time to figure it out.

He squeezed both.

The left barrel exploded, sending fragments whistling around the crowded hallway. Something heavy ricocheted off his left arm, and a burning pain shot clear to his bones. Both ears rang, and it felt like someone was pushing a dagger into his left ear. He gritted his teeth against the pain, but he kept his grip on the gun's trigger. He felt, more than saw, a stream of high-velocity rounds leap from the right railgun barrel.

Even with his armor, Klaus weighed much less than a power-armor-clad Marine, and the railgun was a heavy weapon – the first five shots went down the hallway, more or less, but the sixth ricocheted off of the ceiling above. He grimaced and unclenched his finger from the trigger. He had to control the recoil, or his firing would be pointless.

The searing pain in his left arm was gone, but it was numb now, and useless. He struggled with only one arm to control the recoil and get the railgun pointed back down the corridor. Fire. Wrestle with the gun. Fire again. He could hear nothing over the overpowering ringing in his ears, and his vision blurred. He only knew that the enemy was that-a-way. He hoped that he was helping.

A hand clapped his shoulder, and he whirled, ceasing fire. An armored Marine stood beside him, his opaque faceplate in sharp contrast to the dull blue of the armor. A silver bar insignia sat on its shoulder.

The Marine's faceplate cleared. Antoniy. Still alive.

Antoniy's mouth was moving, but Klaus couldn't hear anything. He shook his head, pointing to his helmet.

Antoniy pointed at the railgun with his left hand, while drawing his right hand across his throat. Stop firing.

Klaus nodded, and looked down the hallway. The smoke cleared slowly, the ventilators pulling it away. Nothing else moved. The corridor was strewn with bodies – and parts of bodies – of enemy troops.

Klaus dropped the railgun, and stood to get a better look. His hand shook, and he pressed it to his side to hide it from Antoniy. Only four of the corpses were clad in power armor. A dozen others were dressed in simple, one-piece suits. The armor blocks they wore on top covered only their torso, not their extremities. Blood pooled everywhere on the deck. Some of the bodies were completely destroyed, their torsos shattered, their limbs missing. Like soldiers shot apart with cannon fire. He looked down at the railgun at his feet, and swallowed hard.

Oh. His chest tightened.

Then he remembered the Marines. His stomach flipped as he tried to ignore the body of the man who originally held the railgun, his left shoulder and arm missing, his head canted at an impossible angle.

Klaus breathed again. It was war, and he had only done what needed to be done. At least his worst fears had not come true. The rebels had military equipment, all right, but only for a few of their men. Made sense for a group of insurgents, but for most of those men, they might as well have entered the battle naked.

He turned back to Antoniy. "NOW WHAT?" he said. Antoniy winced. Probably too loud, then, but he couldn't tell.

Antoniy tapped the side of his helmet, to indicate that he had received a radio message. He typed into the datapad built into his suit's left-hand gauntlet.

A message appeared on Klaus' datapad. "Boarders repulsed."

"WHAT, THAT'S IT?" He had expected more of a fight for such an important compartment.

Another message. "Reactor four down. Needs repairs."

Just like that. Leave it to the engineers to clean up the mess. Klaus nodded to Antoniy. "THEN I'M OFF."

^^*^*^*^*^*^*^*^*^*

"Still no sign of the *Verdun*?" demanded the Captain. It made no sense for the rebel warship to hold back like that. By now their boarding crews were down, both on the *Overlord* and on the *Tannenberg*, but it would have been logical for them to attack during the distraction. That meant that they were up to something else. And she hated not knowing what that was.

"No, ma'am."

As if on cue, the sensors officer called out. "Ma'am! Weak grav signature, bearing one-oh-five by eighteen degrees. Range one point two million kilometers. Target is not maneuvering."

A command ship of some sort, observing the battle? She could think of one likely candidate for which ship that was.

Trying to hide, eh? "Can we hit them?"

"They're outside of effective range, ma'am. Shell flight time is four-eight seconds."

With that kind of time, the target could easily maneuver to dodge. She grinned to herself. But that was not the point. If the enemy ship maneuvered, the *Overlord*'s sensors could get a reading on its unique drive signature. If it was the *Verdun*, they would have positive confirmation that it had been captured. If it wasn't the *Verdun*, then they would have a ship ID that they could hunt down later.

Conagher turned to the helmsman. "Rotate to bring the starboard, bow and dorsal batteries to bear. Fire salvo when all three can hit the target."

"Aye."

The *Overlord* sent twelve shots screaming through space towards the distant target, cruising at 8% of the speed of light. None of them would hit, she assumed, but even so she considered it a good investment.

"Target is maneuvering, ma'am." reported the tactical officer. "Drive signature matches the *Verdun*!"

And the investment paid off.

"*Verdun* has maneuvered out of shell trajectory, ma'am."

Of course. The rebels knew that their shields might have held, but why risk it? "Close the range." She considered for a moment. "Keep the deflectors up at full power. Divert energy from weapons to engines. Full available speed."

So – the *Verdun* had been watching the fight, but had not engaged?

"Ma'am!" *Verdun* is moving away, at speed. We're barely gaining on her."

And now she was fleeing? "Keep up the pursuit. When she jumps, I want to know where to." In the *Overlord's* current shape, there was no way that she could safely pursue the *Verdun* if the smaller warship jumped to superluminal speed.

She kept an eye on the tactical holo as they drew closer. She wondered how well the *Verdun's* new captain knew Navy weaponry, especially the new-generation guns on the *Overlord,* and how close he could let them approach before he—

"Ma'am! The *Verdun* has jumped! We got her vector. On-screen."

"Trace the vector, see if it passes near *anything* recorded." This far out-system, they were nearly to the heart of the Oort Cloud installations. There were plenty of large asteroids and minor planetoids which had not been surveyed, and which the rebels could use as a fallback. It was very unlikely that they'd choose a location which would show up in records, but you never knew.

Worth a try, at least.

She studied the map of the battle, thinking. The *Verdun*'s captain had jumped earlier than he needed to. Earlier, that is, unless he knew about the classified weaponry aboard the *Overlord*. Either that, or he was just being cautious.

^^*^*^*^*^*^*^*^*^*

Klaus' hearing was recovering. He could hear voices, yet couldn't make out words. But that did not concern him much at this point. After all, the reactor would not be talking to him.

The number four reactor — what was left of it — posed a real challenge. The grav foci casing was covered with pockmarks, where coilgun impacts had dug into the structure. One streak of deeper craters — the ones that had likely done the most damage — looked like railgun impacts. He peered back and forth between the reactor and the fortified corridor outside, and shook his head. Who the hell had missed *that* badly?

The coolant pipes themselves were not as strong as the casing. Holes had been blown clean through them everywhere. Pieces hung off the reactor assembly in tatters, but at least the flow had been switched off. The wet deck, and the water pooling around the drains, revealed that the automatic cutoffs hadn't activated perfectly, though. Typical Rockman corner-cutting. Probably not a single priority feedback circuit in the entire scram system.

The four technicians in the room had not seen him enter. He nodded. Good. They were crawling over the access scaffolding, stemming the worst of the leaks. Exactly what they should be doing. With his left arm now taped to his side, he didn't fancy climbing up there after them.

No sense letting them get full of themselves, though. He called loudly, "Right! What have you done to this poor machine?"

One technician to his left put down a wrench the length of his arm, and approximated a very hurried salute. "It got hit by a few stray shots, during the fight. Ah...sir." He did not wait for an answer, but went straight back to what he was doing.

"What? Speak up! I'm still deaf from those damned railguns."

"A FEW STRAY SHOTS, SIR!" The tech stood up and faced Klaus, carefully mouthing the words. Once again, he turned back to his work.

"A few stray shots?!" Klaus grumbled. The turbine feed piping alone would take days to repair!

"Well, yes." This time, the technician did not bother looking up.

At least, Klaus *assumed* he had answered. He couldn't read lips, and certainly not from behind. He had to admire the tech, though, as the man climbed a ladder for a better view. Better for him to fix the thing than to talk.

At the rate they were moving, they might clear the broken pieces within hours. He scanned the console for an in-depth report. And the other damage did not look too—

"Dammit. The detail generators are slagged." he exclaimed. Nobody reacted.

That was a killer. He probably should have expected it, though. All the newer fusion reactors in the Navy used focused gravitational fields to force particles to fuse. They were much more reliable and low-maintenance than the magnetic fields that they had replaced.

The downside was, they were sensitive. And for some reason, the gravity field generators used here were unarmored. Probably the designers did not expect any fighting this close to the ship's core.

But whatever the reason, the damage in front of him would take a lot of time, effort and spare parts to repair.

Did they even have the replacements for those? Klaus checked his datapad, hoping that some enterprising quartermaster would have thought to stock a replacement. He frowned. Of course, that hadn't happened.

"The reactor's deadline." he muttered to the techs, and again nobody listened. "No spares for the detail generator." He strode to the hatch. "I'll check with the 'shops if they can fab us one."

But he would not hold his breath on that idea, either.

Chapter 11: Rebel

In the depths of the *Overlord,* Antoniy sat in a dark, quiet room. Flat neutral colors, solid but bare furniture. The wall behind him was a one-way mirror. A room whose design, he suspected, had changed little over the centuries. The other walls, the ceiling, and the floor were coated to absorb sound, giving the room an unnerving silence.

He gave a long, intense stare at the man across the table. "So. You were expecting a walkover?"

The man raised his head slowly, locking one good eye on Antoniy. His right eye socket was empty, its edges still oozing rivulets of blood. His right arm was no more than a stump – the ship's surgeons had cauterized the wound to keep him alive – and his left was loosely manacled to the chair. He twitched back and forth, as if something gnawed at him under his skin. All over.

He did not look comfortable.

Perhaps this explained the pure rage which glared from his remaining eye: he was beyond the 'yelling' stage of anger, and had proceeded to a preternatural calm. His voice was low and insistent, his teeth gritted.

"We were expecting some fucking *help.* The bastards set us up." He waved the stump at Antoniy, pointing with a non-existent hand. "And it would have worked. We *had* you!"

Antoniy leaned back, and studied his prisoner in the long silence. His valuable prisoner, as there were not many. Of the two-hundred and ten rebels who had boarded the *Overlord*, twelve were still alive, more or less. Seven of those might even live until tomorrow.

Antoniy steepled his fingers, and rested his chin on his hands. "'The bastards, hmm? I can think of a few ways we can get back at them."

"'We'? There is no 'we." he pulled at the chain on his left wrist. "Why the hell should I help *you*?"

"We've cauterized your bleeding arm, patched up your missing eye and pumped you so full of antibiotics that you'll probably survive. We're the only reason you're alive right now. That's on one side." He leaned forward. "What have 'the bastards' done for you?"

"You're the reason I'm in this shape in the first place," came the low growl.

Expected, but at least the man was talking. "Think about it. Who sent you here? Who promised support, only to pull the rug out from under your feet? Who sent brave soldiers to their deaths?" Brave the rebels might be, but calling them 'soldiers' was charitable.

Antoniy stood and waved toward the door. "Look, we could walk out there right now, and look through all the bodies of your dead. How many of 'the bastards' do you think you would find out there?"

He waited a few moments, letting that sink in, and then sat down again. The prisoner's downcast gaze told him what he needed to know. The man might not love Antoniy or the Navy, but he *did* know that his 'leaders' were not with the boarding parties.

Antoniy could use that.

He tapped a finger idly on the table. "Why, do you suppose, did they choose to betray you? And why now?" The Oort Cloud rebel groups, he knew, were highly compartmentalized, and they would most likely not change that, even for such large-scale mission. Each independent cell, often less than a dozen members, had little to no information about the others, much less about who gave them orders. "You saw your friends killed. Not easy to do, I know."

Antoniy's memory jumped, unbidden, to the face of one of his own Marines, killed in the fight. He leaned over the table, poking a finger into the rebel's chest, avoiding the bandages and bruises. "And you think *we* are your enemy?"

For several seconds, the two men stared at each other. One and a half pairs of eyes, unmoving. Then the rebel spoke, voice strained. "I ain't gonna betray my comrades."

"Tough-guy, huh?" Ah, well, that was worth a shot. There were always more traditional methods of extracting information.

First, the 'stick.' Antoniy leaned forwards. "You know the minimum sentence for armed rebellion. You're in for a bad time of it."

"I ain't afraid of dyin'."

"Dying isn't what you should be afraid of. You've killed Federal servicemen."

The rebel kept silent.

"But you didn't kill them all, and *their* comrades would like to have a word with you." On cue, the room was flooded with the most horrible, ear-piercing scream imaginable. A scream so terrible that it could not have come from a human, but engineered to set off every single 'panic note' the human ear recognized. Even knowing that it was a computer-generated sound, Antoniy shivered involuntarily.

Across the table, the man shivered as well. The human hind-brain was very susceptible to manipulation, thankfully. With the rebel unnerved, time for the 'carrot.' "Of course, that isn't set in stone. Tell us where they are, and we can do something for you."

^^*^*^*^*^*^*^*^*^*

Captain Conagher, face impassive, watched the Commodore pace back and forth inside her office. Let him pace, she thought, as long as he held his tongue, at least for a while. Inside she was seething. Her beautiful ship, halfway wrecked because some high-up brass had to leap before he looked. And she had had to let him.

Although, to be fair, the rebels' trick with the IFF would have worked, even without Petrakov's foolhardy stunt. Just not as well. It could have been worse, though. At least he had not ordered a follow-up attack straight away. After all, it could easily have been a set-up. Maybe that's what the *Verdun* had been trying to do, and maybe not. But in either case, the *Overlord* needed time for repairs.

The Commodore waved his arms. "What are we waiting for? Their boarders told us where their *nest* is, so we hunt them down like the rats they are and crush them." He smashed one fist into his open palm.

"Sir. We've been ambushed once, already." She let her meaning sink in. After a few strides, the Commodore stopped pacing, and she continued, her voice matter-of-fact, "On top of that, there's still battle damage to repair. One of the reactors is deadlined indefinitely and we've got key people in the medbay. Our sails have yet to be replaced, and the *Tannenberg*'s not any better off."

She studied the man's face, trying to read it. Was this just his natural aggressiveness, or was he over-reacting out of some sense of shame? After all, it was pretty clear to anyone that Petrakov had made a serious blunder. But he was still the commanding officer. She needed to get him to see reason, before he made another error. "Their base is certain to have heavier defenses, and it does us no good to go in under-prepared. The squadron needs time to rebuild combat effectiveness. "

Petrakov nodded brusquely, not letting up, but at least his tone lost some of its bluster. "Well, yes. But the enemy's taken much heavier losses. We need to hit them again, before they can regroup."

"They lost a number of minor ships. Very little, really." The Captain responded, pointing to the graphic projected above her desk. "They sacrificed those troops, let them die. And to what purpose? Perhaps to lure us into a rash attack?" She toggled up a holo of the *Verdun*. "And now we know they've got this. She could go toe-to-toe with the *Tannenberg*, even without her damage."

She called up an image of the rebel base: a small planetoid, less than a hundred kilometers in diameter, with its own collection of much smaller debris orbiting it. "If their base really is at 1048 Podera, we must assume that they've got defenses ready.

It's perfect for defense: large enough to hold deep bunkers, small enough that the gravity well won't be a problem for weapons platforms."

She keyed her datapad, and a series of blinking lights appeared in the display. "Podera was never scanned in detail, all we've got is a surface-map. But if the rebels have any more military-grade equipment, this is where they would put it. They'd have lines of fire on any approach vector to the planetoid."

"Then we stand off and bombard them from out of their effective range."

"Which would take time. Time that any enemy leaders — anyone with *useful* knowledge that we could extract — could use to escape. While we sit at long range, they fly off into the black before we could possibly intercept. We only have two ships, don't forget, hardly a blockade." She shifted her display to show a list of insurgent attacks in the past five years. "If we want to *end* this, we have to destroy the enemy command structure." She looked away from Petrakov, thinking. "Which gives us the problem of finding them. They *could* be on the planetoid, but that doesn't feel right."

"Care to elaborate?"

"We first heard about their Podera base from interrogation. Intelligence gives it a fifty-fifty probability. We confirmed with trace navigational data on one of the enemy boarding craft. Data that had been deleted, but not overwritten." She drummed her fingers on the desk. "It smells like a plant."

"A plant?" asked Petrakov. He blinked, and sat upright. "Are you suggesting that they sacrificed all those ships and troops just to draw us into a trap?"

"Improbable, I admit," she said, and then she sat forward. "Unless they have some bigger objective in mind, something big enough to warrant such a sacrifice."

"Such as?"

"I admit I don't know." She leaned on her desk. "But it feels wrong. So far, they have not made those kinds of mistakes."

The Commodore snorted. "No mistakes? Hardly. Their attack obviously hadn't expected the *Overlord. That* was a mistake. This ship" he gestured to the room around them "is an unexpected development for them. A monkey-wrench in their gears. If we hit them with both the *Tannenberg* and the *Overlord*, we'll have them. Besides," he flashed a grin "I happen to know that the boarding craft represented most of this rebel cell's space-worthy craft."

"And how do you know that?"

The Commodore tapped on his datapad. "I got a message today from Bill— ah, the miner's union representative." He handed the datapad to the Captain. "They finally managed to get a mole into the enemy command-communications network."

Conagher nodded, but she had strong doubts. The message certainly seemed to come from the union. It even had the proper codes and e-seals. And her mission brief said the union were allies out here in the Cloud.

Then again, these were the same 'allies' who rarely lifted so much as a finger to actually hunt down the insurgents, even with all of the fleet-surplus equipment they had been given. Not if they could get the Navy to do it for them.

She hated doing the dirty work for others, especially if it might cost good men their lives. She tapped the bottom of the screen. "There's no information here about exactly who their mole is, and how they got him into the enemy's confidences." Of course, Navy Intelligence branch had been trying to get their infiltrators into a vital position like that for years without success. So if the union *had* succeeded where the Navy had not, it stood to reason that they would protect the mole's identity. Still, something did not sit right with her. "Besides, it's too detailed to be reliable." Real intelligence would never be this...specific.

"Of course they don't want to reveal their sources."

"That makes no sense, unless they do not trust us. After all, we're on their side." Although she was not too certain the reverse held true. "Besides, this" she tapped the datapad "says nothing about where the rebels got their equipment in the first place."

Petrakov shrugged. "The equipment's probably stolen from the union. No definitive answer yet on that, I understand, but it stands to reason. Even in that case, the union wouldn't want to admit that their security is awful." He tapped the arm of his chair with two fingers. "As for trust, don't forget those IFFs the rebels had. There was obviously a leak somewhere. Maybe the union will suspect it came from us."

Plausible. The union *might* merely have had bad security on their arms, and yet they claimed that they'd landed an intelligence coup that her Navy had not been able to. Were they competent or not? She sighed. "Very well. Accepting that on a provisional basis, we still have the issue of actually pinning down the enemy leadership." She switched her display to show the area around Podera, highlighting the planetoid itself. "They are most likely either well-ensconced in a bunker on the planetoid, or—" a bright red dot appeared on the display "—onboard the captured *Verdun.* She wasn't commissioned as a command vessel, but she's still the closest they'll have to a flagship."

The Commodore leaned in towards the display. "So we have to find some way of both destroying any emplacements or bunkers on the planetoid and preventing any enemy craft from escaping, while fighting the *Tannenberg*'s own sister-ship?" He shook his head. "The *Overlord* may be a great ship, but she can't be everywhere at once." He paused. "Correct?"

She shook her head, wondering just how much the Commodore knew about their trial results. Still, he was flag, and had a high security level. "QMP is not working yet. Our man made some progress. Not enough."

Petrakov frowned. "Wish we had more ships to cover their escape."

"Perhaps. But we do have the advantage of being the attackers here. The enemy doesn't know exactly when we'll be arriving. We can use that. Give us a week for repairs, and we'll have a workaround on the targeting systems. If the enemy has more stolen transponders, it won't help them this time."

She highlighted the very center of the display, expanding on Podera. The image zoomed in, showing a cargo-transshipment station reaching out from the planetoid's surface. "And then we exit FTL right on top of this station. It's got the only proper hangar space on the whole rock. If the enemy has escape ships, they'll be there." Petrakov started to object, but she held up her hand to stop him. "Yes, I know Navy regs call for exiting FTL further away. So far, the rebels know far too much about 'Navy regs', so chances are they won't expect this. That is exactly why we need to do it."

She zoomed the display in closer. "The *Overlord* stands off just far enough from the station so that her batteries can cover it and the planetoid, while the *Tannenberg* moves in closer." She smiled thinly. "While the *Tannenberg* may not be the *Overlord*'s equal, she is an intimidating sight, especially at close range. It'd take a disciplined captain to *not* flee from her. Discipline born from proper training. Discipline that these rebels don't have."

The Commodore nodded. "I see. Simple enough. When any enemy ships leave, the *Tannenberg* disables them for boarding. If the enemy leadership tries to flee aboard their ships, they're captured. If they stay on the planetoid, then they're trapped."

"Exactly. And if it turns out that the enemy leadership was aboard the *Verdun*, then we'd likely not catch them in this attack anyway. Most likely, she doesn't have any real weapons - no way the rebels could re-install the main guns. But she *could* run." Conagher drummed her fingers and grimaced. Much as she would like to capture the *Verdun* along with the base, one step at a time. At least they could cripple the rebellion. "Either way, we *would* have located and isolated a major enemy base, one which we can then destroy. At which point we sit back from Podera, close enough to intercept any evacuation ships but far enough to be outside of the effective range of any enemy weapons emplacements."

She switched the display to a view of a new spaceship. To her eyes, it was not a true Navy ship at all - a long, thin cylinder as opposed to the rounded spheres and ovoids of proper combat vessels. It looked more like a merchantman than a military vessel.

But it was the perfect shape to mount a battery of three-kilometer-long railguns, designed specifically to destroy hardened, fixed targets. The *Artillerist* class was the most specialized naval designs currently in service, with only one ship yet commissioned.

Conagher stabbed her finger at the ship's image. "And then once we capture the enemy leaders, we call in the *Gribeauval* and let her reduce the target to powder. The rebels lose a major base, and most likely their leadership for this cell."

"Excellent point." The Commodore nodded. "Very well. We'll wait a week, and then come down on the enemy like a ton of bricks. See to it."

Chapter 12: Diplomacy

Oh, now they showed up. Captain Conagher rolled her eyes as she watched the repair ship come alongside the Overlord. After all the critical work's done. Would have been nice if they'd shown up earlier and helped with getting the backup masts set up. Of course, she had herself to blame for that. After the ambush, she had insisted on extra vetting. She grinned humorlessly to herself. But if they thought they had missed the *hard* work, they clearly did not know the Navy.

The *Overlord's* replacement sails had been fabricated, but the painstaking task of re-attaching them to their masts was only beginning. A perfect job for a civilian crew, which would free the Navy crew to supervise. The fricsim drive core also needed repairs, having drifted slightly out of alignment on its first voyage out of dry-dock. The core room was cramped and perpetually hot, as her chief engineer had explained, because the drive couldn't be taken offline and re-started in the shallow gravity field this far out-system. At least neither repair required Navy-specific training.

Yet another job that could effectively be left to the civilians. She was mulling through the repair detail, when the intercom on her desk buzzed. She pressed the button. "Yes?"

"A Miner's Union representative just arrived on the repair ship, ma'am. A Mr. Jones. He says he needs to talk to you." There was a muted conversation in the background, which she could not make out. "Ah, that is, he requests a meeting with you."

That did not ring any bells. She assumed that they hadn't notified the ship's liaison officer beforehand, and checked her schedule to be sure. No Mr. Jones. Perhaps he was here to help with the repairs, but she doubted it. Perhaps he was here to explain just how the Union sent the squadron into a trap, but she held little hope for that, either. Whatever the man wanted, she would deal with it.

"I can see him in fifteen minutes. Then send him in."

Arrogant damn bureaucrats. Just because they were this far out-system, they acted like it was their own private country! Would it have killed them to arrange any of this before the last minute? But she couldn't afford to snub them, directly. At least she could make their representative wait a bit longer than protocol dictated. And see how he reacted.

But that wasn't the important question. Why hadn't they asked to meet the Commodore, instead? The Union had enough contacts at Andromeda station that they must know he'd left, and a quick ping of the *Overlord*'s systems would show her Flag status. Either they did not want to reveal what they knew, or they decided that they would rather talk to a less senior officer. She chuckled at that.

She thought about notifying Petrakov, but decided to wait. If the Union wanted to talk to her specifically, they might have a good reason. If she disagreed, she could just as easily inform Petrakov afterward. Besides, it might be easier to get a reading on this 'Jones' without the Commodore in the room.

She brought up the Union personnel file and looked up any representative by the name "Jones." Only one result seemed likely, a nearly-blank file, just a name and a start-of-employment year. Lazy civilians – they didn't keep their records current. She re-read the date, and raised one eyebrow. This guy had only had his job for five months?

She searched the Navy's own records for any interaction with this Jones, and came up empty. She was interrupted by the guard's voice from her anteroom. "Mr. Jones is clean. Credentials check out. No implants."

"Very well. Send him in."

The door to her office opened immediately, and a short, dapper man strode in. He barely came up to Conagher's chin, but was almost as wide as he was tall. His pale, smooth skin and short-cropped hair fit the bill of a person living far from the Sun's rays. He was dressed in one of those anonymous gray business suits, every crease in its proper place, that had never quite managed to go out of style over the centuries.

She stood, giving him her professional smile, revealing nothing. "I am Captain Conagher. You wanted to see me?" She knew she was out of practice at talking to civilians, and might have left out some of the courtesies that politesse required, but decided that it worked to her advantage. Judging by the man's suit, he was well used to playing politics. Better to change the game, and make him play by *her* rules.

"Yes." He remained standing, his smile betraying no reaction to her brusqueness. He stepped forward and held out his hand. "Alex Jones."

She shook his hand, firmly, quickly, the Navy way. "Pleased to meet you, Mr. Jones," she replied, her tone carefully neutral. "Please have a seat."

The captain waited a moment, saying nothing. He leaned forward and cleared his throat. "We - that is to say, the Union of the Workers of the Oort Cloud – believe that it would be wise to have a local liaison go along with your force. To help wherever we can."

"Excellent idea, Mr. Jones. We always appreciate help from the Union." She made a point to check her datapad, then looked across at the diminutive man. "I do not see any communiqué on the matter. What sort of help do you propose to provide, exactly?"

"To ensure that there are no civilian casualties."

'No civilian casualties, my ass'. thought the Captain. If that was their goal, they would have cracked down on the rebels earlier, and not left it all to the Fleet. "A liaison, you say? When will he arrive?"

"I am the liaison." His matter-of-fact tone revealed no emotion.

"Ah." She looked at his immaculately-well-kept suit. She wagered that this was the closest to 'field work' he'd ever been. "I trust, then, that you are familiar with the local area?"

"I've been a full-time employee at our local offices for five months, and a public-relations management intern for thirteen before that."

"I see." His answer was evasive and rehearsed, but was revealing nevertheless.. Five months was not nearly long enough to learn the ropes. Nor to earn the trust of the workers. She had learned they were the suspicious type. The question was, did Mr. Jones realize that? Besides, he was clearly older than such a résumé would suggest. Had he earned the trust of Union management in some other position, perhaps?

She leaned back, face impassive, inviting his impatience to fill the silence, but Mr. Jones volunteered nothing.

"We will, of course, extend every appropriate courtesy to the Union." She brought up the man's credentials. Top-level security clearance from the Union. Odd for a junior liaison. On the plus side, it gave her an opening to find out what the man *really* knew.

She tapped her console. "Perhaps you can start helping us right away. We received a message from your Union a few days ago. It had some rather detailed information about what equipment and numbers the insurgents have. Would you, by any chance, have equally detailed information on what the rebel defenses are?"

"I'm afraid that our information does not cover the insurgent's weaponry. But we do not believe that they have acquired anything to threaten the Fleet." He smiled, a slight movement of the mouth that did not reach his eyes.

"I see," Captain Conagher nodded, and kept any emotion off her face. The man had said absolutely nothing of value, which would actually fit with a junior liaison. But he had not been surprised by the question, and had answered far too quickly, and far too glibly. She could hardly believe that by now, the top Union brass would be unaware of the disappearance of the *Verdun*. Either he really *was* the junior rep he professed to be, but with pretensions far above his station, or he was a more senior rep with instructions to lie. Her money was on the latter.

Captain Conagher stood and extended her hand. "Welcome aboard, Mr Jones. I will have my protocol officer extend you every courtesy while you are on board." With instructions to keep him well away from anything in the least bit important, she added silently. This man had given her absolutely nothing, and that is exactly what he would get in return.

"Thank you, ma'am. I look forward to working closely with you." Jones shook hands, and left her office as smoothly as he had entered.

Conagher stared idly at the closed door. Why had the man come to see her, specifically? For that matter, why had he come at all? They had made no secret of their prisoners, yet he had asked absolutely nothing about them. And he had left her office too quickly, not asking for anything, really. So clearly his mission must be something else. He had also said nothing of any value about the rebel base.

The final tell, though, had been his reaction to being assigned a protocol officer. No reaction. Almost as if he had been expecting it. If so, that confirmed her suspicion that he was *not* some junior liaison. What was it, then, that he wanted?

Not knowing bothered her, so she keyed her datapad, and changed her instructions to the protocol officer. Mr. Jones would not be restricted. Let him go where he wanted. Maybe his choices of what to visit would tell her something. However, he would be accompanied everywhere he went, and he would see only what she wanted him to see.

Chapter 13: O'Rourke

"So, you're assigned to my section?" Klaus walked around the newly-arrived repairman. The man was tall and skinny, normal for a man born and raised in free fall. A local, the file said, a miner.

"Yeah."

He didn't say much, either. Well, another wrench-turner would still come in handy. "I see. What experience do you have?"

The miner shrugged. "Worked on ships most of m' life. Enough experience."

"Uh-huh." Klaus patted the corridor wall next to him. They were just outside the damage control room, and the walls were still scarred and pitted from the earlier combat, but at least the gaping holes had been repaired. "You're on a warship now, not some rock-hauler. The man you're replacing is still in sickbay, getting both his lungs replaced. You still think you're ready?"

"Yeah." No change of expression.

"All right. Here's your chance, then. You're chipped, right?" The miner nodded. "Good. Go find Lieutenant Queridos. His team's working on getting the grav corridors working properly. Something the bridge did to the systems during the fight has them completely futzed." Should take a few hours, a good way to get the new kid worked up to speed. Klaus turned to leave. "By the way, the grav corridors are limited to eight gees, on account of the damage. Don't go over that." Better check with Queridos later. The last thing he wanted on his record was a civilian casualty.

As Klaus walked into the damage-control center, he realized that he hadn't asked for the miner's name.

^^*^*^*^*^*^*^*^*

"What do you mean, 'he fixed it already?' I just sent him down there an hour ago!" Klaus yelled into his datapad.

On the other end of the call, Lieutenant Queridos shrugged. "I mean, he worked through the code for all of fifty minutes, and fixed it!"

"What, he went through the entire program?"

"Yes!"

"And how many lines of code?"

There was a pause. "Thirty-seven thousand."

"Nobody works that fast." Klaus thought for a moment. "I'll come down, I want to talk to him."

^^*^*^*^*^*^*^*^*

Arriving outside the grav control room, Klaus found the miner standing outside, leaning against the bulkhead. The kid seemed relaxed, even after how quickly he must have been working. Klaus caught himself. The 'kid' looked to be more than just another replacement, might actually be skilled. Maybe he should try being polite to the man. "What's your name, again?"

"James." The miner's tone was disinterested, bored-sounding.

"James. Nice name." Civilians liked pleasantries, he had learned. "How did you fix the grav code so fast, James?"

The repairman shrugged. "Was easy. Isolated what the bridge crew changed. Wrote around it."

"I see." Made sense, but Klaus suspected that it could not have been that simple. "Out of curiosity, what did they change?"

"Tracking algorithm set to constantly check positions of anybody onboard against list of crew. Written far too quickly – the error-avoidance code was very basic, not useful." Now the kid – James – was talking more normally, and almost sounded awake. He leaned forward, voice gaining in energy and losing its monotone. He even burred his r's. "See, when the software hiccuped, the grav systems identified everybody onboard as intruders. Only for a fraction of a second, though – the failsafes in the system re-booted it fast enough to keep the glitch from being fatal – but enough of a delay to cause problems."

"And you fixed this in, what, thirty minutes?"

"Well, closer to thirty-five." He shrugged, leaning back again. "Problem was right there."

"Where did you get that good at programming?"

He shook his head "I'm not, plenty of friends are better."

Good Lord. Klaus studied the miner's face. Was the kid putting him on? If not, if that was normal for miners, well it raised a lot of new questions. At least it might explain how the rebels had managed to mimic Navy transponder signals closely enough to spoof the *Overlord* and the *Tannenberg*.

"Come on, follow me," Klaus stood, checking the time. "We've got an hour for lunch break. There's someone you should meet. I've got a friend who'll be very interested in talking to you." He turned away from the miner. "Computer, request flight to crewman Antoniy Gureivich. Execute." The corridors flew past him as he ratcheted his speed up to max. He checked that the miner was following him. Good, the kid not only knew his tech, but he had completely ignored Klaus' '8-gees-only' warning.

Entering the mess hall, Klaus found Antoniy easily enough. The Marine was sitting with his back against one of the walls, with a clear sight of the entry.

Antoniy waved at them, and Klaus wound his way over, motioning for the miner to follow. The kid had been so quiet he'd begun to worry if he'd wandered off. "Antoniy, meet James, one of the new guys assigned to my team. He's a miner, one of the locals." Behind him, he heard James mutter something, but he couldn't make it out, and decided it probably wasn't important. He sat down, leaning forward toward Antoniy. "He just fixed the grav system programming in under half an hour."

"Thirty-four minutes." corrected the miner.

Antoniy gave Klaus a blank stare.

"Thirty-four minutes! Did you hear?" Klaus spread his arms. "That's some kind of system record!"

Antoniy raised an eyebrow. "Impressive." He leaned to the side, looking around Klaus towards James. "How'd you manage that?"

"Was simple. Just a quick check."

Klaus took a seat at the table next to Antoniy, pulling out a seat for the miner. "Seriously, how'd you learn to work that fast?"

"It's my job."

"I thought you were a regular tech, not a computer specialist." Klaus furrowed his brow.

James smiled slightly in response, about the first emotion that Klaus had seen out of him. "We're not exactly working with picks and shovels. I'm a computer-integrity specialist."

"Computer-integrity specialist?"

"Yes. We work so close to the leading-edge of the heliosphere that our electronics need to be shielded against extrasolar radiation and the System's bow-wave aftershocks. When set-up on an active dig site, they're shielded by grav screens at the site itself, but when moving between sites the computers are unshielded. Keeps scrambling the code, an absolute pain to repair."

Good God, that was more words than the kid had said since he'd come aboard. Klaus couldn't help grinning in response. "Believe me, I can identify with that sort of pain. I've been having all sorts of trouble with computers being wrecked by—" right, classified information "—ah, transportation." That was technically the truth, too. "So you got your experience by re-programming whole computer systems? Sounds rough."

James shook his head. "Actually, no. My job is to keep the computer code stable during transportation."

Klaus raised one eyebrow. For the first time since he had boarded the Overlord — in fact, if truth be told, for the first time since he had left Earth years ago — he felt a tingle at the back of his brain. He had to work to remember what it was. Ah, he had it. *Intellectual curiosity.* "What?" He sat up straighter in his chair, leaning over the table. "How do you manage that?"

"Hard to describe, exactly. We use a custom neural interface to link a specialist — me — to the computer during the trip. I, ah..." James trailed off, frowning. "I guess the best way to say it is that I 'monitor' the computer's software. When any part of it starts to feel...wrong, I guess, I correct it."

"You can re-write code that fast?" Klaus' eyebrows shot up in astonishment. "For that matter, you can monitor that much software by yourself?"

The min— *programming expert* grinned in response, a full grin this time. "I didn't say it were easy. And I don't really *write* repair code. It's more like I...tell it how to correct itself."

"Right, that neural interface you were talking about."

"Exactly. Faster that way."

"And this works?" Klaus could not help himself from doubting. He exchanged glances with Antoniy, who had been watching the two of them silently. He tried to read the Marine's face, but to no avail. Klaus was the senior engineer at the table, and he did not like being proven wrong, especially not by some upstart. Surely, there must be something the man — he had stopped thinking of him as 'the kid' — was not telling him.

"Yes. Keeps the computers alive during transport."

Amazing. Was the programmer some sort of savant, or might there be some technique here that could be applied to their own issues with the QMP drive? Klaus suddenly felt uncomfortable. For the past several years, people had always been asking *him* questions. Truth be told, he had always felt that he knew more than others, and that included most of his superiors.

Admittedly, that attitude had led to him being stuck on the *Ad Astra* in the first place.

He rubbed his brow, hiding the beads of sweat that he feared were forming. Now that the shoe was on the other foot, he could not let on that he felt at all uncertain. Maybe it was a false hope, after all, and the kid — the programmer, he corrected himself — had only diagnosed simple processing units. "What sort of computer systems have you worked with?"

"The largest I've handled was a CQ-37."

Not bad. The CQ-37 was normally used on near-Earth stations, to plot the courses of the billions of Kessler debris pieces left in the planet's orbit.

More importantly, it was easily as complex as any of the computers aboard the *Overlord.* "Did you bring one of those neural interfaces with you?"

"Yes."

"Excellent. Kid — I mean, *James* — the Captain has authorized me to move you to my team. Believe me, better than baking in the reactor rooms." Klaus would figure out later how to get that one approved retroactively. He quickly messaged Johann, telling him that he had a promising idea for fixing the QMP system. Turning back to James, he asked "What work schedule are you on?"

"Third shift."

"I'll get you up to speed on a project of mine. It's certainly more interesting than any of the other stuff they've got you working on now." And more important.

Antoniy stood, holding his tray piled with empty dishes. "Well, now that that's settled, I could use some more food. Care to join me?"

As the three men approached the cafeteria line, Klaus' datapad chimed. Message from PO Murphy, who was working with Johann to direct the repair crews that were fixing the damage to the *Overlord's* internal QMP support latticework. A top secret system, and absolutely vital to boot. Or it would be, if they ever got a chance to use it.

Testing pipe repair in bulkhead seven-C outside reactor four. Assume you want to be here.

Lunch could wait. He returned his tray and turned to leave. "Sorry, gotta run. Got work to do that just came up." He looked at James and instructed, "Meet me at auxiliary engine compartment C in twenty — that's minutes. The ship's computer can show you the way. Bring your neural interface."

As he turned to go, he added, "Oh, and remember, this is the Navy. Our work could be important, so don't mention this to anyone."

^^*^*^*^*^*^*^*^*^*

Antoniy and James returned to their table with full trays, and Antoniy took the same seat against the wall. He scanned the room once more, out of habit.

He then studied the civilian, who was shoveling down his food in silence. Klaus seemed to think that this guy was some sort of computer wizard — and to be fair to Klaus, that meant that he *was* — but Antoniy was interested in a different aspect of this 'James.'

He knew that the guy had been vetted by Intelligence section, so he certainly wasn't a rebel sympathizer. But he was still a local civilian.

In Antoniy's trade, that made him either an intelligence risk or an intelligence source. "So, 'James,' right?"

"Yes."

Not a talkative fellow. "Sorry about my friend there, Klaus tends to get caught up in his favorite topics."

"I noticed."

Well, if this fellow tended towards bluntness, then maybe he'd be open to blunt questions from Antoniy. That would save time if he could jump right in. "If you don't mind my asking, why did you choose to work on a repair ship?"

Across from him, the miner barely glanced up from his plate of pasta, which he was doing his level best to inhale. "Wuff a jov." He swallowed. "Was a job. Between contracts. Pay lower than hoped, but at least something." He pointed at himself with a fork. "James O'Rourke, by the way."

"Of course, where are my manners?" Antoniy held out his hand. "Antoniy Gureivich, Marine Corps."

The civilian raised his eyebrows, looking directly at his counterpart for the first time. He shook Antoniy's hand. "A Marine?"

"Yeah."

"Why?"

Antoniy took a small bite out of his sandwich. It was as good as it looked. Was that a real tomato? Amazing. The food here was certainly better than at Andromeda Station. "I've always wanted to serve, and they paid my way through college. Good deal, if you ask me."

"True. M' brother thought it was a good idea, too. He's Navy now."

"Really? Which ship?"

"Dunno. Classified."

"Ah. Still, I didn't know many people off-Earth served. I don't think I've met anyone in the services who's not from Earth or the Moon."

James shrugged. "Well, that's just statistics, I'd say, a result of unequal population distribution. There's far more folks on Earth than anywhere else in the system." He waved a fork in the air to emphasize his point, the large meatball at its end threatening to fly across the room. He popped it into his mouth and swallowed. "I'd wager that a higher percentage of miners join the military than Earthers."

"Huh. That would be surprising." Antoniy took a small bite of his sandwich. The culture of the Navy was certainly Earth-centric, based on what he had seen, and he had always assumed that such a culture would have discouraged enlistment from among others. His time at Andromeda Station, including the intel reports he had read, had only reinforced those assumptions, but maybe he had missed something. "Y'know, I've never had the opportunity to talk much with the locals out here. What's your opinion about all this?" He gestured to the ship around them.

"'bout what?"

"The whole issue with the rebels around here. If so many miners are in the armed services, why is there such support for the rebels out here?"

"Huh? Don't know anybody who supports the rebels, not really. Mind you, the Feds are not exactly popular, either. Wish they would lower the taxes out here – pay enough for fuel imports, already."

"Oh? I didn't realize that the taxes were that bad out here."

"Shit flows downhill." James smiled at the puzzled look on Antoniy's face. "Well, technically the tax is on the Union, not on us, you see. They just pass the cost right on to us. And on top of that, the Union's enacted a special levy to pay for fighting the rebels. So, all told, we end up paying almost fifty percent of our income."

"Fifty percent? Why work for the union, then?"

"All there is. Union or starve."

Antoniy studied his sandwich, speaking over the top. "I'd always heard that the miners pay nothing. Didn't they make some big point on that a while back, about no income tax on hazard pay?"

James finished a glass of juice and wiped his lips with the back of his hand. He smiled. "In *your* media, maybe. Just words. Bottom line, we don't get your Earther single-digit tax rates."

Antoniy nodded, eyeing his empty plate. He wanted to continue, but lunch was done, and he had work to do. Surprisingly, this was the first he'd personally heard of people from the outer System in the Navy — all of his classmates in the Academy were from Earth or one of the established colonies.

He smiled back, "So why don't you side with the rebels, then? If you don't mind my asking. Don't they promise you everything you want?"

James looked to his left, then his right. He cleared the last bit of pasta from his plate, then leaned back in his chair. "There's promising and then there's doing. Out here, we can't live on words. That will get you dead." He sighed. "Maybe we just want what you want. Peace and liberty." He chuckled briefly. "Seriously, make a living. Nobody watching over our shoulders all the time."

"Hmmph." Antoniy mulled that over, looking again at the walls of the cafeteria. Walls everywhere. For all the empty space in the Cloud, the places where people could live were miniscule and far between. All encased in steel. He had always thought of it as the raw frontier, a rough place with little use for law or order or any other trappings of Earth, but maybe that was just an illusion. He stood to leave, shaking hands with James. "Good to meet you, Mr. O'Rourke. I hope you get what you want."

He left, thinking about what the miner had said. During their conversation, he had looked for telltales in the man, for subtle signs of lying. Everything indicated he was telling the truth. If so, how could intel have been so wrong?

^^*^*^*^*^*^*^*^*^*

A few hours later, Klaus sat in the observer's chair in the QMP control room. In the seat next to him sat James, who was fiddling with his neural interface, a slimmed-down helmet which he was painstakingly fitting onto his head.

A veritable rat's nest of wires connected the interface to the control computer, which James would use to communicate wirelessly with the test computer in the actual rig in the teleport box. They had petabytes of stored gibberish in the files, exact copies of the code that had come through on each failed experiment. Though Johann had wanted to start with fresh teleports and let James fix the code in real-time, Klaus had over-ridden him. Technically, all research on QMP was supposed to be halted, per the Captain's orders, and they weren't even supposed to be in here. He viewed those orders more as guidelines, and they might just get away with ignoring them.

As long as they showed results.

And for that, they needed time to experiment. If they requisitioned the ship's precious store of osmium, and tapped into the gigajoules of power the teleport would take, then even some dimwit pencil-pusher in the chain of command was bound to notice and shut them down. And he had no doubt whatsoever who they would blame for this. Not either of the civilians, that was for sure. Better to fly under the radar, at least for now.

Despite his doubts, he was gambling that James could find patterns in the garbled code which they had not. Something about it didn't sit right with him. His code repairs had been good, his approach very thorough. Yet he had not found the answer. How could some Oort Cloud newbie succeed where he and Johann had failed? He shook his head, reminding himself that it didn't matter, as long as they came up with something that worked. If so, all would be forgiven. He would have his once-promising career back, no more scrap heaps like the *Ad Astra.*

Probably. But if they were caught before they succeeded, or if they failed, he could kiss any hope of that goodbye.

He shrugged. Better not fail, then. He turned to Johann, who sat at the master-control chair. "Is everything set up? Everything ready?"

Johann nodded in response. "Aye, we're all set here." He flashed Klaus a quick grin. "Here's hoping all this works, eh?"

He hit the key.

James grunted once, but gave no other outward sign. He sat motionless in his chair, eyes closed, but Klaus could see his eyes moving rapidly back and forth behind his lids. The miner frowned a couple of times, and smiled at others. On the display screen, bits of code spun in circles with larger clouds of gibberish, an entirely incomprehensible mess. Slowly the clouds coalesced, spiraling around the small bits of clear code, and then attaching themselves here and there. The spirals whirled faster and faster, changing colors as they resolved into order.

From Johann's computer, bagpipes played.

"What's that?" asked James, opening his eyes. His voice wavered in uncertainty.

"That, my dear boy," beamed Johann, "is success." He checked his display again, and then smiled over at Klaus. "He beat your best time by half!"

Klaus frowned. It was great progress, but still not fast enough to make jumps useful to the Navy. Which meant no reward.

James smiled, his voice now steady. "Can do better, I think. Takes time to get used to the code." He closed his eyes a moment, lost in concentration, then opened them again. "And to find the markers."

"Markers?" Klaus raised an eyebrow. Then he grinned. "Oh, I see. Well, have at it, James, but I warn you, it won't be easy." He tapped the display in front of him, resetting the computer and bringing up a new trial. "I've looked at dozens of these runs, and my software can't find anything at all resembling a pattern."

James grinned. "That's why we use specialists, not code."

^^*^*^*^*^*^*^*^*^*

Hours later, Klaus leaned back and massaged his temples. He was exhausted, but nevertheless his pulse raced with a glimmer of hope. The trials had gone much better than he had thought possible. "James, I wouldn't have believed it."

"Aye, fifteen trials, each one faster," Johann echoed, frowning at his own screen and tapping some keys. "But we still don't know how you did it, exactly. How am I going to write that up?"

"Forget the damn journals, Johann." Klaus leaned forward. There was no time for the physicist's academic theory, not now. What mattered was getting the thing to work, and getting it to work every single time. "Look, I've been recording where he puts his markers. If I can just automate what he's doing, never mind how, then we can give the Captain what she asked for."

"Uh, can I say something?" James raised his hand, as if asking permission to speak. His eyes were bloodshot, and his stomach growled audibly. "Is anyone else hungry?"

"Hungry?" asked Klaus. "How can you be hungry at a time like this?"

Johann stood and paced, hands behind his back. "But this is only part of the problem, isn't it? Sure, he fixed the code that we got canned in these little boxes." He slapped the top of his display. "But can he do it on a real ju—?"

Klaus made a chopping motion with his arm to stop him. So far, he hadn't revealed any secrets to James, and he did not want to. That would only dig their hole that much deeper. Still, though, the man had a point. "I've been thinking the same thing." He pinched the bridge of his nose. "Unfortunately."

James looked back and forth between them. "What are you talking about?"

Klaus paced, joining Johann. "We're going to have to do it for real. With osmi—" He cast a guilty glance at James, "er, with more equipment, and more power." He faced Johann. "And with Murphy."

"Murphy? What on earth for?"

"Someone has to keep you from killing all of us, Johann." Klaus stopped, checking James' face. Surprisingly, the programmer had shown no reaction to his exchange with Johann. Maybe the kid just didn't understand the stakes. He snapped his fingers as another thought struck him. "And we need someone that the Captain trusts. No offense."

"I warn you, boy, she's a real stickler for the rules. What makes you think she will help?" began the physicist. He paused. "Aye, but she is good, I grant you that. With her help, we could present the Captain with something that works."

Klaus nodded. "Either that, or she'll have us sent to the brig."

Chapter 14: Murphy

"You want to what?" Murphy hissed, looking up from her tray, eyes narrowed.

"Not so loud!" Klaus' eyes scanned left and right. Nobody in the cafeteria seemed to be paying them any attention. Probably all too tired from the repair work. He leaned closer. "Look, you know how important the jump drive would be, right? I mean, the Captain assigned you for a reason, and I don't think it was random."

She said nothing. Just stared.

"So you *do* know. Good." Klaus smiled to himself. He had just made a guess about Murphy, but in hindsight it made sense. PO North had been appropriately uninterested in the actual physics, but not Murphy. She had taken a real interest in what they were doing, had asked all the wrong questions for a random petty officer, and none of the right ones. It made sense, though. Conagher had assigned her, and the Captain seemed to have a lot more up her sleeve than what she had let on.

He spread his hands. "We need you there, Murphy. For one thing, Johann would blow all of us sky high. The man is a menace with anything beyond theory. For another, we need more osmium, and we need power. You know the drill."

She looked up, face neutral. "That's disobeying a direct order from the Captain. I can think of at least three different charges for that one." She tilted her head, a faint grin on her face, and locked eyes with Klaus. "Is that all?"

"Ah, no." Klaus fidgeted in his seat. This was going to be the tricky part. He wasn't so keen on the idea himself, so he was not sure how to convince Roberta. "We have a breakthrough. We've got the code fix and reboot time down to just a few seconds."

"That's great news. Congratulations!" she sat forward. "But I don't get it. If you succeeded, I'm sure the Captain would rescind her orders, and let you..." Her voice trailed off. "Oh, I see. You did it on the old test code?"

Klaus nodded.

"And you need to test it for real. That's why you need me." She frowned. "Even so, why not just ask the Captain?"

"Well, that's the tricky part. We owe the breakthrough to this miner, er, programming specialist, and —"

"I see." She dragged out the words, then paused. "Let me guess, a civilian?"

Klaus nodded again, holding her gaze.

"And you absolutely need all three of us to read him in on the QMP technology? The *top secret* QMP technology?"

Klaus shook his head. "No other way."

She took a bite of her steak, chewed it thoroughly, and then swallowed. She pointed her fork at Klaus. "You realize that's treason, don't you?"

∧∧*∧*∧*∧*∧*∧*∧*∧*∧*

Murphy called from her monitor's chair. "All recording sensors are green, safety interlocks engaged, we're ready to go."

Klaus smiled at her, relieved that she had volunteered to help. More than help, in fact. She had pulled rank and arranged for the osmium they needed, and found a way to divert energy for their tests. Even so, it would not last. They had at best a few hours before some idle busybody on the bridge had nothing else to do, and noticed the missing osmium, or the power they had hijacked. Then they would all be hauled off in chains.

"Got it. Ready here as well," answered Johann.

He turned to the miner. "Last chance, James. You can back out now. If you stay here, you can get into real trouble. Navy justice, and believe me you wouldn't like it."

"For what? You still haven't told me." The specialist swallowed the last bite of the burger that Klaus had brought from the cafeteria.

Klaus drummed his fingers on the desk. He had been dreading this moment. If he told James about the QMP, he would be repeating the same security breach that had killed his career years ago. And since he was on a warship engaged in battle, that would literally be treason this time. No simple tramp freighters in his future, but a nice metal cell for the rest of his life.

If he was lucky.

But there was no other way, not if he wanted his life back. Johann would be okay, being a civilian. Might even publish an article after this was all over. The same for James. After all, what could they do, banish him to the Oort Cloud?

He glanced at Murphy. She knew the risks, but had agreed to help them, anyway. He could not figure out what she had to gain, but maybe it had something to do with why she had been assigned in the first place. She was by the books Navy. So that meant the Navy wanted this working more than they were saying. Or somebody in the Navy.

It came back to success. If this worked, everybody would be fine. If it didn't, the truth would come out sooner or later. Hell, James might spill everything to his friends in the cafeteria. But so far, James had trusted him. He had done everything Klaus asked, without objecting, or even asking why. So now he needed to trust the miner in return.

"It's called a quantum multi-positioning jump," he said, "a controlled test with one of the ship's computers."

"Teleporting, eh? Seriously? That's one for the 'zines," scoffed James, stifling a quick laugh. He looked around. "You really mean it, don't you? And, ah, I don't think you should be telling me this." He shook his head, thinking a moment, and then re-seated his helmet. He gave a thumbs-up "Count me in."

Klaus let out a long breath. For better or worse, they were all in it now.

Everything was set to go. It was all familiar from the numerous tests they had run when Klaus first started the QMP experiments. Except—

"I'm ready, too. I've got a feel for what the code should look like." James added. "This isn't that much software you've got me watching over, by the way. Should be easy."

"So you say." Klaus turned to Murphy. "Let's start this, then."

"Aye, sir." The petty-officer's voice was crisp and by the book as she entered the commands into her console, and the experiment began. No sounds reached to the control room from the actual testing chamber, of course — it was too well insulated. "Test vehicle launched."

Next to Klaus, James suddenly clutched his head and grunted.

"You alright, kid?" The last thing Klaus needed was a civilian injured while they were committing treason. Not unless they had a result to show for it.

"Yeah. Just...ow! That's quite a kick to the brain. Like a migraine, but sudden."

"Is that normal?"

"Never had it before, actually." James frowned. "I hit this really short, very intense moment of nausea."

Johann looked up from his display. "D'y'reckon it's an effect of multi-positioning?"

"I don't see what else it could be." Klaus shrugged. He gave a warning glance toward James. "We'll see if it hits again when the rig returns."

The miner's head snapped up. "You mean tha—sonuvabitch!" He clutched his head.

In a neutral voice, Murphy reported, "Test rig is back," but her expression betrayed her. She looked up at James, concern written in her furrowed brow. "Code is non-functional." In a more hopeful voice, she added "eighty-seven-percent reduction in software fragmentation, though."

James straightened in his chair. "Uh, took me by surprise. Can we run again? Lemme have another shot, see if I can get those programs cleaned up completely. Would be *some* sort of victory. Shouldn't be too long."

After a few minutes of James reclining almost motionless in his chair, eyes closed, he mumbled "There. That oughta do it. Hit it."

Klaus had his doubts, but gave the go-ahead anyway. Sure enough, no sooner had the test rig returned to its proper cradle, it seemed, than Johann's pad started played bagpipes. James clapped his hands to his ears, and Klaus hissed, "Turn that damned thing off!"

"Sorry," Johann apologized — for the first time in his life, as far as Klaus knew. But then the Scotsman beamed. "Success!"

"Not quite. *A* success. Not total success." Klaus shook his head. "We'll need to run more tests, to see if it's repeatable." He chewed his lip for a moment, thinking. "I'll want to change the test code a bit, too." He turned to James, explaining. "I've got a few repair scripts that I've written to automate the markers from each test we've run before. I'll add it to the computer; all you need to do is restore that section of the software, and it should largely take care of itself."

With any luck, Klaus hoped to find some way to remove the need for the organic component — James — to be involved in the cleanup process. He still felt odd about not understanding exactly *how* the specialist had kept even part of the code from fragmenting. It seemed like a miracle, with no rational explanation for how exactly it worked.

Klaus distrusted miracles. They weren't repeatable, weren't analyzable.

Five minutes later, PO Murphy read out the test results. "Test three of active-guidance QMP transition...success. Software re-instated and functioning seventeen-point-five seconds after transition arrival."

Johann shot out of his seat, as the bagpipes played again. "Ha! Another success!" He reached over, patting James on the back. "You're a bloody wonder, Jimmy boy!"

"James," came the curt response. His voice slurred slightly as he added "M'name's James." He dropped his head solidly onto the little remaining clear space on the control table. The wires attached to his helmet rustled. "Lemme...ah...lemme just sit here for a few."

Murphy read aloud as she entered her notes into the log. "Guidance procedure is taxing for personnel involved in active, neuro-connective software repair."

Klaus leaned over to Johann and whispered, trying not to disturb James. "Seventeen-point-five seconds! Told you my programs would improve repair speed."

With humor in his voice, barely louder than Klaus' whisper, Johann responded "Aye, but there's plenty o' credit to go around for this!" His voice rose back to its normal volume. "We've done it! Drinks are on me tonight, lads!"

"No drinks," moaned James, his hands clapped over his ears.

"Sorry to interrupt the celebrations, but even with this" Klaus gestured to the still-head-down James "we just can't move the whole ship. The poor man can move two, maybe three processing hubs, but he's down for the count after that."

"Bah." Johann waved his hand dismissively. "That'll come in time, just see if it doesn't. We've seen a wee bit of success, now we just need t' refine the methods involved."

Klaus hoped that Johann's confidence was well-placed, but he had his doubts. Technology, now *that* he knew how to scale up. Humans, however, were another matter entirely. James wasn't doing anything that a machine shouldn't be able to replicate, yet in less than an hour's work he had blown past any results that Klaus and Johann had managed to achieve with QMP technology. The QMP technology that *they* had invented.

On the other hand, now that they had found something that actually worked, Klaus should be able to analyze it to understand exactly what was going on. He had no doubt that with enough testing, he could find a solution. This was *his* technology field, after all.

But to do that, they had to stay out of the brig.

"We need to talk to the Captain. Now."

∧∧*∧*∧*∧*∧*∧*∧*∧*∧*

"Is there any reason I shouldn't just throw you in the brig?" demanded Captain Conagher.

Klaus, Johann and PO Murphy stood uncomfortably in front of her desk, eyes straight ahead. They had left James in the outer office, under guard. Klaus had not wanted to make the situation worse, and Captains always hated loose ends.

Johann started, "Well, I'm a civilian, you see, and —"

Klaus elbowed him in the ribs. "No ma'am. We disobeyed a direct order."

The Captain turned to Murphy. "And you, Petty Officer. I would expect something like this from these two" She waved at Klaus and Johann, "But you were supposed to keep them out of trouble, not help them get into it."

"Yes, ma'am."

Conagher leaned back, letting the moment draw out. She studied the report that Murphy had given her, then looked up. "Very well. PO Murphy, you will coordinate directly with Commander Li Yat-Sen." She looked Klaus and Johann in the eye. "He is our chief engineering officer, emphasis on engineering. You better make this work. As for you two, I will re-consider the charges against you in four days. That means you have four days to make him happy." She focused again on her console.

Klaus and Johann stared at each other. Murphy smiled to herself.

The Captain looked up, one eyebrow raised. "Dismissed."

Chapter 15: Podera

"Coming in on destination. Fricsim transition to sub-cee in thirty seconds," announced the helmsman.

Captain Conagher steepled her fingers, and rested her chin on her thumbs. After the long days of repair near Andromeda Station, she was eager to finally see action. She and Petrakov had worked on refining their battle plan, although she still had her concerns. Would this be another ambush, despite their unorthodox approach? She turned to Commodore Petrakov, and spoke in a low voice. The Captain's and Commodore's chairs were isolated towards the rear of the bridge, conveniently allowing this sort of privacy. "So we're agreed? Retract sails immediately upon arrival?"

The sails were coming in one way or another, but it was easier if she didn't have to blame a 'computer malfunction.' Her job would also be much easier if the Commodore wasn't trying to override her, too.

"Yeah." Petrakov frowned slightly, but didn't disagree. He lowered his voice so that only she could hear. "I still say they should stay out. The enemy will run."

"Agreed, then." Raising her voice, the Captain added "Engineering, confirm retract sails immediately upon transition."

"Sails in immediately after cee-barrier breach, aye, ma'am."

The *Overlord* slowed to sub-cee speeds, and its sensors began to probe the surrounding area. Emerging this close to their target was risky, but Conagher had convinced the Commodore of the tactical advantage. The planetoid, 1048 Podera, was an enormous blip on the bridge holo-display. The *Tannenberg* had appeared within close range of the rebel station, while the *Overlord* had taken up station farther back. This let the larger warship train her guns over the entire face of Podera, her fire-arcs not blocked by the station itself. But their emergence point put them inside any distant defenses the rebels might have set up to ambush them.

On the downside, it made her a prime target for close-in, planetoid-based defenses.

"Incoming weapons fire, ma'am. Kinetic-Energy projectiles, count six. Velocity zero-point-zero-nine-five-cee, ma'am," called the tactical officer.

"Hold fire," she commanded. If there were more emplacements out there, they might reveal themselves.

Captain Conagher stared intently at the holo-display as the bright-red icons of enemy railgun fire streaked towards the *Overlord.* Less than point-one-cee was slow for railgun fire. Were the rebels not as well-equipped with heavy weapons as she had feared, or had they moved them out to periphery defense?

The icons reached the *Overlord's* blip, and overlapped.

A muted *clang* reached the bridge, and the damage-control console beeped. "Light damage, ma'am! Layer-three armor belt in section O1-45-37 holed at four locations!"

Conagher let out a breath that she hadn't realized she had been holding. That was much lighter damage than she'd expected. Still, the fact that the enemy had opened fire so rapidly meant that

190

the enemy gunnery crews were either very well trained, or they had anticipated her close-in tactic. And there were no trailing salvos.

No sense, then, in holding her fire. Decision made, there was no time to waste. While the enemy weapons batteries were well-hidden on the surface of the planetoid, they had revealed themselves when they fired on the *Overlord.*

"Main battery, return fire. Two rounds per target," replied the Captain. "There's bound to be more emplacements. Fire upon them as they are detected." In the ground-clutter of Podera, even long-barreled high-power railguns would be almost impossible to spot until they fired. That was one of the risks of being this close.

"Return fire, aye. Free to engage weapons emplacements as detected, aye."

Two more emplacements opened fire, and the *Overlord*'s starboard railgun battery loosed a flight of projectiles in return. Their icons on the holo-display raced towards their targets. Their impacts were almost anti-climactic. No secondary explosions, only the silent disappearance of six red markers.

Conagher nodded. That was more like it. The rebels must have armored their magazines, or kept them far from the weapons themselves. They didn't have military-grade deflectors, thankfully, but the enemy had done the best they could to protect their guns. They'd put some effort into this, which meant they valued this particular base. Maybe the Union intel had been right, after all.

The battery armor wouldn't help them, though. The *Overlord* and the *Tannenberg* carried enough ammunition to reduce any surface structure to slag. Without hardened weapons emplacements or docking bays, the rebels would have no way to keep the Navy squadron at a distance, nor to make their own escape if the squadron approached nearer. This close, even two ships could easily keep anyone from escaping, and wait for reinforcements to arrive to clean out the base at their leisure They would have to run for it right away, or give up.

As if to confirm her deduction, the tactical officer called out "Ma'am! Multiple drive signatures detected, designated bogeys one through thirteen. All bogeys are moving away from the station. Bogeys are breaking formation."

The Captain examined her own repeater display, built into the command chair. The rebel ships were accelerating very slowly – less than one gee – and their drive traces matched the patterns typical of the gravity-sensitive engines that were used this far out-System. "Let them go for now. Tag them, and set an alert if they change acceleration." At that rate, they would take hours to clear Podera's gravity well far enough to jump.

Most likely cargo carriers, not personnel transports. Most likely a distraction, as the rebel commander would never put their leaders onto craft that slow. She'd hunt them down later, after the base was reduced.

"Sure enough, they're running." The Commodore crowed. "They didn't expect us."

"And they're certainly letting us know it. I can't believe that they didn't expect us here. They must have gotten a report of their losses at Worzik." She highlighted the disabled weapons platforms so that the Commodore could see. "There's no way this was their entire defense."

"Perhaps. But they obviously haven't expected us." He highlighted an icon on his own display. "Over here, at the station we discussed. They're already evacuating."

Conagher focused where the Commodore was pointing, toggling the pre-programmed location to her display for closer detail. She zoomed in, revealing a space elevator extending from the planetoid. A spoked-wheel station, less than a kilometer across, perched halfway up. Three transports hovered near the station, faint grav signatures indicating shuttles running back and forth between the spacefaring ships and the station.

Sure enough, as she had predicted, the enemy were evacuating. And given the tendencies of the enemy so far, she had no doubt that any enemy leaders would be among the first onto the evacuation vessels.

Commodore Petrakov seemed to have reached the same conclusion. He keyed the ship-to-ship comm on his console. "*Tannenberg*, eyes on this location." He toggled the highlighted station on his detail display to send it to the squadron-wide datanet. "Disable and board these ships, prioritizing taking enemy prisoners. Be on the lookout for ambushes or traps."

"Aye, sir" came the reply, the station icon in the squadron holo pulsing green to acknowledge the target. "Targeting hostile craft for capture."

Petrakov turned back to the captain. "Congratulations. Your plan worked, Captain. Their weapons emplacements here aren't anywhere near as well-shielded as expected. We can afford to go after prisoners rather than shoot them as they flee."

She'd realized that whole minutes ago, of course, but it was nice to see that the Commodore had as well.

The *Tannenberg* accelerated towards the enemy craft. As the *Tannenberg* loomed closer, the larger enemy ships accelerated away from the station, leaving the dots of their shuttles behind. Their high-gee acceleration revealed them as personnel transports.

Excellent. Drive cores that could pull that off this far out-system were damned expensive. Those must be high-priority transports for the enemy. Hopefully, for enemy officers.

The enemy had to realize that they wouldn't escape the *Tannenberg,* not with it so close to their fleeing ships. They'd need to make a distraction. Captain Conagher's eyes shot back to the main display just in time to see another rash of red dots flare, around the base of the station's elevator.

"More weapons platforms firing, ma'am. They're targeting the *Tannenberg.*" The tactical officer's voice was calmer now. The *Overlord* was not in danger.

The *Tannenberg* did, however, have to maneuver out of the path of the enemy shots. This let the evacuation ships put a few hundred kilometers more between them and the *Tannenberg.* Unacceptable.

"Main battery firing, ma'am." announced the weapons officer. A few seconds later, "all target batteries destroyed, ma'am. No secondaries."

The *Tannenberg* was almost within grav-beam range of the enemy shuttles trying to escape their station. She was nearly on top of the station itself, maneuvering slightly to avoid outright collision with the giant chunk of rock to which the station was anchored.

Her attention moved back to the black-marked icons of the destroyed weapons emplacements. She hoped the rebels kept firing those half-hearted salvoes. Neither the *Tannenberg* nor the *Overlord* were close enough to the surface to be threatened by such low-velocity cannons. The more enemy weapons lost for no gain, the better.

All the same, the attack felt almost *too* easy. Doubt tickled at the back of her mind. The enemy had competent commanders somewhere. The earlier fighting had shown that. But where were they?

No sooner had the thought crossed her mind than the holo-display pinged red again. But this time the new weapons emplacements were — *on the station?* Still low-velocity weapons, but much larger than the earlier batteries. But the station couldn't be stable enough — or large enough — for railguns of any meaningful size. They would just tear it apart!

"Ma'am! Enemy railguns firing on the *Tannenberg*!"

Yet there they were. Firing point-blank into the *Overlord's* squadron-mate. Captain Conagher gritted her teeth. At that range, the deflectors wouldn't stop much.

Eighteen shots burst forth from the maws of the cannons on the station. Seven missed the *Tannenberg*, even at that range, as the small station bucked under the recoil of the huge guns. But eleven shots slammed into the warship.

Most of the Marine complement of the *Overlord* was on the *Tannenberg*. It had seemed like a good idea when planning the attack, as the combined force would make boarding rebel ships easier, but now she regretted putting the bulk of their fighting forces into unnecessary danger.

She realized that the combined Marine complement would have staged in the outer hangars of the *Tannenberg*. Standard military procedure. Faster to get into their own shuttles, faster to board the enemy. But more exposed to enemy fire.

"*Tannenberg* reports damage to main reactor. They're venting it. *Tannenberg* reports main power lost!"

Damn! That barrage must have destroyed many of the hangars where the Marines were staged if it had reached deep enough to hit the reactor. Worse, the *Tannenberg* had only the one reactor, to the *Overlord*'s eight. Losing it was critical. She focused her display on the rebel station. The recoil of the large railguns — they must have taken up most of the interior room, a Potemkin disguise — had crumpled it and launched the whole mess away from the *Tannenberg*. As she watched, the elevator stalk snapped halfway up from the planetoid, unable to hold the strain, and broke away.

"Acknowledged," she answered, biting back a strong curse. She would not let herself break protocol, not in front of the crew. She looked to the Commodore, her mouth set in a flat line. She would give him exactly half a second to give the right order, or *she* would.

"Oh, Hell." Petrakov grimaced. "Helm, move us closer to the station, flank speed. Prepare to run a grav tether to the *Tannenberg*. We'll pull her back to stand-off distance."

"Aye, sir."

That was really the only thing to do under the circumstances. Without power, the *Tannenberg* was a sitting duck for any remaining enemy weapons. She would have to be shielded and rescued by the *Overlord*.

But that would mean letting the enemy transports — and their presumed valuable passengers — escape. Then again, if the enemy had planned enough to hide one-shot railguns in the station, those ships were probably decoys anyways. Almost a waste to destroy them, but targets were targets. "Guns, disable all enemy escape ships and shuttles. Destroy them if you have to."

"Aye, ma'am." The small vessels disappeared in flashes on the display, most replaced by blinking gray icons, others vanishing completely. Some would be damaged more than others, some destroyed outright. But that couldn't be helped. She knew that if there were high-value rebels on those ships, they no doubt had priority on the life-support pods.

She felt a slight tug as the *Overlord* accelerated, closing the range between her and the stricken *Tannenberg*. Less than a thousand kilometers, almost within grav-tether range—

The room lurched, throwing the Captain against her seat's restraints. The overhead lights, the console displays, even the gravity blinked out for a split-second before returning.

Thankfully, the ship's software coasted over the power interruption. The consoles and display still functioned, green status lights flicking to red.

"What the hell was that?" asked the Captain. Nothing had shown on the display, no warning of inbound weapons fire.

Engineering Officer Li looked at his console, shot out of his seat, and dashed over to one of his junior staffers' console. Brushing the crewman aside, his hands flew over the keyboard. He turned, looking the Captain in the eye, all blood drained from his face. "Ma'am! The fricsim drive has overloaded! It's down, ma'am!"

"What!?" That was one of the most reliable systems on the ship!

Li put a finger to his ear, listening through his headset. "Fricsim crew chief says it looks like sabotage. Primary and secondary coolant channels were drained, and the safety restraints were all jammed open."

"Who's in charge there?"

"CPO Torstensson, ma'am," Li shook his head, "one of my best. If he says sabotage, then it *is* sabotage."

Damn. She didn't want to believe that they had been betrayed, but she had to. But by whom? She'd personally vetted Li and his entire senior staff, and nobody else had high-enough level access to the drive. To get past *all* of the safeguards, you'd need to remove all of the cover panels, which never happened except when – her eyes widened as a realization struck her – it was being *repaired*.

There was still a glimmer of hope. Maybe the saboteurs did not fully know the system's weak points. "Can the drive be repaired?"

"We've got a damage-control crew en-route to see if they can, ma'am. But we're short-handed. I wouldn't bet on it."

"Navy crew?" she asked, and got an answering nod. Good. The Miner's Union repair crew had worked on the fricsim drive. They were the only probable saboteurs. What the hell were they playing at? Could that have been the real purpose of the 'liaison' they had sent aboard earlier? But how the hell had they managed it? He'd been watched by her crew ever since he came aboard, and he hadn't been anywhere near those drives. Besides, there were layers of failsafes and double-checks on everything the repair crew did. Maybe Jones had just been a distraction. She saved that train of thought for later – for now, she had to contain the problem.

Most of the Union repair crew had disembarked the previous day, but a few of them had been retained aboard to finish repairs. Including liaison Jones. Turning to the bridge Marine officer, she barked "Secure the remaining Union crew, search them and take them to the brig. Double the watch on Mr. Jones. He is not to leave his quarters. For his own safety."

It wasn't really a lie. If word got out, someone in the crew might kill him. Discipline only went so far. She would deal with the saboteurs later. But right now, the *Tannenberg* was in danger. "What is our maneuverability without the fricsim drive?"

"Barely there, ma'am. We can brute-force the deflector screens to move us, but we won't get above ten gees of acceleration."

That was practically nothing compared to what the *Overlord* could do normally, faster than civilian transports, but not much use in combat. Still, it was enough for basic maneuvering, at least. "Better than nothing. Move us in."

"Aye, ma'am."

This whole attack was turning into an embarassment. The rebels, supposedly on the run, if the Union were to be believed, had managed to sucker-punch a Navy squadron. And if the *Overlord* couldn't reach the smaller warship very soon, the enemy might even destroy a Navy capital ship. That was the sort of propaganda victory that brought in yet more support to this sort of insurgency. Maybe that was the rebels' 'bigger goal' she had suggested to Petrakov.

The engineering officer interrupted her thoughts. "Ma'am! Damage-control crew at the fricsim drive report primary engine coils are half-melted! The drive's down for good!"

Of course. When it rains, it pours.

Before she could respond, the tactical officer announced, "Ma'am! Gravitational trace, coming out from behind the planetoid. Designated bogey fourteen."

"Any I.D. on the trace?"

"No, ma'am. It's partially shielded by the planet's grav well."

"Very well. Estimated tonnage?"

"Five point eight gigatons, ma'am."

Larger than any rebel ships yet encountered. As big as the *Tannenberg*, or—

"Ma'am! Bogey fourteen emerging from behind the planetoid. Target identified as the *Verdun!* She's firing on us, ma'am! Four rounds incoming, one kilometer spread, velocity zero-point-three-five-cee. Impact in eight seconds."

"Full screens!" she called. The better choice.

"Aye, ma'am."

With her drives crippled, diverting screen power to maneuver out of the way was not an option, because they would never dodge in time. But at least that left plenty of power available for deflectors. The ship's computers automatically re-routed deflector-screen power to the emitters on the side facing the *Verdun.*

The enemy salvo struck the *Overlord.* Again, the sound of the impacts was barely audible on the bridge. "Three impacts on section O3 – 02 – 27. Minor damage to outer armor belt."

"Hah!" exclaimed one of the bridge crew. "They'll have to do better than that!"

Captain Conagher glowered at the crewman for breaking discipline, and then smiled humorlessly to herself. The problem with saying that sort of thing is that it tended to come true. Obviously, the commander of the Verdun would know their main guns were pointless. So what was their strategy, and how could she interfere with it? "Main battery, return fire at the *Verdun.* Target her external weapons."

The *Overlord*'s coaxial, fixed railguns were really a better choice for destroying such a large enemy ship, but they could only aim within a limited angle from the bow of the *Overlord,* and with the maneuvering drive down, the ship was slow to turn. The main battery guns, mounted on turrets, were a more flexible choice.

"Aye, ma'am."

The *Overlord*'s bow railguns battery fired a salvo towards the smaller warship, spread to nullify the target's evasive maneuvers. Twelve bright orange icons split off from the *Overlord* on the holo-display. The projectiles screamed through space at over half the speed of light, but on the display they moved slowly, taking agonizing seconds to cross the screen and intersect with the *Verdun*.

"Target hit, ma'am." Announced the weapons officer. But the enemy ship's icon on the display did not change. "No effect. Their deflectors are up."

Damn. But of course, expected. Their engineers must have been top-notch to re-install military-grade deflectors on the frame of the *Verdun*. "Can we hit them with missiles from here?" The missiles carried aboard had their own fricsim drives. No deflector could stop them. They would be able to cripple the *Verdun* without destroying her.

And that might be necessary. Captain Conagher eyed the battle display warily. The *Tannenberg* was unshielded and unable to maneuver, making her a sitting duck. If the enemy destroyed her — and Conagher was not certain why they hadn't done so yet — then capturing the *Verdun* might be the *Overlord*'s only way out of this mess.

Most of the squadron's Marines may have been killed aboard the *Tannenberg*, but there was no way that the rebels had enough manpower to fully crew the *Verdun* with soldiers trained for boarding actions.

The weapons officer shook his head. "Out of range, ma'am. This far out-system, they're largely ballistic. Their homing drives won't work well enough outside our grav field."

"Noted. Helm, rotate ship to bring the co-ax to bear. After firing, we'll close with the *Tannenberg*." It would bring them closer to the *Verdun*, too, but the enemy ship was too much of a threat not to neutralize. It would have to be destroyed, then, unless it could first be rendered combat-ineffective. "Weapons, full power. Destroy the *Verdun* on first co-ax salvo."

Before the weapons officer could confirm the captain's orders, the tactical officer interjected. "Ma'am! The *Verdun* is changing her course, ma'am. She's maneuvering around the planetoid; she'll have line-of-fire to the *Tannenberg* in thirty-seven seconds!"

Worrying, but expected. If the enemy knew that the *Overlord*'s drive was sabotaged – almost a certainty – then they must realize that the *Tannenberg* was the *Overlord*'s only ticket to safety. "How soon can we hit the *Verdun* with the co-ax?"

The tactical officer looked at his console. "Ten seconds, ma'am."

"Fire as soon as it bears."

"Aye. Firing on *Verdun*...now."

The *Overlord*'s coaxial railgun battery fired as one, the massive recoil causing a barely noticeable hiccup in the ship's acceleration. On the display, eight orange icons flew forth from the *Overlord*, racing across the screen towards the *Verdun*. At seventy-percent of the speed of light, twice the speed of the enemy's batteries, the enemy ship would have almost no warning of the incoming fire. For this reason, the salvo was a tighter spread than the main batteries had been, to maximize the impact.

"Ma'am!" The tactical officer called out, drawing her attention from the display, "The *Verdun* has dropped her deflectors!"

"What?" came Commodore Petrakov's startled reply. The Captain had almost forgotten that he was there.

How could the rebels know about the co-ax battery? It was — supposed to be — top-secret! Regardless, the enemy had come up with the only real way to 'defend' against its high-velocity projectiles.

The shells were hardened to pierce through the enemy's deflector screen, the force of traveling through the field converting the projectile into a ball of super-heated plasma as its velocity slowed. This would then impact the enemy hull and carve through the interior of the ship, expanding as it went, wreaking massive damage. It was a weapon designed specifically to destroy armored, purpose-built warships.

But with the *Verdun's* deflectors down, the shells would impact at full velocity. With that much kinetic energy, they would pierce right through the enemy hull like paper, destroying anything in their path – a comparatively small, one-meter-diameter path.

Damn them. She found herself leaning forward in her seat, studying the display. Would the co-ax projectiles get lucky and hit something critical within the *Verdun*? She crossed her fingers. Maybe the heavy armor of the ship would spall, or the percussive effects would rupture something critical.

"Target hit, ma'am. *Verdun*'s grav signature is fading! They're drifting, ma'am! Her drive must have been damaged!"

Captain Conagher leaned back, eyes cold. The non-functional QMP drive may have been the most secret innovation aboard the *Overlord*, but her coaxial battery had turned out to be the most useful. Their three-kilometer-long barrels took up a great deal of space – the capacitor banks and coolant tanks even more – but it was worth every cubic meter.

"Their deflectors are still up – looks like we missed their reactor proper."

She examined the holo-display. The *Tannenberg* was still shielded from the *Verdun* by the mass of Podera, and now the enemy was slowed to deflector speed. Good. There was still the risk of enemy emplaced weapons on the planetoid itself, but those, if they existed, were holding their fire. They must be at least somewhat cowed by the destruction of *every* weapons battery to open fire so far. The Captain turned back to her weapons officer. "How soon can we reload the co-ax?"

"Next salvo available in six-eight seconds, ma'am."

"Good. Helm, keep the bow oriented on the *Verdun*, and close the range on the *Tannenberg* at maximum speed. Weapons, hit the *Verdun* with the main battery. Time salvoes to impact along with the co-ax."

"Ma'am!" tactical officer announced. Now what? "Enemy small craft are launching from the planetoid!"

"Where are they heading?" Was this the real evacuation? Launching shuttles from hidden hangars?

"They're heading for the *Tannenberg,* ma'am."

Damn. There's only one thing that can be. "Label those craft as boarding vessels. Can we hit them from here?"

"The *Tannenberg* is between most of them and us. We can only hit a few, and even then our shots would be cutting it rather close."

"We'll have to take that chance." The *Tannenberg* could survive a few glancing shots. She looked at her data repeater. The *Verdun* was out of the fight for now: the crippled ship was maneuvering towards the other side of the planetoid, hiding from the *Overlord*'s guns. Moving slowly, at that, using their deflectors for propulsion. But fast enough, judging by the plot, that the co-ax guns wouldn't be reloaded in time for a second volley.

Captain Conagher examined the holo-display, running through the few options left to her. The *Tannenberg* drifted, without power, near 1048 Podera. A flotilla of red icons – the enemy boarding group, one-hundred and twenty-eight in all – approached the disabled warship. More than they brought last time. Much more. It would be a close fight aboard the *Tannenberg,* especially given the casualties they had taken from the original broadside.Thankfully, the enemy's false IFF transponders wouldn't help them this time around — the extra week of preparation had seen to that.

So far, the attack had shown the rebels to be highly prepared. So why then did they have the *Verdun* engage? There was very little she could do against the *Overlord,* even in her disabled state, and the rebels must have realized that. Could it be desperation?

On the other hand, so long as the enemy's plans didn't work out for them, that was all right by the Captain. While the *Verdun* was now out of the *Overlord's* line of fire, that meant that the rebel warship couldn't fire on the *Tannenberg*, either. Pretty sloppy maneuvering, actually — it was reassuring to see that the enemy could still make *some* mistakes in this battle.

It was almost a stand-off, but her superior firepower should let them grind out a victory, even if their mobility was shot to hell. It would be grim, but as long as the rebels did not come up with another —.

"Ma'am! Grav sensors picking up a large contact!" Announced the tactical officer. "On display now."

A new target indicator flashed onto the holo-display, red and very large. Its meta-data showed it slowing to match speed with the *Verdun*. The tactical officer did a double-take at his detail display, and announced in a puzzled voice, "It's a rock-cracker, ma'am. Er – it's a mobile mass driver, for breaking asteroids apart for mining. But they carry only slow projectiles – no threat."

Commodore Petrakov spun the holo-display to get a better perspective at the newcomer's relative position to the tactical situation. With his pointer, he highlighted some trace lines. "It's put Podera between us, so we can't hit it. Of course, it can't hit either us or the *Tannenberg*, either.

A bright red ring flashed around the rebel rock-cracker, indicating that it had fired. The holo-display plotted the trajectory of the slow-moving projectile.

"What the —?" exclaimed one of the tactical-section ratings. "They've fired on the *Verdun*!"

"No, not quite." Captain Conagher magnified the view on the holo. "It'll just barely miss, but…" her voice trailed off. Suddenly she turned and barked at the helmsman. "Helm, shift maximum power to the deflectors, get us moving along this vector." She highlighted a new course, perpendicular to the vector linking the *Overlord* and the *Verdun*.

Commodore Petrakov turned to look at the Captain, brows furrowed in puzzlement. "They're no threat. That shot is nowhere near us, and it's moving at less than point zero-one cee."

The tactical officer gasped slightly, and looked at the Captain. "They're going to slingshot around the *Verdun*." Conagher grunted. Close. The officer knew his physics, at least. The gravity beams of the *Verdun* could be used to dramatically accelerate the projectile, and sling it around the planetoid towards the two Federal ships. But at what cost? If they accelerated the projectile to useful speeds that way, it could easily cripple their ship. Grav tethers simply weren't that robust, and no ship of *Verdun's* size could take that kind of asymmetrical stress. Not repeatedly, anyway. The enemy captain was gambling with the lives of his crew.

The enemy projectile reached the *Verdun* just as the *Overlord* began her slow dodge. It slung around the *Verdun*, leaving the much smaller ship's artificial gravity field at a frightening velocity.

"Ma'am! Round velocity at zero-point-six-three-cee! Impact in four seconds!"

There was barely enough time for her to clasp the armrests of her seat before the shot hit them. Point-six-three-cee! Their captain must be mad!

The hull rang like a gong, a gong five kilometers across. It struck the Captain as more of a physical *force* than a sound, driving the air from her lungs. The seat restraints bit into her shoulders as the entire bridge shook. Loose debris flew around the compartment, but thankfully none of the crew were thrown from their seats.

Conagher blinked the stars out of her eyes and forced in a breath of air. "Damage report! What did we lose?"

"Deflectors burned out in octant three!" cried the damage-control officer.

"Ma'am! The number-three reactor's down!" The engineering officer's face was bone-white. "Current spike. It failed hot!"

Damn. She pinched the bridge of her nose. The poor crewmen. The gravity-field containment for the reaction had failed before the machine had shut down, venting hot plasma into the compartment. There wouldn't be many survivors from that reactor's crew. "Shift main battery fire to that rock-slinger! Cut through the station if you have to. Make them maneuver!"

At this range, a narrow ship like a rock-slinger stood a decent chance of dodging the *Overlord's* fire. But to do that, they would have to put everything they had into the drives, which would throw their aim off.

The damage pattern from that impact showed that the *Overlord* had been hit by what was effectively a simple rock. A very large rock, moving very fast, but a rock nonetheless. Its sheer mass had burned out the deflectors, and based on damage estimates, had delivered more energy than the *Overlord's* own railguns could. A lesser ship, such as the *Verdun* or the *Tannenberg,* would never have survived. But the impact itself had not penetrated to the ship's structure.

Hopefully, that would continue to be the case.

Chapter 16: Repairs

Klaus grunted as he forced the badly-mangled cover back over the number-three reactor. It had taken the brunt of the damage, and it showed. Bits of metal that had once been machinery lined the compartment. At least the cover itself was recognizable. It was ugly, but at least with the help of some electro-pneumatic jackhammers the key anchor points had been forced to line up properly.

His datapad showed that the deflector screen for this octant was down, which made him hurry as best as he could. His neck and back ached from the tension, and sweat ran down his back. All that stood between enemy fire and his fragile body was thirty meters of heavy armor plating.

That might be a lot for some people, but Klaus was a Navy engineer. He knew plenty of natural hazards that could cut through protection like that, let alone military-grade weapons fire.

He didn't want to end up like the crew of reactor three. When the deflectors burned out, the overload surge limiters on the reactor's grav foci had failed almost immediately, hyper-condensing the fusion core before the containment field died completely.

Steam flashed into plasma, metal melted into liquid, and the poor damned crew boiled into ghosts. There were discolorations here and there that might once have been engineers. At least it would have been quick.

It was little consolation. He felt regret that he and Johann hadn't finished their QMP trials. Sure, they had stabilized the code and had even modified the ship's mission-critical systems to survive the jump. Even Commander Li and the Captain had been pleased enough to keep them out of the brig, but they just couldn't scale it. The *Overlord* was just too big. And with the drive sabotaged, and no QMP, they had been sitting ducks for whatever had hit them.

Klaus turned to the grease-streaked engineering NCO who was assisting him, and kicked the reactor cover. "That'll keep the bulkheads from melting. Might even work for as much as an hour before it blows out and takes the whole section with it." he groused, almost shouting so that he could hear himself over the howl of the suit's cooling fans.

The crewman nodded, his deep, rasping breathing audible over the helmet comm. Behind him, the compartment bulkheads still glowed white-hot from the reactor's initial failure, so both Klaus and the crewman were fully suited up, their visors opaqued. Cooling systems in the suits spun at maximum, yet he was still drenched in sweat. He could not see the other man's face, and could barely hear his voice above the whine of his own suit, but the scowl in the man's voice was clear enough. "And I'll need to find a replacement crew for the compartment. Poor bastards."

Klaus swallowed, and clapped the man softly on his shoulder before turning to leave the compartment. There was nothing he could say. They all had to press on as best they could. Out in the relative cool of the corridor — thank god for thermal shielding — he removed his gloves, and wearily checked his datapad to see where he was needed next.

Capacitor bank D61-NW-87. He sighed, "Computer, request flight to—"

His communicator chimed.

Odd. Any of the ship's officers could have — would have — overriden the ringtone and gone straight to voice. He couldn't see who was calling, either - the hands-free headset built into his helmet didn't have a caller ID display. Shoddy product. "Accept call."

He was almost deafened by the voice on the other end. "KLAUS! Where are yeh, lad? I've got an idea, and I need yeh to come look at it."

Klaus winced. "For God's sake, Johann, turn your volume down. My ears are bleeding." He shook his head, and thumbed down his own volume control. Just in case. "I'm needed with the repair crews right now - I can't leave my station."

"Nae, look - I been talkin' to the Captain. Remember, she asked me ta see iffn' I could nae get the QMP fully workin'. Movin' the whole ship an' all that. Seein' as we're getting bloody *shot at* and all, I reckon that it'd be useful t' finish that task, y'see."

Oh, no. Klaus reflexively reached to pinch the bridge of his nose, but only singed his gloved fingers on the still-hot faceplate of his helmet. Johann's accent only got that strong when he was drunk. Very drunk.

It seemed that the battle hadn't interrupted Johann's celebrations after the partial successes on the QMP project earlier.

Muting the call for a moment, Klaus finished the request for a flight to the capacitor compartment, where he was needed next. The corridor walls began to fly by, as the display on his databank promised a flight time of eight minutes. Much longer than it should have been. The route-finding program must have been forced to detour around battle damage.

"Johann, you're drunk. But look, I've got eight minutes before I'm needed next - go ahead and talk."

"I'm not bloody drunk! That was yesterday!"

Klaus checked his datapad. "It's barely past midnight, ship's time."

"Aye, which means it's a new feckin' day!"

Oh Lord. "All right, all right. What's your idea?"

"Weel, I was talkin' to some o' the other folks stuck in here." Here? Ah, yes. When the *Overlord* moved into combat, all civilians onboard were confined to the civilian section, near the middle of the ship. "One o' them — real nice lass — and I got to talkin'. See, she used to work with some o' the big, in-system mining platforms, the ones what they used fer crackin' open Mercury. She was sayin' that they often didn't have 'nuff engines to move the whole bloody platform at once, see? So they'd move the thing in sections, and piece it back together at each new rock!"

"Makes sense. For mining, anyway. Your point?"

"So what is the big feckin' problem we're havin' with the QMP? We canna' move the whole bloody ship at once!"

Oh, for the love of — "Are you seriously suggesting that we cut the single largest, most expensive moving object in the history of mankind into *pieces*, and hope it comes together properly at the other end?"

"Precisely, lad! And theoretically it's easier. The way it works, the slices will come back together at atomic distances within picoseconds, so they'll just fuse where they were, give or take an electron or two. And for the computers, we just sit Jimmy here in the first compartment t' make the jump, and let him get all the systems sorted!"

Klaus shook his head, before remembering that Johann couldn't see him. Johann wouldn't have seen the Captain's order to confine the miners, which probably included James. Of course, as the miner was key to a QMP jump that had to be working in the next few minutes, Klaus could no doubt get him sprung from the brig. But there was another problem. "Still wouldn't work, Johann. As good as James is—" and as good as Klaus' repair-assistance programs were "—he still couldn't possibly get the whole ship's systems up and running fast enough."

"Aye, and so we use your idea!"

"My idea?"

"Those bloody repair programs of yours, o' course! We'll put 'em in every system on the ship! We just need t' wire a computer into each compartment, and then have each one work over the code o' the next one in sequence! Jimmy'll need to see the first few off himself, but they'll cascade from there!"

Hmm. Johann might be onto something here. "Have you run the numbers on just how long that would take?"

"Aye. 'Tis nothing, barely a few seconds."

A few seconds in which the *Overlord* would be crippled, its control systems down. Klaus hoped to God that it would never become an attractive option.

"Hold on a moment." Klaus winced as he rocketed past a fire - an inferno, really - still burning white-hot in the corridor. With the ship as beaten-up as it was, isolated fires didn't warrant a response so long as they weren't near anything too important. Even at the speed he was going, he felt the searing heat through the shielding of his suit. That fire would melt the local bulkheads soon. He checked his map. No worries. They could afford to lose the ship's number three movie theater.

"You know, that just might work." He thought a moment. "But that would take a full-up quantum-core computer. How many of those do we even have, onboard?" Johann probably hadn't gone far enough to actually look that up, and Klaus didn't know the number, offhand. He looked down to his datapad, preparing to search through the engineering database himself.

"Err, plenty." Huh. Johann's answer surprised Klaus. It looked like Johann was determined to see his idea through, and had actually done his homework. "Sort of."

"*Sort of?* What do you mean, 'sort of?'"

"They're used right now fer calculating the deflector fields, aimin' the guns, 'n whatnot."

Klaus blinked. "Now you want to rip out the ship's aiming computers, and the deflectors to boot? How much did you drink, again?"

"Not enough, mate. But aye, I'm telling ye it would work."

Klaus grinned wryly. Well, if testing his theory kept Johann distracted and out of trouble, maybe it would be worth it. Especially if he even got it to work. "Sure. Go ahead and see if you can write the code for all that. And have James and Murphy check it." Johann might be able to come up with some pretty good ideas while drunk enough to faze a sailor, but there was no way that Klaus would trust his programming abilities under the same circumstances. "If you can get the QMP drive to work, that'll be—" " a damn miracle "—a good backup." But who knew? By some stroke of luck, it might actually work.

^^*^*^*^*^*^*^*^*

Captain Conagher drummed her fingers on the armrest of her command chair. The reports out of the *Tannenberg* were sporadic, and not always coherent when they *did* arrive. With its main power down, everything had to be relayed verbally.

And there wasn't anything she could *do* about it. Not for— "Helm, what is our ETA to the *Tannenberg*?"

"Thirty-seven minutes, ma'am."

—damn near forty more minutes, and that's if they used the deflectors solely for propulsion. And if the rebels fired any more of those giant mass-driver payloads, they'd have to maneuver either to dodge or to block. That would slow them down. The loss of her engine really had crippled the *Overlord*.

And with it, doomed the *Tannenberg*. There were two possible outcomes of the fight underway on the smaller warship: either the enemy managed to seize control of the ship, or they didn't. If they did win the boarding action, then the whole battle was lost.

And even if the Marines repelled the boarders, their problems were far from over.

The *Overlord* was the strongest warship ever built, but she was not invincible. Not quite. If the enemy had more mass-driver ships and more ships to sling the projectiles, they could defend Podera from any further attack by the *Overlord*. The ship would have to limp away from the planetoid at her frankly embarrassing acceleration under deflector propulsion. And that's assuming that the rebels *let* her escape without following and harrying her with long-range fire.

And even if the *Tannenberg's* Marines successfully defended their ship, the situation would hardly be any better. The *Tannenberg* still floated right next to what remained of the cargo-transshipment station, and with her shields disabled, was completely unable to maneuver. Given that this all seemed to be one massive ambush, Conagher had to assume that the enemy still held more weapons batteries in reserve on Podera's surface. The only reason that they — or the *Verdun*, or the enemy mass-driver ship — had not yet destroyed the *Tannenberg* was because the rebels hoped to capture her. And once they decided that capture was no longer achievable...

She cursed the immobility of her ship. The situation was desperate enough, that even a long shot like the QMP technology touted by that crazy academic MacDougal would have been worth a try, but they had not been able to scale it up to anything useful.

Captain Conagher balled her hands into fists. When she got her hands on the saboteurs, the *skulking rat bastards* that had hamstrung her ship—

Her communicator chirped. She frowned at the caller ID. Dr. MacDougal? She shrugged. Quite a coincidence, but she did not want to hear anything more about theory. She reached for the 'cancel' button, and then stopped. At this point, she was grasping at straws. There was a lull in the battle at the moment, as the *Overlord* slowly moved towards her crippled squadron-mate. If anything important came up, the captain could just cut the call. She hit 'accept.'

"Captain Conagher here. Speak."

"Cap'n! Err, ma'am. I've, ah—" The physicist's voice was slurred – was he *drunk* in the middle of a battle?

"Out with it. You have fifteen seconds." She couldn't waste time listening to some civilian's tongue stumble around his mouth. Drunk on a battlefield was no way to be.

"Aye." He spoke faster now, but his words tripped over each other, overlapping slightly. "I can get t' QMP system workin', teleport the whole ship. Sir-ma'am, ah, sir."

"Are you certain?" Her head snapped up, but she held her thoughts in check. With Dr. MacDougal, she wanted confirmation. "Has this been checked over by—" She paused. Who would know enough to be sure? This could save the *Tannenberg* — save the battle — but if it was just the drunken ramblings of a civilian too far from his university classroom, then she wanted it shut down right away."Did you run this by CWO Ericsson?"

"Yes, ma'am. He an' I worked on it, together!"

That was good to hear. Klaus Ericsson might have difficulties understanding the *classified* part of classified R&D, but he knew the technology — and its limitations — better than anybody else she trusted. "How soon can you have it operational?"

"D'pends. We'd need a few, ah, hundred quantum-capable computers."

"We don't have that many to spare. Can you work with less?" The Captain didn't know off-hand how many such computers there were on-board, but it couldn't be more than three hundred. And almost all of them were sorely needed; fire control, reactor monitoring, deflector control, all depended on hyper-rapid computation.

"I canna' perform miracles, cap'n. I'm a physicist, not a miracle worker! I've run the calculations, and two-hundred fifty-two is the absolute minimum. That's the smallest number o' parts we can split t' ship into."

"Split the—?" The sensor officer's warning called the captain's attention back to the sensor display. "Hold for a minute." Two more red ship-icons had appeared, glowing dully on the far side of Podera from the *Overlord*. More rock-throwers, like the one that had hammered her ship.

These new ships had approached from a new direction — they could sling their huge projectiles close enough to Podera to hit the *Tannenberg*. Not very fast, of course, but they wouldn't have to. The smaller ship was a sitting duck. Hopefully they'd hold their fire as long as the enemy had boarders on that ship, but still a dangerous threat. The *Overlord* needed the *Tannenberg* alive in order to escape. Ironic that mining vessels were proving to be more of a threat than the *Verdun*.

For the moment, the new arrivals posed no threat. But she knew that the enemy was already making preparations to destroy the *Tannenberg* in case their boarding attempt failed.

The *Overlord* had the deflectors and the armor — her sheer *bulk* almost helped more — to survive a few hits from projectiles of that scale. The *Tannenberg* did not, and she had already been crippled by the barrage which disabled her reactor.

But for now, there was nothing that Conagher could do but keep advancing towards the *Tannenberg*. She re-opened the comm channel with Dr. MacDougal. "You said something about 'splitting' my ship?"

"Aye, we'd need ta move the ship in a few hundred pieces t' move it. Too big otherwise."

"Is that even remotely safe?" Or sane? It sounded crazy, but then again combat command was just balancing levels of risk. If it let the *Overlord* reach the *Tannenberg* in time to save the battle, then it might be worth the risk.

"Aye, it is. Err, I think. I haven't got t' programming ironed out yet." In a smaller voice, he added, "or tested for this sort o' scale." His voice rose again. "But there's no reason it shouldn't work and be perfectly safe, ma'am."

Captain Conagher massaged her temples. The man really *was* an academic, not the person she needed to be talking to right now. "I'll contact you if the plan is approved." She cut the call, and opened a new channel to CWO Ericsson.

Without preamble, she asked, "MacDougal has told me his plan for making the QMP drive useful. Is it realistic?"

221

"Yes and no, ma'am. The *theory* behind it is solid enough. I'd say that it's a choice of last resort, though; it really should be tested under safe conditions first."

"I see. And what would you need to get the ship ready to use it, now?"

"Now, ma'am?" She could hear him cursing over the comm. "If we absolutely *needed* it operational..." His voice trailed off, then came back stronger. "We'd have to start by checking the ship's osmium piping for leaks. The damage-control parties would be able to tackle that, themselves — no specialized equipment necessary, just a routine integrity check. Then I'd need one of the civilian repair crew — James O'Rourke — and as many quantum-core computers as possible."

"Most of the repair crew civilians are under guard in the brig." she interjected. "At least one of them was involved in sabotaging the fricsim drive."

"Him?" There was a pause. "Mr. O'Rourke wasn't involved in the fricsim crew at all, ma'am. He's been working with us since his arrival on board. Ah, improving our QMP methods."

"What?!" she shouted. Then her voice became quiet and menacing. "First you give him access to classified machinery *before* getting my approval, and now you want to spring him from the brig?"

"He, ah, didn't actually touch anything classified, ma'am. We haven't shown him any, uh, restricted information. Ma'am."

Oh, for the love of—

She growled softly. She should have known that putting the Ericsson and MacDougal team back together would have led to history repeating itself. MacDougal was drunk when he shouldn't be, Ericsson was discussing classified — classified with good reason! — materials with potential security leaks.

She'd handle *that* later. Wrestling her frustration back under control, she barked, "All right. I'll court-martial you later. What else do you need?"

He sighed. "We'll probably have to cannibalize half the fire-control systems, and maybe some of the deflectors, too. We'd have to get the computers distributed throughout the ship, one per compartment. If we press-ganged the damage-control parties, that'd give us enough spare hands."

Captain Conagher rubbed the back of her neck to relieve the tension forming slowly but relentlessly. That was quite the shopping list that CWO Ericsson had laid out. Cripple the ship's weapons, possibly her defenses as well? As far as danger to the ship went, maybe O'Rourke wasn't the one she should be worried about.

"I see. Get teams working on checking the piping, then. Pull them from damage-control if necessary." Nothing too critical on the *Overlord* needed repair at the moment. "When that's been arranged, go help Dr. MacDougal with whatever he needs." She let some of her anger slip through into her voice. "I can't spare Li right now, so you have to see that he does things *properly.* I'm trusting *you*, of all people, to keep him under control."

"Aye, ma'am." Klaus' voice sounded almost meeker, with none of the bluster normally attributed to a veteran engineer addressing the officer who happened to be in command of the *engineer's* ship.

No sooner had she closed the channel, her finger over the button, when—

"Ma'am! Incoming fire coming around the planetoid!"

On the holo-display, a large orange blip was closing rapidly on the *Overlord*. One of the rebel rock-cracker projectiles, but they hadn't seen it coming until now. The enemy must be firing from the sensor shadow on the other side of Podera.

It was slower this time, but they still had very little time to react. "Helm, hard to starboard, vector high."

They dodged the projectile easily enough, but each second they spent dodging was slowing their approach on the *Tannenberg*. If they reached the *Tannenberg*'s position, they'd be shielded from most enemy fire, but to reach that location they would have to run the gauntlet of point-blank fire, where they would have much less warning of enemy shots coming around the planetoid.

She checked the ETA to the *Tannenberg*. Twenty-eight minutes, and counting backwards now. The QMP drive was looking like a better and better option. She opened a channel to Dr. MacDougal. "We have a crew checking the Osmium piping. What other resources do you need?"

"I could use some good programmers. Any you've got — this is a big bleedin' job here!"

The Captain checked the ship's roster. A few civilian contractors were still aboard from the shipyard, and eleven of them were marked as computer specialists. They'd have to do.

"I've got eleven to spare. Where do you need them?"

Chapter 17: *Tannenberg*

"Ha! Look at 'em come in, all fat 'n' happy." The helmeted Marine next to Antoniy on the Tannenberg gloated. He patted the heavy railgun which anchored the improvised defensive line across the corridor. "They won't know what hit 'em!"

Antoniy — like the rest of the Marines — watched the image relayed to his helmet HUD from the Tannenberg's exterior sensors: Rebel boarding craft slowing as they closed on the ship. Preparing to deploy their troops. Retro-rockets fired, slowing their approach, laser drills deploying to cut entry holes into the sealed outer hatches.

With the Tannenberg's main weapons disabled, only the low-power point-defense lasers had been able to engage the small enemy craft. Those were designed to destroy lightly-armored missiles, not dedicated assault shuttles! Barely a dozen of them had been neutralized before they reached the ship, their half-melted husks shattering upon impact with the warship's hull. That still left scores.

Antoniy slammed his fist into his thigh-armor in frustration. The Navy tech geeks had fixed the IFF issue that the rebels had been taking advantage of, only for the insurgents to come up with yet another damn trick! What the hell had that even been, that hit the Tannenberg? The communications channels had been too crowded afterwards for him to ask anybody who might know.

Turning to face the Marine who had spoken, Antoniy growled, "Don't count on it, kid. They suckered us into this attack quite well, and timed the ambush perfectly - they have to know better than this."

"Not our problem. We just get to punish them for their mistake."

Antoniy shook his head. "Here's hoping you're right." He knew better, though.

The unit's Major broke in on his override channel. "Lieutenant Gureivich, looks like they'll hit your position first. You've got two minutes to prepare. Out."

Antoniy double-checked his defenses, wondering for the hundredth time if there were something he had missed. Their heavy railgun commanded the center of the line, with the best arc of fire. Around it, whatever bits of scrap the troops could find – mostly service equipment from the nearby mess hall – provided reasonable cover. The line was emplaced just after a bend in the corridor, so that advancing rebels would meet his troops at point-blank range. All by the book.

The Marines' armor and barricaded position would be a massive advantage in that sort of slugging match. This time, at least, the entire Marine contingent were in full power-armor, heavy weapons ready at hand. Even if the enemy had more of the stolen heavy equipment they'd brought to the last boarding action, Antoniy's team were ready.

Of course, it should have been a more defensible position, but he had had to improvise. Closer to the outer hull of the *Tannenberg* had been compartments specially designed for defending against boarders: they were chokepoints controlling access to the interior of the ship, with hardened fortifications already built in.

But enemy fire — the same salvo that had cored the *Tannenberg's* reactor — had destroyed most of those specialized compartments. Including the one Antoniy and his troops had been heading for, in preparation to leave the ship to board disabled enemy ships.

He had been forced to fortify this corridor instead, one of the very few leading into the *Tannenberg* from the destruction out closer to the hull. The only chokepoint left in his sector of the ship.

"You reckon they believe that they caught us in the staging compartments, sir?" The same Marine asked. "I mean, if it weren't for the Major, we'd have been out there." He gestured down the corridor.

Antoniy nodded, grateful to have a CO with combat experience. Their mission, after all, had been an offensive boarding attack. SOP dictated that boarding troops stage in the outer defensive chokepoints. These were large compartments, which sped up the process of getting troops out the hatch. The rebels were obviously evacuating: why not get the Marines in as fast as possible, stop as many rebels as possible from escaping? Daltry was one of the veterans they had picked up at Andromeda Station. He'd been fighting the rebels for years, and he had smelled a rat.

So instead of SOP, the combined Tannenberg - Overlord boarding party had staged in the corridors deeper behind the chokepoints. At the time, it had seemed a needless waste of time.

But now, it had been a stroke of genius. They were still breathing. Even if most of the perimeter defense was gone -

including chokepoints, murder holes, cameras and everything - they still had almost their full complement of Marines.

A loud, sharp 'CRACK' echoed from around the corner, breaking Antoniy's thoughts. Shrapnel whirred through the air, harmlessly against the side wall in front of them. The first of the anti-personnel mines in the staging compartment had detonated. Contact.

He checked the sole remaining camera feed for confirmation. Nothing. What? He slapped his helmet, as if jarring the HUD would make any difference in the camera feed. Still nothing, a blank hallway. The image's timestamp was stuck on ten minutes ago. Damn Murphy! Of course the only seemingly undamaged camera broke down.

This would have to be an old-fashioned ambush, then. The whites of their eyes, and all that. He'd left the hand-thrown deployable camera pods behind in the armory, because their presence would have warned the rebels of the Marines' presence. His coilgun pointed down the corridor, finger on trigger, Antoniy waited for the first targets to appear. And waited. Nothing.

Come to think of it, there had been no sound since the mine had detonated. No screams of wounded soldiers, no breaking ordnance, nothing.

Another 'CRACK' sounded down the corridor. Another mine. Still nothing followed it.

By the timing and distance between the charges, the rebels would reach the bend in the corridor in less than thirty seconds. A damn fast advance for troops who must be rattled by the mines going off in their faces. Antoniy suspected that these wouldn't be the same pushovers that had attacked his ship last week.

A third, and then a fourth 'CRACK' came down the corridor. The last of the camouflaged mines had detonated. No sound followed.

But the Marines had stacked the deck in their favor, though, with a little help from engineering. The air systems were blowing away from them, to keep the corridor clear of any gas weapons the rebels might use. When the shooting started, the ship's grav systems would project a steep gravity field, facing away from the defense. This would speed up friendly projectiles, and slow incoming rounds. Hopefully, it would be enough to tip the balance.

He tensed, waiting for combat. The corridor remained quiet — he should have heard the rebels' footsteps by now, for goodness' sake.

After all, he was close enough to smell the primer from the mines on the incoming breeze. His armor's sensor suite took in all available data from his environment, and then faithfully replicated all the senses, and then some, inside his helmet. He read no IR of burning ordnance. Heard no sound in the wavelength of human screams. The breeze told him nothing. — Wait, *incoming* breeze? What could have caused...oh, Hell.

A dark grey, rectangular wall of metal came around the bend. A pair of stubby quad-mounted railgun barrels on ball mounts flanked the rounded, jet-black hemispherical boss in the center. The whole arrangement almost filled the corridor with its side-panels extended flush with the forward face, but Antoniy could see green-suited rebel troops behind the contraption.

His breath caught. How the hell could the rebels have an assault gun? Antoniy had rarely faced them, and then only in basic! Those things were for training missions where the review officers hated the trainees!

For a moment, the corridor was silent, as Antoniy's Marines paused a moment in stunned silence.

But only for a mooment. A single, flat 'crack' rang out as a single railgun bullet spat forth from the Marines' line.

It bounced harmlessly off the assault gun's armored front. The grav field of the Tannenberg shifted, but it had little impact on the assault gun, which had a grav projector of its own. It hesitated only a moment, and then came on again.

One of the quad railgun mounts swiveled. A roar filled the corridor, and the HUD icon for Antoniy's railgunner went black. KIA.

They couldn't hurt the assault gun, nor could they escape. Its grav projectors prevented the Marines from using the Tannenberg's systems to retreat from the corridor at high speeds. The corridor was arrow-straight for nearly a hundred meters behind him - that direction would be suicide.

They couldn't hurt it from its front, either. If they blasted away at the assault gun with their outclassed weaponry, they'd accomplish nothing but throw their lives away. But even two quad-mounted weapons couldn't kill them all before they got too close for their firing arc.

"Fix-bay'nets-and-charge!" In his haste he made it just one word. As he ran, he slapped the toggle on his coilgun, and the titanium-alloy blade snapped into position. Twenty centimeters long and polished to a shine, it could pierce through any suit's armor. Even more importantly, the bayonet remained an excellent terror weapon.

He scrambled forward, over the barricades, followed by the rest of his Marines. They were all either very brave, or smart enough to realize that staying put was suicide. Together, they stood a good chance. They could not shoot at the troops behind the assault gun, because the vehicle was blocking them. Which meant that those troops could not shoot them, either. And the massive guns on it were meant for really heavy armor, and did not have the rapid-fire mode needed against infantry.

He was almost level with the assault gun now, gauging how best to climb around it, when a sharp pain exploded on his hip. He was flung aside, flying into the blue-painted wall to his left.

Blue? Ceilings were blue, not walls! He blinked, trying to clear his head. Of course, the grav generators. They would spin, trying to impede the assault gun, which would also mess with his 'down'. He stood, and winced. The armor over his hip was buckled, melted and creased where a railgun round had just barely ricocheted.

The gravity fields shifted again as the armored vehicle's gravity generators fought the Tannenberg. Two of his fellow Marines scrambled through the gap between it and the wall, barely making it before the heavy vehicle slammed home. The crew of the assault gun were clearly not fools. They must have realized that they were about to be flanked, and were attempting to crush the Marines as they squeezed past the multi-ton vehicle. But they were evidently not experienced enough to move their heavy weapon quickly, and Antoniy's Marines were well-trained.

His hands scrabbled for purchase on the side of the armored behemoth. This close, its guns could not reach him, and the narrowness of the corridor kept it from throwing him off. Even so, it was a close thing. The pain in his hip burned up his spine, and he fought to claw his way forward. The walls of the Tannenberg would be no help to him. While they were rougher from long service than those of the Overlord, they were still too smooth to provide enough traction.

As if to highlight his fears, the assault gun lurched sideways and crushed two Marines against the opposite wall. Two sickening, wet crunches, and a dark red smear of blood and oil on the wall. Two lights on his squad display going black.

Damn.

Over the low-pitched rumbling of the enemy's railgun fire, came the higher-pitched crackle of coilgun fire. His Marines — a good number of them, by the sound of it — had made it past the vehicle, and were engaging the rebel infantry.

He frowned, happy that they had made it, but concerned that they had not followed orders. That could put all their lives at risk. He had called for a bayonet charge, and his well-trained soldiers knew full well that stopping to fire sustained bursts was just wasting momentum. His Marines would be very closely-packed as they squeezed past the assault gun. All it would take was a single rebel trooper holding down the trigger, and half of Antoniy's squad would be down. His troops needed to get in close, so that the enemy wouldn't have a shot at them. So why were they stopping to fire?

Finally managing to get a solid grip, he pulled himself along the side of the assault gun with one hand, coilgun held in his other. The gravity fields shifted, the vehicle moved under him, and one of the Marines screamed in pain over the comms circuit. On his heads-up display, one of the Marine icons was outlined in red, but only its right leg was shown in black. Just lost a leg. No blinking red, so the suit's auto-medic was handling it. Non-fatal. He pulled himself past the assault gun, which had stopped dead in its tracks, and saw two of his Marines prying at the rear hatch.

And lowered his weapon. Now the coilgun fire made sense.

Of the dozen or so rebel infantry whom he had glimpsed following the assault gun, two were curled on the ground, wriggling like worms on a hook. They'd had the misfortune to be in the front ranks of what passed for a formation. The blood pooling around them, smearing across the green paint, bore testament to the effectiveness of the Marines' bayonets.

Behind them stood seven green-suited rebel soldiers, their hands in the air, weapons on the deck at their feet. They were coilguns, but short-barreled models. No penetration, useless against suits. Civilian weapons.

The enemy must have figured that out early, and dropped them the instant that they saw the armored Marines coming at them with fixed bayonets. The best option available to them.

"Sergeant," he commed, surprised at how thin his voice was. "Set two men on recon. Make sure we haven't missed anyone."

"Sir!"

Antoniy fought to catch his breath, and he muted his mic so that the others would not hear. He forced his shaking legs to hold him upright, when all he wanted to do was sit and catch his breath, and rest his burning hip. But he was in command, and there were enemy to attend to.

Behind the surrendered troops, four corpses lay unmoving on the deck further down the hallway. Must have been trying to run. Antoniy sneered. He'd picked the ambush position in large part because it was twenty meters to the next bend in the cover-free corridor. Those cowards had never had a chance of running away, and were too stupid to realize it.

Well, that wasn't quite fair. They were likely enough just green troops — appropriate enough, Antoniy smirked, given their armor color. And he had deliberately played on the fear factor. It took thorough training — and then some — to keep a man from running from an armored soldier wielding nearly two feet of 'cold steel.'

"That's all of 'em, sir." reported his sergeant. Antoniy started, realizing that his troops had been almost completely silent over the – only fifteen second! - engagement. Good training.

"Good." he replied, watching as the squad's medic — thankfully not one of the troopers harmed by the vehicle — tended to the soldier who had lost his leg. Antoniy's HUD updated — the man was stabilized, would survive, but he was combat-ineffective for the time being.

"Shit." The muttered curse in his headset made Antoniy turn around. "Goddamn cowards." The two Marines had finished forcing open the rear doors of the assault gun.

"Bastards offed themselves before we got the door open."

Antoniy peered inside the vehicle. The brightly-lit interior made the two helmet-less corpses inside all the more striking. The driver was slumped over the steering panel, and the gunner still twitched on the floor of the vehicle. White foam flecked their lips. Cyanide.

"These two were probably the only hard-core rebels." Antoniy said. It took one right-hard soldier to go out like that. Or a zealot. He gestured to the surrendered troops. "I mean, do these other guys look seasoned?"

His sergeant grunted. "Probably the only ones who knew anything, too."

Antoniy searched the bodies, looking for any paper, any live electronics that could tell them something. It was certainly an unusual battle squad. Fanatical soldiers driving military-grade hardware - and obviously experienced enough to maneuver it down those hallways - "supported" by a mob of "soldiers" who surrendered at the drop of a hat?

Antoniy shook his head. The soldiers certainly behaved like conscripts, but conscription had been out of military fashion for more than a century. Were the rebels this short on manpower, then? He looked at the idling assault gun. And how did that square with such advanced military hardware? Maybe the rebels had good finances, but couldn't find any mercenaries worth a damn this far out-system. Made sense. The only people out here in any numbers were miners.

A priority message pinged over his comm. The voice was rushed, not one he recognized. "Rebel troops outside command deck. Need backup, urgent. Sealing entrances." Antoniy heard a loud explosion through the system.

In the background came another voice, faint but panicked, "They're through the blast doors!"

The first voice returned, the words jumbled together. "Lieutenant, get your section here ASAP. We'll try to hold them, but we're locking the systems all the same." The sound of coilgun fire erupted on the other end of the link, and it went dead.

Antoniy gritted his teeth. "Sergeant, recall the scouts. We move out in one." He pulled up the ship's schematics on his HUD, tracing the fastest approach to the bridge. That explained why he had faced such green troops. They were a diversion, he supposed, as the more veteran unit advanced to the core of the ship.

It made sense, of course, for the rebels to bypass the main opposition. Almost all of the troops on board the Tannenberg had been readied for boarding near the outer perimeter of the hull, and the rebels would have expected that.

But even so it should have been impossible to slip through and get to the ship's command deck, at least without hitting another Marine squad. He had heard nothing over the comms, so how had they managed it without any engagement?

Thankfully, as long as the bridge crew had locked the ship's systems, the rebels at least couldn't control the ship or its gravity systems. Only someone with command-level access codes could unlock the ship. So at least his troops wouldn't have to fight the Tannenberg's own gravity systems on the way to the bridge.

But the rebels could easily do a lot of damage. If they were thinking fast, they could execute enough higher-level officers so that the Tannenberg's systems wouldn't be working for anybody for hours.

It all depended on how desperate the rebels were to put the Tannenberg out of action. Their tactics implied that they meant to capture her, and that meant they would do the least damage possible. If they were well trained. Of course, their desperation would depend on how the Overlord was doing. Either way, getting to the bridge fast was key, and his HUD notified him that the ship's grav systems were now offline. Of course they would be, with the bridge systems on lockdown.

Antoniy cursed briefly, inventively, but then grinned. The rebels had thoughtfully brought them just the tool they needed.

He waved his troops closer to the assault gun. "All right, new plan. Rebels got through to the bridge. We're needed there yesterday. Everyone grab hold of the tank."

"Assault gun, sir," corrected Gutierrez, who was the squad's best pilot.

Antoniy ignored the comment. "Gutierrez, you drive. We'll ride it until we hit rebels."

"Literally, sir?" one of the Marines joked.

"If necessary." The assault gun's own gravity systems could be set to hold people against its hull, and if unopposed it could move almost as fast as the ship's grav system could have transported them.

Of course, that carried a risk. They'd be bunched up while riding, and the assault gun would have to partially retract its shield to move quickly. If they ran into a rebel ambush, the troops riding the vehicle would be sitting ducks. But if he was right, and the rebels had very few trained troops, there might not even be any organized ambush. He had to run the risk. "We'll run 'em over if possible. Can't stop to fight." Speed would be their best defense.

"What about the prisoners, sir?" the sergeant stood over a dozen seated rebels, their hands bound behind their backs. Their eyes were bloodshot from the acrid smoke that hung in the scorched, dimly lit space. Several of them started shaking, and one gave a stifled sob. No, not seasoned soldiers at all.

"The only combatants died in that gun," he replied, pointing back over his shoulder. "These are civilians. Snap their guns, double-check their cuffs, fry their electronics and leave them here."

"Sir!" came the reply, accompanied by a crisp salute. Antoniy turned back to the assault gun, so that only his own men could see his face, and grinned. No true soldier wanted to kill civilians, and the sarge was a true soldier.

Antoniy deployed his best pilots into the assault gun, and clambered into position on its exterior. His hip ached, and he fought to keep the pain off his face. He took a hold near the front, of course — a Marine leads from the front — and gave the command.

"Gutierrez. Go."

He glanced over his troops, hanging all over the outside of the modern 'tank'. One of the soldiers started humming softly, almost under her breath. A tune that Antoniy recognized. "And I swear that the first person I hear singing 'Katyusha' is *walking* to the bridge! I'm looking at you, Sergeivich!"

A wave of strained laughter swept the section, and Antoniy grinned, despite himself. The squad needed the break. It was the only one they'd be likely to get for a good while. He watched the walls blur by to gauge their speed, but could not manage to be any more precise than 'scary fast.' His HUD showed that they occasionally hit eighty kilometers per hour. He fought to keep his hold on the vehicle, his injured hip screaming at him as the gun shook violently. Assault guns were *not* built for speed.

Still, they were fast enough that it was a severe shock for the eyes whenever they turned a corner at speed. The vehicle's grav systems kept his Marines from being thrown off, but the inner-ear didn't know that. Antoniy thanked God that he had never suffered from motion-sickness.

They passed another battle scene, walls scarred and floor littered with shattered equipment and broken bodies. He could not tell who had won the engagement, or where the survivors were. On the other hand, the fact that the enemy had pierced all the way to the bridge told him that it hadn't been the *Marines* who won every firefight.

Had his section gotten off light, even with a God-damned *assault gun* to deal with? What had the enemy hit these other fire-teams with? As they got deeper into the interior, he passed a scene of massive damage. An assault gun lay on its side, tendrils of smoke still pouring from it. Bodies littered the floor. A whole squad of Marines, none moving from the quick look he got. He swallowed hard, but kept his own squad moving.

He would have halted the vehicle and detached his squad's medic, but they could not afford to slow down. And frankly, Antoniy knew his own troops would need their medic soon enough. Rebel resistance at the bridge would be stiff.

Antoniy did not allow his thoughts to distract his eyes from scanning the corridor in front of him alertly. Line-of-sight identification would be all the warning he'd get of an enemy roadblock — with the *Tannenberg's* systems locked down, the ship's internal sensors wouldn't help him one bit.

As they moved further towards the bridge, the deep scarring and scorches of pitched battle disappeared. The lighting became brighter and more regular, and the haze of smoke and vaporized metal thinned out until it was all but gone. Antoniy felt as if he were emerging from a deep, dusty coalmine, into the crisp relief of daylight.

Chapter 18: Long Shot

"Klaus!"

"What is it now, Johann? By the way, I am headed your way. The osmium piping looks good to go." Klaus was supermanning back to Johann's lab, as the damage repair crews could function well enough with one less supervisor, and he could do more good if he helped Johann get the QMP drive operational.

"This is goin' along well enough, but there's too much bloody code to write! Dammit, I'm a physicist, not a programmer!"

Klaus rolled his eyes. This was Johann's weakness: practical problems. "Ah, I see. So what's holding up the progress? The captain sent you a whole crew to help."

"Aye, a few. But they're green, new t' the field. It's takin' too much time to get each o' them up to speed, and there's half a million bloody lines to run through! The physics is sound, your replicator idea might even work, but we just canna' get everything ready fast enough. We'd need a much larger crew to get this done in less than days!"

"All right. I know the people who can help. I'll get them down there ASAP." Klaus broke the connection. He checked his datapad, looking for the people he was thinking of.

He checked the brig. James' co-workers, the techs who remained aboard when the union repair ship had left. "Dammit." He muttered.

He didn't trust them — after all, they were the prime suspects for sabotaging the *Overlord's* drive system. At the same time, they were the best programmers on-board, according to their records and his conversations with James.

But could Klaus trust them with his *life?*

He shook his head. The Captain had said that the QMP system might be needed to save *all* of their lives. Maybe if he got that into the miners' heads, then they'd be trustworthy enough.

And they were not in the brig. Instead they were deployed — under armed guard — as repair crews on the damaged warship, working on isolated systems far from any critical access. Klaus found the contact number for the ship's Marine commander, and silently thanked the Captain for reinstating his rank. He should have the authority to re-assign some of the prisoners. Enough, at least.

LtCol. James T. Wood - Contact Lost. Hm. Next would be...

Maj. Alex Stevens - Contact Lost. Odd. Then there's...

Maj. Nareen Majarendran - Contact Lost.

Klaus pinched the bridge of his nose, forcing back a growing headache. He was afraid of that happening. With so much of the Overlord's Marine complement transferred to the Tannenberg, their command structure had been decimated by the fighting there. Worse, it was most likely the experienced officers who had been transferred. That left...

Lt. Shigeo Yashimoto. Good grief. According to personnel records, Yashimoto was one of the most junior officers aboard. He must not be that well-regarded, either — judging by the fact that he had been left behind while the rest of the Marine officers had been shipped to combat, on the *Tannenberg.*

And probably passed over for a reason, knowing Klaus' luck. This might be a hard sell. If the man could think on his feet, he wouldn't have been left behind in the first place. And Klaus couldn't just pull rank on the Lieutenant, who was senior to him, even if it was a different service. Taking a deep breath, and promising himself to be as diplomatic as possible, he made the call.

"Lieutenant Yashimoto here. What do you want, ah..." The disdain in his voice was clear before he even finished his sentence, "Senior Warrant Officer?" Klaus was certain he heard a muttered *"squid. "*

"Sir, I request that you detach ten of the local civilians working with the repair crew. Sir, we need them for work on the QMP system. They're the only qualified personnel aboard. Sir." Unless Klaus missed his guess, the Lieutenant would be quite specific about the usual military punctilio. He sent his authorization code, and the coordinates of Johann's lab. He toggled a cc to the Lieutenant's command, and to Commander Li on the bridge. He didn't have time for formal escalation, even though he was certain he would win, and hoped that Yashimoto would have the sense to realize the same thing.

"Impossible." Came the flat reply. "They're needed for the repairs here. We can't possibly let them go on the say-so of some trumped-up—"

"Captain Conagher's orders, sir." Klaus interrupted. He was trying to pull rank, but diplomatically. Although he was right, technically. Sort of. He hoped the magic words would be enough.

"I don't care what the—" The voice quieted, as if interrupted by another person. The lieutenant's voice was muted, but he could make out the off-mic conversation. "What did you say, Gunnery Sergeant?"

Klaus held his breath. He'd been hoping that the Marines would have left a competent senior enlisted with an officer like that. Even the Marines should realize that too much could go wrong, otherwise.

"Very well." The Lieutenant's voice was back, stronger this time. He barked the words, as if he needed to take out his temper on someone. "We can let three of these men go. The Gunnery Sergeant—" Klaus could almost *hear* the glare "—will accompany them as guard. Out." The channel closed.

"Thank you." Klaus answered to the dead mic. He let out his breath. Three was less than the five he had wanted, which was why he had asked for ten. Still, he owed that Gunny a drink when this was all over.

^^*^*^*^*^*^*^*^*^*

Antoniy clung to the outside of the assault gun, his forearms and hip burning from the strain. "Command, we've nearly reached the approach corridor. ETA thirty seconds."

With the ship on lockdown, the only remaining entrance to the bridge was along a hundred-meter corridor, arrow-straight and kept clear of obstacles. It was designed as an effective killing ground for the defenses lining the hatchway leading to the command deck.

Had the rebels managed to get inside the bridge itself? If that were indeed the case, then the vessel would be in very dire straits. The Marines' low-energy weapons were back in the armory. Firing their coilguns — let alone the assault gun's railguns — anywhere inside the bridge would likely cripple the Tannenberg.

If the enemy had posted any competent defense, the whole corridor would be a death trap. No way would Antoniy send his troops into that killing zone without eyes. He contacted command. "Should we proceed or hold for backup?"

"Proceed, lieutenant. Rebels in possession of bridge. Avoid damaging the controls as best as you can, but neutralize all enemy presence in the bridge."

Well, so much for hoping that the fight was going well. He swayed briefly, blinking away his dizziness, and straightened. When he had transferred to Intelligence, he had never imagined himself in this position. He wasn't trained for it - hell, none of his troops had this kind of combat experience - and that made him nervous. He put the distraction aside. For better or worse, he and his squad would have to do. "Confirmed. Advancing. Ship's systems are down. Request status of friendlies."

"Friendly forces in bridge area un-reachable." With the communicators being built into the suits' helmets, that meant the troops were either KIA or captured. "Nearest reinforcements ETA over five minutes." The voice was strained. "You're it, Lieutenant."

He swallowed, hard. Thirteen seconds until they hit the bend in the corridor. If rebel troops had slipped this deep inside the Tannenberg without being noticed, they couldn't be the green conscripts whom Antoniy had fought earlier.

"Halt the tank!" he commanded.

"Assault gun, sir." muttered the driver, as he brought the vehicle to a stop.

"Everybody dismount. Gutierrez, deploy the shield. Infantry to follow behind the assault gun down the corridor.

It struck him that this was almost exactly the reverse of the earlier skirmish. An assault gun advancing around a corner, supported by infantry. But Antoniy's Marines were a cut − several cuts − above the rebel troops they'd faced earlier.

Antoniy linked his helmet HUD to the gun cameras of the assault gun. At least there was one advantage of the rebels using stolen mil-spec weapons. The corridor beyond was clear. They'd set the assault gun's grav systems to project a stasis field ahead of it, so that no sound escaped to warn the enemy. Nothing but a slight breeze, and if their Commander was not experienced enough to recognize what that meant...

"Move up." With the infantry following, the assault gun rounded the corner.

To his surprise, the wind changed direction, blowing hurricane-force the wrong way past the vehicle, sending the men scrambling into the lee behind the lumbering vehicle. The assault gun itself slowed to a crawl, fighting against literally tons of pressure. At this rate, it would take several minutes to reach the other end.

"I'm not doing it!" shouted the driver. "It's the ship!"

Antoniy swore. That must mean the bridge crew hadn't had time to scram the systems, after all. But it was only a quick procedure to do that. Had they been betrayed from the inside, or had the rebels somehow gotten the systems back online that quickly?

He needed a Plan B, and yesterday. His HUD showed no rebel forces in the corridor. The defensive weapons flanking the hatchway at the other end were half-melted, obviously out of commission. His main enemy, then, was time.

The assault gun could move down the hall faster, but it would have to redirect all of its grav systems to propulsion. This would mean that they would not be able to boost friendly projectiles heading down-range, so a firefight in the hallway would be risky. If that happened, they would have to halt the vehicle to re-direct the gravity systems. The fight would be in their favor then, but at the cost of their forward progress.

But maybe they wouldn't have to fight in the corridor. After all, it looked like the rebels expected the ship's wind and grav systems to hold them at bay. If he hadn't captured the assault gun earlier, the enemy plan would have worked perfectly. That explained why there were no troops.

Even if the enemy were expecting them, there was no option. "Re-set the systems. Retract the shield and keep advancing." That would move the tank as fast as possible. He glanced behind him. "The rest of you, close formation behind the tank."

"Assault gun, sir."

Their goal was to reach the bridge hatch. Once through, the fight would be easier, as there were only environmental-support grav projectors within the bridge itself, far weaker than the defensive projectors in the hallway. They just had to get there.

^^*^*^*^*^*^*^*^*^*

"Damn!" What the hell was that?! The Overlord shook wildly around Klaus, the corridor walls lurching at him and threatening to collapse the magnetic cocoon of the transport system. The envelope flared a reddish-brown against the encroaching walls, and Klaus gritted his teeth and swore, fighting to pull in a breath as the overload burned at his ribs. He could just picture himself ending up as nothing more than a red smear on the impersonal, gray metal of the corridor.

Fortunately, the shaking stopped and the transport field stabilized. Klaus quickly ran his hands over the outside of his suit. No damage.

Bless the engineers, he thought, for over-designing the system. Any engineer worth his salt knew enough to allocate at least an over-build factor of two to Murphy. No way that a jolt like that would be anywhere in their design specs.

A warship, a capital ship no less, shaking this hard under fire was an idea found only in the pulp adventure books Klaus had loved as a child. An ancient, seagoing man'o'war might rock as she was hit, but the Overlord massed in the gigatons!

The earlier hits to the ship hadn't been anywhere near this powerful. So what were the enemy hitting her with now?

The fire in his ribs subsided. Thank God he was carrying his cargo on the other side. He quickly checked the computer strapped to his suit for damage. It looked intact, but he would have to check it when he arrived. He checked the mission map on his datapad — his was the last computer needing to be hooked up.

But was his destination still in one piece?

He keyed up the engineering's damage assessment. Ordinarily, the damage map of a warship was eyes-only for officers and those in charge of damage control parties. But bless the engineers, again. Their staff had wisely realized that such secrecy would only hinder the real workers, the ones who mattered. Engineering crews needed those data to hack workarounds, so they had made the damage maps available to all Engineering personnel. Which included data on just *what* had hit them.

Klaus winced as the datapad scrolled through page after page of red and blinking schematics – thankfully, his section's control compartment was not among them – and stopped at the hull integrity report. He adjusted the scale, hardly believing his eyes. Red-marked gashes reached far into the ship's interior, well into sections the designers had designated "green," safe.

Those could not have been any normal mass-driver rounds. The first ones that the rebel ship had slung into the Overlord were what he would have expected: large chunks of rock, the slag produced en masse by any mining operation. Enormous, true, but still not capable of surviving the ship's shields.

The last round, though, judging by the incredible damage, must have been some kind of purpose-built armor-penetrating projectile. To run through the deflectors intact, the projectile must have carried its own gravity projectors, carefully arranged to counteract the Overlord's defenses. And to plunge that deep into the ship upon impact, it must have massed scores of tons, bigger than anything the *Overlord's* own axial guns could deliver!

Klaus grudgingly gave a degree of admiration to the rebels. Rock slingers were slow, so they must have sling-shotted for speed. Only a mil-spec ship like the Verdun had the kind of grav systems needed for that. Even so, they must have radically modified the grav systems. Not easy to do without burning them out and killing everyone on board. And either they had designed and fabricated such ammunition in the blink of an eye, or they had prepared this ambush months ahead. Neither option seemed likely, and both had worrying implications.

For one, nobody had intel that good. Or, more to the point, nobody would invest the kind of resources needed to build a projectile that large, based only on intel. No matter how good. So why *had* they gambled all of their resources like that?

Which really made him think, his eyes not even seeing the corridor walls as they flashed past. What was really going on here? The Overlord had been a closely-guarded secret months ago, and no other warship near her scale had ever had her keel laid. Even if there had been a security breach, she had not even been tasked to the Oort Cloud until a few weeks ago, as far as he knew. And the rounds being fired at the Overlord now would be massive overkill on any other ship in the system, on any ship known, period, when the rounds were made.

Any other ship, period. Klaus' eyes widened in a growing suspicion, and no small amount of fear. He did some quick mental calculations. Andromeda station was around the right size for these rounds. He poked at the new idea, trying to convince himself he was wrong. But he couldn't.

He now doubted what he had heard about the rebellion, all the assurances from civilians, all the casual assumptions of other servicemen. The rebels were on the run, they said, on the ropes. Just needing the final offensive to finish them off. Sure, every now and then some small patrol would get bushwhacked, but everybody knew that the days of the rebels were numbered.

But targeting Andromeda station, a Navy stronghold? An organization like that, on its last legs, couldn't possibly be ready for that scale of undertaking.

It would be surprisingly simple, though. Klaus played out the scenario in his head. An unidentified vessel, the same one now slinging rounds into the Overlord, drops out of warp near Andromeda station. No alarm would be raised: it's just another rock-hauler, probably with a transponder gone dead from lack of maintenance. The crew standing watch at the station would never see them as a threat.

Suddenly, the purpose-built penetrator round – possibly many of them – would come screaming in towards the station, fast enough to get inside the outer reaction loop of the defenses, and the station certainly could not move out of the way. Klaus looked again at the damage wrought on the Overlord, a capital warship. Andromeda's structure would have been no match for such an attack. It would have been ripped apart.

And with Andromeda Station, the hub of its patrols in the Oort Cloud gone, the Government would be hard-pressed to maintain any sort of presence in the outer System. That would have let the rebels consolidate and shore up their support. Given such a fait accompli, Earth might easily have negotiated, rather than send out further forces and risk a larger war. After all, the Oort Cloud was a rich resource.

But the rebels hadn't counted on the Overlord, the first capital ship designed from the keel up for combat: the first true warship. And if he was right, if they had made the armor-piercing projectile to ambush Andromeda, most likely they only had the one. They certainly would not have needed a second. He breathed a bit easier at that, notwithstanding his burning ribs.

As if to prove how wrong he was, the Overlord once again rocked violently. The maglev cocoon flared again. Dammit! Did he have to keep tempting Murphy like that?

The blanket of red on the damage-control screen was different this time. It was superficial, but spread all over the upper-starboard quarter, aft of the beam. That was not consistent with any sort of anti-armor projectile. Had the rebels only had the one shot, after all? He mentally crossed his fingers. Could this be good news? Klaus brought up more detail on the new damage.

He blanched.

Wrong again. A full quarter of the Overlord's defensive force-field projectors were burnt out, completely out of service.

The Captain's voice cut into his intercom circuit, an all-hands. "That jolt was one of the enemy's larger rounds missing us. We're still in the fight, people. Carry on."

That explains things, even if it was not good news. Unlike Andromeda station, the Overlord could move. The Captain must have realized the same thing, and used the deflectors to provide one brief burst of acceleration and shove them out of the way. But the deflectors were never designed for such a load transient.

Klaus smiled thinly. He supposed that losing a fraction of the ship's primary line of defense was preferable to taking another of those station-killer rounds on the nose, in the sense that being shot in the lungs was preferable to being shot in the heart: one would most definitely kill you; the other would only *probably* kill you.

^^*^*^*^*^*^*^*^*

Antoniy flinched as something hurtled towards him. A resounding 'CLANG' came from the front of the assault gun, and he realized that he had reacted to the image displayed on his HUD. Rookie mistake, he berated himself. The gun's cameras showed a chair: badly bent, padding charred and burned almost to the core. But bulky.

"What the hell was that?" one of the Marines mocked. "They're throwing furniture at us now? They leave their bullets at home, or what?"

"You might be right." Antoniy replied. "Look at that light spalling. Coilgun damage. They probably left their railguns behind, didn't want to hurt the bridge—"

Gutierrez chuckled. "Ha! So they got nothing that'll hurt our suits?"

Another chair came hurtling down the hallway, and fell next to the other one. Both were easily pushed along by the assault gun. Still eighty meters to go.

"Hopefully, no. They don't know yet what our troops have, and they're not wasting coilgun fire on an assault gun. That means they aren't stupid, and they have to know that furniture won't slow the tank."

Half a desk joined the pile of debris. He thought for a moment, and the reason became obvious.

"Gutierrez! Suppressive railgun fire on that hatchway! Keep it up 'till we reach the door or the barrels melt!"

Sparks flew from the hatch where the rebels were hidden, as the Marine opened up on it. Rolls of dark smoke from melting metal blew past them. None of it bothered the tank, or the Marines.

Antoniy shouted, to make himself heard. "We can't drive this thing into the bridge, and they know that. They're trying to build up a debris field, so we'd have to pick our way over the junk to get to the hatch. Without this thing," he patted the assault gun. "we would be easy targets if they have heavy weapons."

"So," the sergeant added, hefting his own coilgun, "we have to assume they have something heavier than coilguns, then."

"Any commander worth his salt would bring something, even if he didn't plan to use it, so yes." Then he added, "And remember, even a coilgun can hurt you, if they aim it well enough."

The roar of sustained railgun fire filled the corridor. The hatchway ahead — and the wall around it — sparkled with the muted flash of railgun impacts. A split-second later, a red-orange fireball blasted out of the doorway and struck the opposing wall.

"Got one of 'em!" shouted an exultant Gutierrez. One of his heavy projectiles must have penetrated through the bulkhead near the hatch, and set off the power-pack of a suited rebel soldier.

Antoniy smiled. With a weapon as powerful as the tank's railguns, even 'misses' often had useful side-effects. Or possibly bad side effects, given what was backstopping the rebels. But at least he was mostly sure that nothing important on the bridge was directly opposite the entrance.

Mostly sure. But then, this was war.

Chapter 19: Jump

The holo-display flashed red and a warning klaxon sounded. Captain Conagher shot forward in her seat.

"Enemy firing on the *Tannenberg*, ma'am!" called out the tactical officer. "They're arcing the shot around the planet, ma'am. Extreme-low-velocity."

Damn. It looked like the rebels had given up on capturing the smaller warship, and now only sought her destruction. Maybe their boarding parties had not been as successful as they had hoped. But it didn't change the *Overlord's* situation. She needed the *Tannenberg* in order to get back home.

At least the two enemy rock-slingers which had fired so effectively on the *Overlord* earlier were at the edge of the engagement, far from both the planetoid and the *Tannenberg*. That necessitated their shots' odd trajectory, and the slow speed. The *Verdun's* grav generators must be starting to burn out, and the planetoid must have had no grav generators. Therefore they could only use its minimal gravity well to deflect the shots. Their fire came at a fraction of the speed they had achieved by slinging around the *Verdun*.

Yet even though it would take much longer for their projectiles to reach the immobile ship, the result when they got there was not in doubt. "ETA to impact?"

"Six minutes, ma'am."

The Captain drummed her fingers on the command chair as she stared at the two orange icons moving slowly towards the *Tannenberg's* green. Almost certainly they would be simple dense-rock conglomerates. Only rock. Not that fast. The Overlord's thick armor and deflectors would laugh off such a projectile, but the *Tannenberg*....not so much. "Helm, our ETA to Tannenberg?"

"Seventeen minutes, twenty seconds, ma'am."

Far too slow. If the *Tannenberg* were crippled, or even destroyed outright – both likely possibilities – then the *Overlord* would be stranded, and most likely unable to run fast enough to escape the rebels and their out-sized ordnance.

They had to reach the *Tannenberg* in time to intercept those projectiles. There was simply no other option. That meant...

^^*^*^*^*^*^*^*^*

The Captain's voice erupted in Klaus' helmet, more brusque than normal. "ETA on the QMP?"

Klaus checked his flight-time to his destination. Two minutes. Add a bit to get the computer hooked up, and—"Four minutes, ma'am."

"Your QMP jump is a go. You've got three." The Captain cut the connection.

Shit. This would be very, *very* close. He had to set up a sensor rig – computer, sensors, cables – in under a minute. Or else, he suspected by the Captain's tone, he and thousands of others on the *Overlord* would die.

He wondered whether the captain realized just how much was at stake. Maybe he was the only one who had realized the real significance of the enemy's purpose-built projectiles, and what they meant to do with them. A lot more could die if the *Overlord* were lost. Possibly tens of thousands, if the rebels followed through with their attack on Andromeda Station.

His hands were not quite as steady as he would have liked, as he checked his cargo the fifth time. The small targeting computer, complete with its portable power source and QMP sensors, looked undamaged. Thank goodness he had not crashed into a wall with it. That would have doomed all of them. Every one of these units needed to be carefully placed and networked. Everything depended on this computer – and every one of the dozens like it - working perfectly, using untested code, on its first try.

And every one of those computers had just taken a giant jolt of acceleration as they dodged enemy fire. He commed Johann. "I'm nearly there, but this computer and I almost became a smear on the wall in that last attack. Have your team run a confirmation diagnostic on all the others, make sure they have no damage."

"Already done, lad. You're the last."

"Got it. Thanks." Klaus broke the contact and smiled. That had been very good, practical thinking on Johann's part. Must have been Murphy or one of the miners who put him up to it.

A warning buzz sounded in his ear, only a moment before he decelerated at what felt like at least ten gees. There was barely enough time to clench his abdominal muscles so that he did not pass out, as the transport system set him down hard outside his destination. In combat, comfort was an abandoned luxury.

No sooner had his feet hit the deck than he squeezed through the opening hatch. He had never before noticed just how slow the hatches were. The words "Processing Node 112-84-29" emblazoned on the hatch seemed to slink slowly into their recessed slot in the bulkhead. One minute left.

Klaus almost filled the small, dimly-lit compartment, barely two meters on a side. There was supposed to be a crewman on duty, but he had been pulled to staff a damage-control team. Probably happier there, anyway. Klaus didn't envy the crewman his station. The heat generated by the exposed light and floor-to-ceiling server racks filling the compartment made this a real hardship posting.

Mounting his computer on one of the open slots, he looked around for an available cable, but none were in sight. Forty-five seconds left.

"t'Hell with it," he mumbled, reaching to disconnect one of the other computers in the rack, "nothing here's as important." He pulled the cable.

His stomach lurched as the room became weightless, and he heard the air-conditioning – what there was of it – turn completely off. The room, dim enough to begin with, darkened further as the lights died. Now only the red glare of emergency lighting gave the room any illumination. Combined with the heat, this made the compartment hellish in every sense of the word.

Oh, for the love of—! He bit off a curse. What were the odds he'd yank the Environmental computer for this section? No matter. He could work without it. Thirty seconds left.

He plugged in and powered up the computer he'd just mounted, counting out the precious time. Twenty seconds.

The preliminary check showed green – the program was ready to go. Ten.

He commed the Captain. "Last computer in place." He leaned against the hatchway, breathing the cool air coming from the corridor.

"Confirmed." Came the Captain's voice. "Standby." Now her voice shifted to the all-hands announcement channel. "Attention all hands, engaging QMP drive in ten seconds. Hold your positions until all-clear. Sealing hatchways."

The hatch slammed shut only a foot in front of Klaus. Dammit, why had he not thought of that? Now he was stuck in here with the heat. His interior-service suit was designed to keep him alive in case of a hull breach, no temperature control provided…and the reading from his datapad showed 52 degrees Celsius.

Klaus shook sweat from his eyes, and braced himself against one of the racks. Six…five…four…

The heat should have been the least of his worries.

^^*^*^*^*^*^*^*^*^*^*

Captain Conagher gasped reflexively as the *Overlord* disappeared around her. She was alone in the universe — no ship, no Podera, no stars, only bone-chilling cold. Time expanded, and although she knew that it was only a split-second — at least that was what she tried desperately to tell herself — her mind refused to believe it.

She floated, alone. No senses, no light, no touch, just cold. Forever.

Her mind filled her head, pressure growing, trying to escape. Then her consciousness flew into the void, seeking in vain to fill it. She screamed in silence, fighting to hold on to the essence of herself, fighting to grip it firmly to her, to hang on to the memories, the dreams, the visions that were Emily Conagher. And losing.

And then, just as fast as the sensation had appeared, it was gone. Light flooded back into her eyes, revealing the familiar bridge of the *Overlord*. Her crew were speechless, exchanging wide-eyed glances, some reaching out to pat their faces, arms, consoles, chairs, or even the deck beneath them. As if verifying that these things were indeed real.

She forced herself to release her fingers, which clutched the armrests of her chair in a white-knuckled deathgrip. She took a deep breath, smiled and gave the chair a small pat. Solid as ever. She held up her hands. Ten fingers. Check.

So that was how teleportation felt. It had always looked much more comfortable on old-time TV...

"Holy shit!" called the helmsman, voice unsteady. "What the hell was that?"

Conagher was too shaken to reprimand him.

She shook her head, focusing on the urgent task at hand. She would contemplate the downsides of teleportation later. There was work to be done. The displays on all of the consoles were black, but as she watched they started their re-boot cycle.

Even though she had been assured that the bridge's computer systems would re-boot within fifteen seconds, it still felt like an eternity. She gnashed her teeth until the last of the essential controls came back online, and the holo-display flickered back to life. She blinked and did a double-take to confirm what it told her. "Helm. Confirm position."

"Thirty kilometers to *Tannenberg*, ma'am." His voice was steady this time.

"Hoo-yah!" cried the weapons officer, and the rest of the bridge crew joined in.

Conagher gave a thin smile. "Hoo-yah indeed. ETA on incoming fire?"

The tactical officer clambered back onto his chair. "Forty-two seconds, ma'am!"

That should be enough. "Helm, move us to intercept the enemy fire. Grav-tether us to the *Tannenberg* once we are in position to block." To the engineering officer, "All power to deflectors facing the incoming fire. Overload them at impact."

She could not be certain that the *Overlord's* structure hadn't been compromised by the jump, and she could not afford to take any chances. The deflectors would die, but they'd almost completely dull the shock of the enemy rounds hitting the hull. Hopefully, that would be the last shot the *Overlord* would take.

"Impact in ten seconds, ma'am!"

And there was no way to tell if this next projectile was another of the super-shells they'd hit the *Overlord* with earlier. She could only hope that it was not, that the enemy had felt that such power was overkill for finishing off the wounded *Tannenberg.*

'CLANG'! The hull resounded again, and the bridge shook around her. Conagher's eyes darted to the damage-control readout on her repeater display.

"Ma'am! We've lost the last of our forward deflectors!"

She let out a long breath, and leaned back. But that was all that they'd lost. A few more armor sections had been holed, but they had served their purpose well.

^^*^*^*^*^*^*^*^*^*

Klaus stumbled onto the *Overlord*'s bridge, helmet off, still gasping for breath as smoke curled out of his suit. He had long ago lost his ability to smell its acrid, metallic odor. The charred outer surface, showing little of its original blue & gold coloring, stood in stark contrast to the gleaming, unblemished interior of the ship's bridge.

He was grinning from ear to ear. It had worked! He counted his arms and legs for the twentieth time - they were all there.

"CWO Ericsson," said the Captain, her voice crisp. "You will brief Commander Li on your technology, as soon as we are done here." She smiled in his direction, the first real smile Klaus could remember her giving, and added, "And by the way, congratulations, on behalf of me and my crew."

With that, she turned back to the Commodore. Klaus raised one tired eyebrow and grinned. Coming from the Captain, that was high praise indeed. He made a note to remember it for as long as he lived, or at least for the next few hours, whichever came first.

He glanced down at the lump of melted plastic clenched in his fist, and sighed. He did not drop it, though. That datapad had stayed with him since he'd started working on the *Ad Astra*, and had survived the ship's destruction. One of the last mementos of his time aboard. He swayed.

"Are you all right, sir?" asked one of the Marine guards flanking the entrance. The man wrinkled his nose at the smell, but his voice betrayed none of the casual haughtiness of Marines around Navy personnel. 'Squid' or not, walking in a suit that fire-damaged must have earned Klaus the man's respect.

"Yeah. Electrical fires. Not fun. Release latches melted. Can't get it off." His voice was clipped and strained as he made his way to the engineering console. "No permanent damage. I'll live. Work to do."

He put his report out of his mind, and brought up the damage schematics first, ignoring the other activity on the bridge. They were all too busy with the same thing he was — damage assessment. As the last wisps of smoke left his suit, Klaus chuckled. "Here's some advice: next time we jump, stay away from the server rooms."

"Next time, sir?" The Marine shifted from one foot to the other, and his voice had a slightly higher pitch now. "We're doing that again?"

Klaus gave him a look. What would he have to be so worried about? He was safe in the bridge, not in an electrical fire-trap. Not only was the bridge an integrated design, letting it be teleported as one unit, but it also had its own, dedicated reserve power. There weren't any suddenly-cut-off electrical lines to start fires. He pulled a strand of melted wiring off his suit. Not like the server room.

All the same, Klaus had to admit that the feeling of teleporting — like being dunked into a tank of liquid nitrogen, so cold that it had burned worse than the actual fire — was enough to get to anyone.

And he had to tell the Captain what he had figured out about Andromeda Station. It kept slipping his mind, and maybe he was wrong. But if he was right, she would really need to know. There was an endless supply of rocks out there that the rebels could throw. Then again, he knew the Navy well enough not to blurt it all out in front of the entire bridge crew. Maybe he could talk the Captain alone, somehow.

The communications officer interrupted before Klaus could say anything. "Captain! We've got audio from one of our shuttles on the *Tannenberg*."

"Patch it through," replied the Captain.

Klaus looked up from his work, as a familiar voice came over the bridge speakers. "—enant Gureivich, we've retaken the bridge here, but the systems are locked down tight. We're bouncing our signal through one of the ships in the hangar. The rebels got into the ship's systems somehow — they were using them on us coming in. They scrammed the systems as we came in, though, and none of our codes work."

Commodore Petrakov spoke first. "What about Captain Irakopolous?" Captain Conagher raised an eyebrow at him, but said nothing.

"The rebels didn't take any prisoners, sir." Antoniy's voice was flat.

"Are any of the captured rebels talking?"

"Most of 'em dropped their weapons at first sight, but they don't know anything useful." Antoniy coughed. "The other four - officers by the look of them - took cyanide. Can't exactly question them."

Commodore Petrakov paused for only a moment. "Lieutenant, we need those systems. I'm forwarding you my access code. Patch in the *Tannenberg's* communications console. We can control her from here."

"But, sir!" the *Overlord's* communications officer exclaimed. "This channel isn't secure!"

"It's lose the code or lose the *Tannenberg*," Petrakov cut him off. "The code can be changed later." He typed a command into his console. "I'm authorizing you to bypass protocol."

A few moments later, Antoniy's voice again. "Code received, sir. Entering it now." A second later, his voice returned, a note of stress underlying it. "Sir, I've entered the code, and the system isn't accepting it!"

"What?" barked the Commodore.

What? Klaus gasped, looking up from his damage console. Maybe he was still in shock, but what he had just heard didn't make any sense. He thought about the comm protocol, and ruled out carbon-based error. Antoniy couldn't have garbled it. A Commodore-level access code could override any ship-level lockout. At least in the Navy he remembered.

Commodore Petrakov continued, his voice regaining its calm. "I'm re-sending. Confirm entered correctly."

A nerve-wracking few seconds of silence, background conversation, and then— "Re-entered and checked, sir. Still nothing!"

Impossible. Everyone in the Navy had heard of Petrakov. Only a half-dozen admirals in the fleet had higher-level codes. And each security code was unique. Even if one of those admirals was crooked, either working directly with the rebels or just with a middleman, they couldn't possibly have been stupid enough to allow such flagrant use of a code which would pinpoint exactly who gave it. So why didn't the Commodore's code work?

"Could the systems have been damaged, not working properly?" asked Captain Conagher.

"No, ma'am. Double checked. All system diagnostics green."

Klaus smiled grimly. Coming from a Marine, it wasn't exactly an iron-clad guarantee of system functionality.

"I see." continued the Captain. She drummed her fingers on the armrest of her command chair.

Klaus studied the Captain. He could almost hear the wheels turning in her head. The Navy had always built redundancy, backup and fudge factors into everything, in order that their systems would work in a crisis. And now, despite all that, the most critical system of all was *not* working. To be honest, the whole thing had him deeply worried as well. Their lives were still on the line. His bones still ached, and his stomach knotted as a fear grew in him. All his hard work — *everybody's* hard work — might now be for nothing. The Commodore's control-override code should have started the systems on the *Tannenberg*, yet it hadn't. And without access to the *Tannenberg's* functional main drive, the *Overlord* would be stuck where she was, facing down the rebels. Almost none of her deflector screens were still active. Given enough time, even the *Verdun* could cripple her now, if the rebel warship came out of hiding from behind Podera.

But the Captain's lack of a reaction puzzled him. She must have realized the same problems, but she did not look as worried as she should be. Maybe she was thinking up some way to bypass the codes and get the *Tannenberg's* drive working manually, but Klaus was pretty sure that would not work.

A full scram was *supposed* to disable a ship in case it fell into enemy hands. It hadn't worked against the rebels, but it seemed to be working all too well against the *Tannenberg's* proper owners.

After all they had been through, Klaus did not want it to end this way. Against all the odds, against Murphy himself, they had delivered the Overlord to where she needed to be, had rescued their ticket home. Just to be undone by the Commodore's faulty code. .

So yes, the Captain should have looked more worried. At the very least, as worried as he himself felt.

He sighed, and his aches re-doubled. He sagged to the floor, his exhaustion catching up with him. In his head, he was already outlining some way to get a secure communication to earth. At the very least, he wanted to share what he and Johann — and James, of course — had learned about the QMP drive, and how to make it work. And the danger to Andromeda station. But he did not want to share their knowledge with the rebels. He came up with one scheme then another, settling on one he thought would work.

It was the best he could think of, to salvage something from their deaths. He picked bits of burnt fabric from his uniform, and tossed them onto the deck. He gazed up at the Captain, and wondered idly what *she* would try to salvage.

Yet Captain Conagher did not look defeated at all. Her voice was calm, but very forceful as she keyed the comm. "Lieutenant Gureivich, I'm sending you a higher-level override code. Try it." She clicked a sequence of commands into her console, and then sat back, eyes locked straight ahead.

What? Klaus couldn't have heard her properly. Petrakov's Commodore-level code hadn't worked, so why on Earth — or off it, for that matter — would a Captain have a code higher than that?

Behind the captain, Commodore Petrakov snapped his head up, frowning. "Where did you get—"

"Long story. I'll explain later."

Antoniy's voice came back quickly, a hint of confusion evident from the bridge's speakers. "Er, confirmed, ma'am. Entering new code now."

The bridge went silent, and Klaus held his breath.Everyone knew what was at stake, and also knew all the reasons why the Captain's code couldn't work. Klaus caught several crewmen exchanging glances. Maybe they wondered the same thing he did. Petrakov stared at the captain's back, his expression unreadable, but all other eyes turned to the holo-display.

For now, they had maneuvered the rebels into a stand-off. The *Overlord's* act of teleporting next to the station had placed Podera between the squadron and its most dangerous enemies.

Add to that an unpredictable target. Conagher had grav-tethered the *Overlord* to the *Tannenberg,* and now the two were slowly orbiting each other, using the bigger ship's momentum to race away from where the *Tannenberg* had been just seconds before. The rebels' firing solutions had been changed in the blink of an eye.

The *Verdun* was still skulking around on the other side of the planetoid, the rock-throwers were awkwardly positioned relative to the Navy ships, and so their projectiles would still have to arc around Podera in an indirect — and slow — trajectory. Another rock, launched minutes before the *Overlord's* jump, flew harmlessly past its former target, missing by tens of kilometers.

Even so, time was not their ally. It would only take minutes for the enemy rock-throwers to move to a better firing position, and to use the *Verdun* to accelerate the rocks. That is, if the *Verdun's* grav systems were still operational. Klaus shook his head at the audacity shown by the enemy captain. He would have staked his reputation on their grav systems failing long before this. What kind of crack engineers did they have on board, anyway?

If the *Verdun* were still in action, and if any of their shots hit the deflector-less *Overlord*, the battle would be over. Or if the *Verdun* came over the horizon and fired point-blank from her batteries, grav systems working or not, the battle would be over.

Everything rested on mobility, which meant on the blinking red icon next to the *Overlord*: the *Tannenberg*. Would the Captain's codes work?

An hour passed in the next five seconds.

The *Tannenberg's* icon turned green!

"Hoo-yah!" erupted from the bridge crew.

The Commodore drew himself up in his chair, and managed a grim smile. "Impressive," he acknowledged. His voice lowered, and Klaus barely caught the rest. "You'll have to tell me later where you got that code."

"Of course." responded the Captain. Klaus saw the corners of her mouth turn up in a quick smile, and then fade again. She began barking orders at the bridge crew. "Engineering. Get an umbilical across to the *Tannenberg* ASAP."

Klaus listened with half an ear. Everyone would now be busy getting the *Tannenberg* operational, but he had nothing left. The damage control crew didn't need him right now, and he was totally spent. At least the crew had the presence of mind to see that, and they left him alone. He sat up, and leaned back against the wall, thinking. The holo-display showed no threats, no incoming fire.

Yet.

For now, their objective had to be to keep the *Tannenberg* out of enemy hands. He wondered whether the crew understood just how important that had become. The Captain had given an access code which apparently had priority even over the highest-ranked members of the military, and now that code was on the *Tannenberg.*

God only knew where she had gotten it, but Klaus knew what the rebels could do with such a code, if they could only re-capture the *Tannenberg* and read through her systems. It had been a big risk for the Captain to deploy her ace-in-her-sleeve, but there had been no choice.

Not if she wanted the *Overlord* and the *Tannenberg* to survive.

Chapter 20: Set Them Up The Bomb

On the holo-display, a red marker emerged around the white of the planetoid.

"Ma'am!" called out the tactical officer. "The *Verdun's* moving up!"

Damn. Klaus checked the engineering readout. Less than a quarter of the deflector screens were still online, and those only afforded sporadic coverage. Some had been crushed under enemy fire, some overloaded to stop enemy fire, and still more had been burned out just moving the huge warship.

With the *Overlord's* deflectors down, the *Verdun* was no longer a smaller, obsolete warship to be laughed at. She was a real threat, now. A very dangerous threat.

"Then we'd best move quickly." said Captain Conagher. "Engineering, get power across to the *Tannenberg*, as much as her drive can take." She toggled communications with Antoniy. "Lieutenant Gureivich, we've slaved the *Tannenberg's* controls to ours. Just keep the rebels out of the bridge and the engine compartments, and we'll be out of here shortly."

"Aye, ma'am." responded Antoniy, and cut the channel.

A warning klaxon sounded, and the holo-display flashed three red icons from the *Verdun*. Incoming fire.

"Ma'am!" the tactical officer called out. "The enemy's targeting us! Railgun impact in nine seconds, ma'am!"

Now that the rebels had fully — hopefully — played their hand by using their admiral-level override code, they must be truly desperate to stop the *Overlord* and *Tannenberg* from escaping. The *Verdun* was taking a big risk by exposing herself to the *Overlord's* fire. They were either desperate, or they somehow suspected that the *Overlord's* fire-control systems had been disabled.

After the hammering the *Overlord* had taken earlier from the rock-slingers, Klaus reflexively braced his arms against his console. This was going to hurt.

"Five, four, three, two, one."

He almost missed the impact. The incoming projectiles hit the *Overlord's* armor at an angle, ricocheting off harmlessly. What? The *Verdun* had missed? Klaus looked to the holo-display. Of course — the *Overlord* was now maneuvering, heading away from the planetoid. Slow, but enough to almost dodge the *Verdun's* first salvo.

But they couldn't outrun the *Verdun*, not with both ships tethered together and using one drive. If the enemy ship approached to close-range, each salvo would be harder to dodge. It would take time, but the end result was not in doubt.

"*Verdun* is closing the range, ma'am." announced the tactical officer.

Klaus groaned. Murphy again. Why couldn't the *Verdun's* captain be incompetent for a change? He quite deliberately did not wish that they would be stupid enough to miss the idea of dodging around and going for the *Tannenberg*. The smaller ship lacked the *Overlord's* armor, and was the only key to both ships' survival.

"Main battery, prepare to fire." called Captain Conagher.

"Railgun crews report their weapons are non-operable, ma'am! It looks like their impeller-field emitters were fried when we teleported. The railguns can't operate without them."

The Captain shot a quick glare at Klaus, who looked away uneasily. He'd warned her that he hadn't had the chance to test the QMP drive on all of the ship's systems.

"I see," she growled. "Torpedoes?"

"Too shallow, ma'am! Range is too far, and the chemical drive refit not complete. At least thirty minutes left, ma'am."

Far too long. Might as well be years. What other options did they have? Klaus wracked his mind, searching for a solution.

"Helm, close us up to shield the *Tannenberg*. Nudge them if you have to." Conagher turned to the engineering officer. "How many hits can we take?"

"At close range, ma'am? Between six and fifteen main-caliber rounds."

Klaus did the math. The *Verdun's* main battery could bring four railguns to bear on a target. Five minutes to reload each barrel. They had twenty minutes at the outside. He gritted his teeth. It was so damn ridiculous that they couldn't deliver a simple warhead to a target which wasn't even trying to dodge.

Warhead.

Klaus' heart skipped high into his throat, as a surge of adrenaline hit him. With a groan, he forced himself to his feet and leaned on the weapons console. "Lieutenant Billings," he addressed the officer sitting there, reading her tag. For some reason, he felt it was important to address her by name. Maybe he had sustained a serious injury, after all. "What are the torpedo warhead dimensions? Just the weapon itself."

"Eighty centimeters by forty by forty," she replied after only a moment's hesitation. "Why?"

"I've got an idea. Hold on a second." He said in a voice loud enough for the Captain to hear. He commed Johann, hoping that the intra-ship comms system wasn't too damaged by the jumping. It was mostly wireless, so—

"Eh? Ah, Klaus, good to hear —" Johann's voice was almost free of accent. Good, that meant he must have sobered up.

"QMP test rig still set up in the labs?"

"Aye," Johann seemed to catch the urgency in Klaus' voice. "Why? We're not going to jump again, are we? I've got a yeoman mopping up last night's dinner, and —"

"Get down there ASAP." He almost shouted.

"Wha—?" Something in Klaus' tone must have gotten through to him, because he added simply, "—all right, on my way to the lab."

Klaus thought for a moment. Eighty centimeters by forty by forty. That would just barely fit inside the test rig launcher, with only a bit of adjustment. "Re-size the launch equipment. Use any of the spare parts you need. We've got a package we *need* to send, and it's eighty centimeters on its longest axis. The rest'll fit."

Klaus cut the connection, and faced Lieutenant Billings. His heart pounded, either in fear or hope, or both. He couldn't tell, and it didn't matter. His words were clipped. "We might be able to use the QMP test rig to move a warhead onto the *Verdun*. How soon can your people get a warhead off the torpedo, and delivered to the lab — er, auxiliary engine compartment C?"

"Ten minutes, but—"

Captain Conagher interrupted. "Do it. And you better mean seven." She turned to Klaus as the weapons officer got busy. "How quickly can you get your system ready to fire?"

"After Johann gets there, two minutes to fire it up. Five more to get the system zeroed in on a point ahead of the *Verdun*." Klaus pointed at the display. "If the *Verdun* keeps accelerating like that — I mean predictably — we'll be able to hit her."

"Good. Get to it."

Klaus stumbled to the *Overlord's* auxiliary console, which had been set up to control the QMP rig remotely. For their earlier jump, the QMP controls had simply been slaved to the ship's navigation computers. In order to hit the *Verdun*, however, they would need manual control. He sat down and brought up the third-level displays. With a few quick commands, he diverted the QMP command from the navigation system.

Then the full realization of what he had to do hit him. His fingers stopped, his hands balled into fists . Dammit, why had he brought up the idea? It just wasn't going to work. He slapped his forehead, which was a mistake. The room spun for a few seconds, before settling down.

He should have seen it! For teleporting the *Overlord* itself, the only significant external gravity well nearby had been Podera. But for placing a torpedo warhead inside the *Verdun*, there would be three. The planetoid, as well as the deflector screens of both the enemy ship and the *Overlord* itself.

The really tricky part, though, was getting the working warhead *inside* the target ship intact. It was orders of magnitude more complex that delivering it to the vacuum of space. From a relativistic perspective, it would involve several times more calculations than they had needed for the entire QMP jump. He let out his breath, deflated. Put simply, his QMP systems just couldn't calculate fast enough to place that warhead inside a moving target.

Think! He couldn't just announce that their last-ditch plan wouldn't work. There had to be a workaround. His eyes widened as an idea struck him. It sounded crazy, even in his own head, but yes, it would work. This, he thought, would definitely require the Captain's approval.

Without moving from his chair, Klaus opened a private communications channel to the Captain's earbud, speaking softly. "Ma'am, I'm sorry — we can't teleport a warhead inside the *Verdun*. But I think I have a workaround."

"Out with it." Her clipped tone betrayed nerves, but her voice was steady.

He swallowed, wondering how to present his idea. If he cut down on the accuracy calculations, their computers could easily hit the inside of the Verdun. But the object being teleported would be spread out inside the entire volume. Not good for a piece of precision engineering like a fusion warhead.

But exploding particles, or a blast wave? Accuracy wouldn't matter with those. It had one really tricky drawback, though.

"Ma'am, we can't get the warhead inside the *Verdun*, intact." This would need some explaining as to why it was the only remaining solution. "Its mass would be spread throughout the ship, and it would not detonate. What we *can* do is send, essentially, the explosion itself. The kinetic energy would be preserved through the teleport."

The bridge shuddered as a fresh volley of railgun projectiles slammed into the Overlord. Klaus barely noticed. His systems still worked, the bridge was undamaged. He had to focus.

The Captain responded, "You mean—"

"We detonate the warhead in the laboratory, and then teleport the exploding particles into the *Verdun*. Enough of them will land inside the ship to gut her."

"And that means...oh. Any better ideas?"

"None that I know of, ma'am. I wish I did."

"I see." Captain Conagher's voice was slow and clear-cut. "You're proposing that we detonate a ship-killer warhead *inside our own vessel?*"

"Well, yes, ma'am."

Captain Conagher closed her eyes and pinched the bridge of her nose. Hard. She mumbled, "Well, at least if it fails, we won't have to scuttle." She looked up, and in a strained voice she replied, "Get your systems set up, I'll inform the weapons team."

"Aye, ma'am." Klaus spun back to the QMP console. It was a quick job to strip out much of the target-point refinement code, and to link the target coordinates to the data passed from the ship's weapons computers.

Of course, that was the easy part. The hard part would be moving the warhead before it destroyed the *Overlord*.

He turned to the weapons officer. "Lieutenant Billings, I've got the targeting slaved to your console. Tell your weapons team I'll meet them at the lab."

"A-Aye." The young lieutenant stammered.

Stammered, eh? He studied Billing's face, which was pale. Ah, of course. The Captain would have informed any crew who were needed for Klaus' plan. Made sense, but he hoped she hadn't told the whole ship that they'd be detonating one of their warheads onboard. If it worked, they could learn about it afterwards. If it didn't — well, then it wouldn't really matter.

There was no way that he was leaving this sort of programming to Johann. This he had to do personally. He raced for the hatch, just as the tactical officer shouted "Verdun has fired another salvo, ma'am! Time to impact eight seconds!"

He couldn't help one last look at the holo-display. Four more projectiles were rushing towards the Overlord. Just like last time, with one crucial difference.

The Verdun was closer now. Much closer.

Too close.

"Helm, translate up, maximum!" ordered the Captain. "Seal bulkheads!"

Without deflectors, there wasn't much else that could be done. The emergency blast door slammed shut, sealing everyone in. Stuck on the bridge, at least for the time being.

The deck jumped under his feet, and the hull rang with a subsonic boom that shook his bones. By the sound of it, that was right on top—

The blast door buckled inwards, the overpressure threatening to shatter Klaus' eardrums. The Marine sentry next to it flinched away, holding his ears. That was fifty centimeters of alloyed steel, and it had deformed at least ten centimeters inwards.

"Reactors two and six offline, ma'am!" reported the engineering officer.

Klaus ignored them. His attention was drawn to the sentry by the hatch, who was frantically pounding at the blast door's manual controls. The Marine had no success, and pounded the door with his fist. "We're locked in!"

Klaus swore under his breath. Now he wouldn't be able to get down to the labs in time. He ran through his options. He couldn't do the necessary programming by himself from the bridge — the QMP test computers were isolated from the rest of the ship's systems.

But who could he trust to get it right, of the people that were available? It had to be someone who was familiar with the QMP software. Obviously not Johann. That left...

Klaus brought his communicator online. They had gambled absolutely everything on one person when they had jumped to rescue the *Tannenberg*, and that person had come through. "James, are you up for some programming work?"

"Yeah, sorta. Gimme a moment." A low groan punctuated his statement. "What do you need?"

"I need you to re-program the QMP trigger to slave it to a torpedo warhead's detonation signal."

"Okay — wait, we're setting *what* off?"

"You're the most competent person available. Get to the lab. Johann's there. Just get it done." Klaus ended the call, and turned to the Captain. "Ma'am, I've got the best programmer on-board en-route."

"I heard. O'Rourke, yes?" She fixed Klaus with a stare. "Are you sure about trusting him? He's from the same group where the rebels' support comes from."

Technically true, admitted Klaus. The rebels' main power base was among the Oort Cloud miners. Supposedly, at least. After talking to a number of the local civilians, though, Klaus was beginning to have his doubts about that.

It hadn't really been within his authority to entrust James with the top secret program in the first place, but he hoped that the Captain would continue to overlook that. After all, it had worked. And the miner had proved himself. "If he was a threat, he would have sabotaged the QMP jump earlier. He's trustworthy, I'd bet my life on it."

Her lips parted in what could not quite be called a smile. "'Bet your life?' That's exactly what you're doing, Mr. Ericsson. All of our lives. Keep it in mind."

"Aye, ma'am." Damn! She had said it. Maybe the Captain didn't believe in Murphy. Of course! That was the answer. Murphy.

His communicator pinged. Johann. "Klaus, I've got the QMP rig warmed up!"

"Damn good job, Johann. James should be finishing the code soon. Have Murphy double-check everything. And keep your mouth shut about it." Klaus breathed a sigh of relief. That had been the biggest worry he'd had about the plan. Murphy would ensure the plan wouldn't fail because of, well, Murphy. "There's a Navy crew on the way. They should be there any moment. Help them get the warhead ready to 'port, and then your job is done."

"Aye. Ah, here they — bloody hell, that little thing is a warhead?"

There was a murmur in the background. An answer, Klaus supposed. Johann continued, "If you say so. This'll be easier than I thought! Now, let's get this done!"

Klaus smiled. Of all the people he'd heard during this fight, the only person who actually sounded happy was the ivory-tower academic. Maybe Johann should get out into the field more often. Klaus looked at the holo-display in the center of the bridge. Then again, maybe Johann was happy because he wasn't paying enough attention to anything outside the academics of it all. Maybe he was taking notes right now for some journal article. Klaus could almost envy him that level of focus.

As if on cue, the Verdun's icon again pulsed a brighter red, as another salvo of railgun shells closed on the *Overlord*.

"Impact six seconds!" shouted the tactical officer.

Too close to maneuver out of the way. Klaus scanned the engineering readout: the forward-quadrant deflectors were largely burned out. They'd be little help here.

This was going to hurt. Klaus quickly ducked under the QMP console. It wasn't exactly armored, but it was better than nothing.

The hull rang once more. The lights flickered. Another of the reactors must have been hit. The deformed blast door cracked and flew apart into a shower of debris. Someone screamed as they were hit.

He winced and clapped his hands to his head as the over-pressure hit his eardrums. Jagged shards of ice-hot pain sliced through his head, and he fought to stay conscious. The bridge crew wore only basic vacuum suits. No armor to speak of: any near hit would deal terrible damage to a soft human body. He grabbed the edge of the console and pulled himself to his feet. One of the crew — rather, half of him — was pinned by a meter-wide disc of metal to the bulkhead opposite the hatch. Klaus gulped. The lower-half of the deceased crewman was still vomiting blood all over the sensor console. The sensor officer sat staring, mouth open and frozen in shock.

The Marine guard rushed over and shoved the half-a-corpse onto the floor. He pulled the stock-still sensor officer away from the sight, and laid him flat along the wall. Figures that a Marine would keep his head — their training was the best for staying calm under intense, personal danger.

The Captain drummed her fingers on the command chair, her eyes fixed on Klaus. "How much longer?"

"Any minute now." Klaus barely heard the question. He swiped at his right ear to hear better, and his fingers came away red. Klaus grinned, a bit self-conscious, and turned to the monitor to confirm that he hadn't lied. A chunk of debris had smashed right through the screen projector. The computer itself was not in the console, of course, so it should still work properly. All the same, now Klaus really had little more that he could do. He couldn't even monitor what was going on — his personal datapad had been melted in the fire from the QMP jump, and he had lost its remains sometime during the attacks. Nothing to do but wait.

His communicator chirped again. James. "Almost done here. Ready in under a minute."

"Good. Will your programming work?"

"I'm risking my life on it, so it'll damn well work." There was a pause, keys clattering in the background. "At any rate, I'm done now. Flagged the system as ready. Here's hoping this works." He cut the connection.

A moment later, the weapons officer called out "Ma'am, we've got the *Verdun* targeted! QMP auxiliary crew reports green to fire!" At least that part was working well. Now if only the rest of it worked—

"Fire." came the instant command.

Klaus held his breath. He was dying to actually see the *Verdun*, to see with his own eyes the instant that their tactic worked. He wanted a viewscreen, an optical image, hell, even a window. At least he was still breathing, which meant the fusion warhead had not exploded onboard the Overlord. So far, so—

He bit back the thought. It did not pay to tempt fate. The holo-display showed the *Verdun's* red glowing bright, closing swiftly on the *Overlord*. This was going to be close...

A bead of sweat stung his eye. If this first try didn't work, they wouldn't have time for a second.

Without so much as a sound, the *Verdun's* icon simply...vanished.

"Is that it?" asked one of the bridge crew.

The tactical officer whooped loudly, his voice excited. "Ma'am! Energy spike from the *Verdun!* She's burned from the inside-out, destroyed!"

"Hoo-yah!" exploded the bridge crew. They were going to live. Their cheer died as quickly as it had come, and even Klaus could see why. They were going to live, to be sure. But only because hundreds of others had died.

Commodore Petrakov stared at the holo-display, jaw hanging slightly open. He pounded the arm of his chair once, smiled, and then closed his eyes as he leaned back into his chair. Blood dripped from a red gash down his leg, but he seemed to pay it no attention. The Marine guard — doing a damn fine job as a medic — knelt by the Commodore, and opened his first-aid kit.

Chapter 21: Withdrawal

"All right." The Captain's voice sounded tired. Klaus could certainly empathize with that. "Helm, get us the hell out of here." She highlighted a trajectory in the bridge holo-display. Heading almost directly away from the planetoid, it kept the two warships shielded behind the station for the maximum amount of time.

Klaus nodded. No sense in taking risks they didn't have to – it was almost certain that no enemy weapons emplacements remained, and the rock-slingers posed little danger without the *Verdun*, but there was no way to be sure. The Captain continued, "What's our acceleration?"

"Twelve point four gees, ma'am."

She nodded. "Very well. Divert available crew to repair and medical teams."

Without the *Verdun* to chase down the fleeing *Overlord* and *Tannenberg*, the battle was over. The rock-slingers couldn't accelerate enough to catch up with the federal squadron, even as damaged as they were.

"Time to MSD?" Conagher asked. The minimum safe distance from the nearby gravity well for the two ships to activate their faster-than-light drives.

"Sixteen minutes, ma'am."

In the meantime, Klaus had to stay busy, even as exhausted as he was. He was too keyed-up — trying to 'relax' now would be impossible. His hands shook, and he collapsed into his chair. He glanced over at the bridge's small spare-parts cache.

293

Located near the destroyed hatchway — at least they weren't trapped on the bridge anymore, a corner of his mind noticed — it was surprisingly intact. He checked the mounting for the QMP console's display. Just a standard holographic projector. Should take no time at all to fix.

What the hell was he thinking, repairing the holo-mount on his console? Just look at the bridge! The blue and green paint of the bridge was now covered with pockmarks and gashes, portions missing where smaller fragments of the hatch had impacted. The Captain's chair had a twenty-centimeter-long shard of metal jammed right through the back — by some miracle, it had missed the Captain herself.

The wounded had already been transferred to sick bay. He imagined Lt. Baker running himself ragged, arms red to the elbows. He tried his best to ignore the unmoving bodies, and parts of bodies, that remained on the floor of the bridge. Given the physical damage he saw, it was a wonder so many of them *had* survived.

The sensor console was covered in blood. The engineering console was halfway-detached from the floor. A large piece of debris wedged underneath it must have barely missed the crew. The tactical console seemed undamaged, except that one of the two seats in front of it was missing. The stump of the chair column — and the two stumps of feet, still in their boots, nearby — showed where a sizable shard of steel had cut through.

The helm console was hit hardest. Only half of it was still in working condition. The other half — and the former helmsman — was a crumpled mass of steel and flesh leaking blood in the corner of the bridge. A large chunk of metal, glistening with red, was embedded in the weapons console. On the floor behind the console lay half a body. Its nametag read Billings.

Klaus swallowed hard. He was hollow inside. He would live, sure. Hell, *most* of the crew would live. At some level, it all must have been worth the cost, but right now he couldn't see how. He tried to remind himself of all the people on Andromeda Station that would live, but it didn't help much He himself would either be rewarded for getting the jump drive working, or jailed for revealing Navy secrets. He didn't care. He could have done better. If only he had worked faster. Even five minutes would have made the difference.

Commodore Petrakov had been laid unconscious on the floor next to his chair, blood soaking through the bandages wrapped around his leg. Whatever hit him must have nicked an artery, but he had demanded to stay on the bridge, and not be evacuated with the other wounded. He looked pale, but at least now he had an IV running and the medic treating him didn't look too worried.

Thankfully, the ventilation system was functional, pulling smoke — and the stench of blood and internal organs — out of the air. Klaus could see just how few of the bridge crew had come through the fight unscathed.

The open nature of the bridge, designed to ease communication among the crew, meant that the blast door had been the only real impediment protecting the compartment from critical damage if the hull was breached this deeply. When it had failed, the crew had paid the price. But at least the hatch was open now — trained medics and corpsmen flowed through, seeing to the casualties.

Klaus turned toward the parts cache but tripped, catching himself against the bulkhead. One of the medics braced him up, holding him under one arm. "Where are you hit?"

Klaus waved the man away. "I'm alright, haven't been hit." With his suit burned all the way through in places, he must have looked like one of the casualties. But he felt fine, just weak and a bit dizzy.

Klaus shook his head, watching the medics go to work on people that he had written off as corpses. Any machine could be put back together, sure. He knew that. But it still amazed him how true that was becoming for the human body. Remembering the amazing machines in the ship's sickbay, he gave a silent prayer that they would do their job.

He really should go to his quarters and lie down, but he couldn't muster the energy. For all he knew, his room was gone, anyway. But the bridge stank like Hell itself, and his charred suit wasn't helping. His sense of smell was finally returning, which he decided was not a good thing. There was no escaping the sickly-sweet smell of charred flesh.

His hip throbbed, and he noticed, with mild surprise, that his suit had a large hole over the epicenter of the pain. The edges of the hole were cracked and blackened, and the material crumbled away when he brushed it.

Huh. So he had been hit, after all. Funny that he hadn't noticed it earlier. He probably needed a medic, but saw they were all busy.

The pain grew stronger as he stared at the wound, and his stomach heaved, so he turned away. But the more he stared at the broken bodies around him, the queasier he became. A tight knot formed above his stomach, rising and burning up his throat. He did the only thing he could think of.

He opened the spare-parts cache, and picked through the tools. That would take his mind off of the...mess.

The overhead light dimmed slightly. Someone standing behind him. He tried to ignore whomever it was. "Sir, can you lend a hand with the repairs out here?" Hell, just when he was losing himself. With a sigh, he turned to see the Marine sentry who had greeted him when he had entered the bridge, hours – *fifteen minutes ago?* The soldier gestured toward the blasted-open hatchway.

"What's the — oh, hell. Thank you, son." The hallway beyond was absolutely filled with debris. There was no way that an injured crewman headed for sickbay could get through that. "This'll take some time." The sentry's request was much better than his idea. It would get him off the bridge, and give him something meaningful to do, something that might actually help those casualties he was trying so hard to ignore. Better than tinkering with the damn display. He grabbed his tools and limped through the doorway. "Grab anybody on the bridge who isn't needed. We'll need all the hands we can get."

Klaus grabbed a piece of debris to clear it, whistling softly to himself. Then it all went black.

Chapter 22: Denouement

Within an hour, the *Overlord* and the *Tannenberg* jumped away from the battlefield at Podera. Within a day, the *Overlord's* engine was repaired enough for her to move under her own power. Within a week, they hoped to reach Andromeda station. Most of the miners had been interrogated and then released from the brig, but were confined to the civilian sector.

It all passed in a blur for Klaus. He had woken up late this morning on a cot outside sickbay, apparently too low on their list to warrant a real bed. The nurse had told him that they had patched up some kind of internal bleeding, and urged him to rest. Klaus had left as soon as she turned her back. They probably needed the cot space, anyway.

He had limped his way onto the nearest repair team, where he tried to make himself useful. He didn't remember much, but he just hoped that he hadn't committed any irreversible mistakes.

Ignoring the insistent ache in his hip, he sat on a hard chair in a crew mess hall, picking at a plate of sausages and sauerkraut that he barely recalled ordering. Maybe he hadn't. He scowled at his plate. It could just as easily have been the chef's idea of a joke. He pushed the rest away, most of it untouched. He feared he would fall asleep in his chair if he finished it, and he still had his evening shift to go.

Opposite the hall sat Johann, his food piled in front of him, untouched. He was bent over his datapad, furiously typing away. Every so often he would look up, wink at Klaus, then go back to his work. A brilliant journal article, no doubt. One that might even earn the physicist the Nobel Prize. Klaus shook his head slowly. Sure, in twenty years' time. He didn't have the heart to tell the old Scot about the Navy Secrets Act. Out of kindness, or out of vindictiveness, he wasn't even sure himself.

Klaus had his own problems. He had tried to contact Murphy, to make sure she was all right, to hear her voice again, whatever. But he hadn't reached her. Most likely, he told himself, she was just as busy as he was. James, too, probably. After all, the miner's duty log was full, when he had pinged it earlier in the day. Johann was Johann; he would be fine on his own, as long as he stayed away from moving machinery. And Antoniy had emerged as the hero of the *Tannenberg*. He shook his head, recalling the stories he had heard, some of which might even have been true. That must have been some piece of work.

All in all, a pretty decent outcome, given what they had all just been through. He grinned tiredly. Maybe he had made some good choices, after all, despite his history stepping on the wrong toes.

All of the repair work — and tending to the casualties — had worn him down. And he was not alone. He blinked the acid cobwebs out of his eyes, and scanned the mess hall. Tired faces everywhere, the usual background noise of the mess replaced by low murmurs and the sharp clink of cutlery.

"Good morning, Klaus." A weary voice rasped behind him.

He barely recognized the voice. "And good evening to you, James." He waved tiredly to the seat opposite him. Because of all the casualties, everybody's work schedules had been scrambled, and so Klaus and the miner were now on different day/night cycles. Even more annoying, Klaus was stuck on standard repair duty while James's unique programming ability got him the far more interesting assignments. "What's on your plate for today?" He realized the double meaning only afterwards.

"Lots." Klaus couldn't tell which question the miner had answered, and was too tired to care. James set down his plate. Half-pound hamburger with a side of cheese tortellini. Apparently the food menu was just as scrambled as the crew schedules. "Couldn't get the communications pulsers working, but I've an idea."

"Sounds interesting. What's your idea?"

"Well, they can't actually repair the pulsers themselves. They're scrap. But my idea..." James took a bite of his burger, talking around the edges, "It turns out the number-six reactor only lost its fuel feeds. The grav foci still work."

"Ah, I see where you're going. But the code on those is proprietary, and quantum-encoded. We don't have the tools to re-write it above base level."

"Yeah, Rockman's always been tight-lipped when it comes to programming. Never heard of anybody even reading their code, much less editing it." The miner grinned. "But, as you said, they didn't block access to machine-level programming."

Klaus did a double-take. He'd never known James to be so long-winded. Not unless something was on his mind. "So? Nobody can write —"

James' smile grew.

"Oh, you must be joking." Klaus continued. He grinned, shaking his head. "You can actually write base-level?"

"Yep. Learned it years ago. Have to, really, out here. Can't be soft, like you Earthers." He smiled to take the edge off his words, then shrugged. "Others I know out here who've done the same."

"Huh. Well, that makes sense." Klaus shook his head. "Still, though, what an enormous pain. Just the thought of looking at all that binary makes my eyes hurt."

"That's 'cause you read it with your *eyes*, not your *mind*."

Klaus snorted. "That's cheating."

"Perhaps."

"Heh." Klaus leaned back, looking around the compartment. This mess hall was the one nearest to the civilian section, and so the majority of the remaining civilians on board ate here. Their heads were down, and they ate largely in silence. And he did not understand it. He waited till James looked up, then asked, "Look, could I ask you a question?"

"Shoot."

Klaus waved his hand to the room around them. "This is the first time I've eaten down in the civilian decks, and everybody seems so glum. D'you know what's got everybody so down? I mean, we're alive, for God's sake! We survived an ambush, a pitched battle, and the first mass-scale teleportation ever!"

"What, you can't figure that out?" James looked back at Klaus, head tilted to one side. .

"I can't think of a reason. I figured I'd ask you, since you'd know the people here better," he paused, uncomfortable in the sudden silence. He added, quietly, "Being a local, and all."

"No, I'm from the Asteroid Belt. Born and raised there. Not a local." James pointed down along the table they sat at. "There are people from a dozen different colonies here, each colony as different from the others as they are from Earth." James shook his head and stood to leave. "You Earthers aren't going to be any more popular off-planet if you keep thinking we're all one group. Sure, *I* disagree with the rebels' actions. That doesn't mean that all of the folks here feel the same." He paused, looked down at the table, then back up. "Some of 'em are pretty shook up about what happened to the *Verdun*, too."

"But the rebels attacked us." Klaus frowned. "Hell, when they ambushed us a week ago, they threw their own men to their deaths just to lure us into attacking. Then they tried to kill us. All of us." He pointed. "Them, too. How can people feel sorry for the rebels after *that*?"

James balanced his tray in one hand, pointing to himself with the other. "Look, *I'm* happy enough that we survived. But in order to do that, we had to 'cheat' as you would say, a weapon of mass destruction aboard the *Verdun*." His voice hardened. "*I* had to, God forgive me."

He sat back down, and leaned forward. His voice was serious. "Did you hear? There weren't any lifepods leaving what was left of her. And I can guarantee that some — Hell, most — of the crew on the *Verdun* were just people, conscripts or near enough to it, doing what they had to do. *They* didn't deserve that sort of destruction."

His gaze bored into Klaus', eyes tinged with red.

Klaus blinked. "Er, I never thought about it that way. I'm, ah, sorry that Johann, Murphy and I got you into —."

"Did you know Roberta is Oort Cloud?" interrupted James, his eyes hard.

"What?" blurted Klaus. "I never knew that. If so, I never would have asked her to double-check the code that you were —"

The miner laughed, a dry sound that held absolutely no warmth. "Check my code?" he hissed, "I checked *hers*. She would have landed that explosion outside their hull, just far enough that your checking software wouldn't spot it." He hung his head. "But *I* did. God-dammit, I did."

James looked up, eyes glaring at Klaus. Then he shook his head, and added in a low voice. "I dropped it just inside the forward section. Where the officers would be, as far from the crew, from my friends, as I could."

Without another word, he left his tray, stood, and walked out of the room.

Klaus sat still, stunned. He felt bad for James, and for Roberta, now that he knew. But it had all been necessary. Hadn't it? If the rebels hadn't been stopped, they likely would have used their plan to attack Andromeda station, which would have lead to thousands more casualties, even *more* miners dying. And if they had managed to destroy the main Navy base out in the Oort Cloud, the situation could easily have spiraled out of control, maybe even all-out war. Everyone might have died.

The only way to avoid that had been to destroy the *Verdun*, and all aboard her.

Of course, nobody in the room, besides Klaus himself, had any idea about the rebels' presumed plans for Andromeda station. And Klaus couldn't tell them, either. Not if he wanted to remain a free man. The Captain had made that clear enough.

He stared at the doorway through which James had left. He had an amazing talent, that miner. Had even tried to find a solution where most everyone could live. It had never occurred to Klaus to fine-tune the warhead's destination as closely as James had. But for someone as skilled as James, it was easy, though. And it might have worked, at least against a more modern ship. Except that the *Verdun* had an anti-matter drive. It wasn't the warhead that killed that ship, and all aboard her. It was her drive.

It occurred to him that maybe James didn't know that. He was a gifted programmer, to be sure, but that didn't mean he knew anything about drive engineering. Even so, Klaus did not think that the exact mechanism of how the *Verdun* exploded would make that much difference. Dead was dead.

Still, their actions *had* saved lives, whether or not they realized how many.

Small consolation for James, though. Or Roberta, for that matter. He was shocked to think that she had nearly gotten them all killed. No wonder she had not returned his calls. Truth be told, if Roberta had sat down right in front of him at that moment, he would have had nothing to say to her, either. It seemed that family and friends were what the Oort Cloud miners truly valued. Duty third, maybe. He would probably never see her again. Logically, he should report her betrayal, but he didn't have the heart for it.

He smiled wryly to himself. Was he also guilty of putting friends — former friends, at any rate — above duty? So be it.

Review complete, Klaus sighed. That question wasn't so important now. What mattered was the big picture, the rebels and their plot. He clung to the fact that he had acted logically. They had all done the right thing.

He stood to leave, giving the room one last look-over. Every so often, one of the civilians would give him a blank, unreadable stare, and go back to eating. Klaus shivered, his rationality and reason suddenly of little comfort to him. How much did they know, and what did they truly think of him? Maybe he would eat at a different mess hall from now on. He did not feel welcome here.

But that wasn't right, either. One of these miners had saved them all. At a great personal cost. His earlier smugness was gone. True enough, Klaus' choices had worked out well enough for him, for Antoniy, for Johann, but certainly not for everyone. With a painful knot in his stomach, Klaus realized that he had much to learn. He took a deep breath, and decided that he would keep eating here, where he *could* learn.

He'd spent his life focusing on what made machines work. And he was good at it. But it was people, not machines, who had saved his life. Maybe he should focus more on what made *people* work.

^^*^*^*^*^*^*^*^*^*^*

Antoniy entered the Captain's office, and stood painfully at attention as the door closed behind him. His hip and leg had been treated well enough in sick bay, but he had refused the pain meds. He needed all his wits about him. "You asked to see me, ma'am?"

Captain Conagher only glanced up briefly from her work. "Yes, have a seat, Lieutenant." She turned around the display on her desk. It showed the security code extracted from the *Tannenberg's* systems. The one that the rebels had used to wrest control of the ship "Any progress on identifying where this came from?"

"No, ma'am." Antoniy shook his head. "Our security files had nothing on it. It's not a recognized Navy passcode, and yet the *Tannenberg* accepted it. I just can't understand it."

"Did you test it on the system emulator?"

"I thought you'd ask that. Yes, I did — the code had no effect on the *Overlord's* computers. They simply ignored the code the rebels used." Antoniy leaned back in his seat. "But that makes no sense, either."

Antoniy waited for the Captain to say something, but she only returned his gaze, face unreadable. He fidgeted, feeling once again like a schoolboy while the professor waited patiently for some insightful answer. But what did he have, other than a host of unanswered questions? Still, the Captain had summoned him for a reason. He had to venture something.

"You told us this mission was to suppress the rebels, Ma'am, and destroying the *Verdun* and Podera pretty much accomplishes that. I would guess that even Petrakov believes that was the mission."

"But?" she encouraged.

"But if that wasn't the mission — or at least not all of it —
then that means you know something the Commodore does not."
He paused. "And there is a bigger game." A flash of insight hit
him. "This has something to do with why I was sent aboard the *Ad
Astra*, doesn't it?"

She smiled at him, a thin smile that gave nothing away.
"Possibly. Go on."

He pondered. "My boss sent me as decoy, supposedly in
secrecy. But somehow you knew that, and the rebels knew that.
Which means, if there was a bigger game, then it was aimed at the
Andromeda intel section." He snapped his fingers, leaning forward
in his seat. "But even that would not explain why they sent the
Overlord. It had to be something bigger yet, somebody behind
everything. Somebody on Earth, most likely, and very high-level.
So the true mission was to find out who is behind..." he pointed at
the security code they had captured from the rebels, "that."

"Exactly. If we use this, plus the origin of the pirates who
ambushed the *Ad Astra*, we now have a starting point for our
investigation."

"Once we crack the code, of course." Antoniy stroked his
chin and stared at the ceiling, remembering his own mission, and
the ambush that nearly got him killed. "There's one more piece, I
think. I've learned a lot about who the rebels are, and who they are
not. Hell, I think some of our supposed allies were the ones who
betrayed me in the first place."

"Glad to hear you figured that out," Conagher smiled,
steepling her fingers. "Somebody else did, as well, someone you

know." She brought up a schematic for Andromeda Station. "The rebels had plans to destroy this. With simple rocks."

Antoniy whistled softly. He had read the classified report on the damage to the *Overlord*, which included details on the hardened projectiles. The station would have been a sitting duck. "They aimed high, didn't they?" He sat back again, thinking. That report had been filed by Commander Li, the engineering officer, which made sense. Except that Antoniy did not know Li. So who had really figured it out? Someone on the *Overlord,* most likely, since the *Tannenberg* had not been hit with the projectiles. Someone with access to classified material.

"Do you mean Klaus?" he asked.

Conagher said nothing.

"I'll be damned," mused Antoniy. "Who would have thought that old gear-head would have come up with that?"

"You may have to get used to that 'old gear-head', as you say, Lieutenant. I have some special plans for him. A unique individual. Creative, too, especially when it comes to orders. Did you know, for example, that he set off a nuke in our engine room and teleported the explosion into the *Verdun*?"

Antoniy's eyes widened. "He really did that? I thought that was just a story." He chuckled. "Let me guess, he'd always thought it would work in theory."

Conagher raised an eyebrow. "How could you possibly know that?"

"Oh, just something he said to me when we first met. Almost got us killed then, too."

Conagher said nothing for a moment, then tapped the display on her desk. "We still need to find out who's behind all this."

Antoniy rocked forward in his chair and leveled his eyes at the Captain. "Ma'am, I would welcome an opportunity to talk with our former, er, *allies*. In person."

Conagher smiled at that. "No need to wait, Lieutenant. We have some of the miners in the brig, some of whom sabotaged *my ship*."

Antoniy raised one eyebrow in surprise. The Captain's voice had risen on the last two words, and he had never known her to lose her temper.

She pounded one finger on her desktop. "I would like to find out who sent them."

"Yes, ma'am"

Her voice grew quiet and even. "And when you are done with the miners, we have another resource for you. The Union sent us a liaison, purportedly to help with communication and protect civilian lives. I believe he can be very useful to the Navy, but not in the way he thinks." She steepled her fingers. "His name is Mr. Jones."

Antoniy smiled. He liked where the discussion was going. This time, his answer was more animated. "Yes, ma'am."

"You are still a Marine, Lieutenant," she added, "but as of now you are re-commissioned back to Intel." She stood and proferred her hand.

"Welcome aboard, Lieutenant. Again."

Glossary of Terms

CEE	light-speed
cislunar	between the Moon's orbit and Earth
CO	Commanding Officer
co-ax	short for 'co-axial'
CPO	Chief Petty Officer
CWO	Chief Warrant Officer
ECM	Electronic Counter-Measures
elint	electronic intelligence
ENV	ENVironmental
ETA	Estimated Time of Arrival
EVA	Extra-Vehicular Activities
fobbit	slang for soldiers who try to avoid dangerous assignments
fricsim	reactionless space drive
FTL	Faster-Than-Light
FUBAR	"Fouled" Up Beyond All Recognition
grav	gravity
HUD	Heads-Up Display
humint	human intelligence
ID	Identification
IFF	Identification Friend-or-Foe
ITB	Interceptor Torpedo Boat
KIA	Killed-in-Action

klick	Kilometer
LIDAR	Light (Laser) Detection and Ranging
LOS	Line-Of-Sight
MRE	Meal Ready-to-Eat
NCO	Non-Commissioned Officer
PO	Petty Officer
Potemkin disguise	an object made to look like another object
QMP	Quantum Multi-Positioning
sitrep	situation report
SNAFU	Situation Normal - All "Fouled" Up
SOS	Save Oour Ship
SOP	Standard Operating Procedure
STL	Slower-Than-Light
supermanning	"flying" using the ship's gravitational transport systems
WO	Warrant Officer
'zines	magazines, electronic format

The author welcomes all questions and comments at:

OortRising@gmail.com

www.ingramcontent.com/pod-product-compliance
Lightning Source LLC
Chambersburg PA
CBHW071103250626
47159CB00002B/586